PENNSYLVANIA STATION

"Horrigan's novel is convincingly at home in its time period, full of wonderful details and forthright opinions about architecture and art, family dynamics, and the fight over civil rights."
—*Kirkus Reviews*

"Horrigan has the sublime ability to wed history to visceral emotional experience, architecture to relationships, and sorrow to sex and love. Whether it is flirting with a sexy stranger who sits next to you in a Broadway theater, public sex in a dressing room in Rome, or seeking emotional solace in Palladio's La Rotonda, *Pennsylvania Station*, with its echoes of Henry James and E. M. Forster, amazingly collapses the profound grief of losing the past with the fear of gazing into a new future."
—Michael Bronski, author of *A Queer History of the United States*

"*Pennsylvania Station* is poignant and provocative. By exploring the conflicted relationship between a closeted middle-aged architect and an impetuous young activist at a pivotal point in New York City's geographic and cultural history, Horrigan thoughtfully employs the past to reflect complexities which face the LGBT community today."
—David Swatling, author of *Calvin's Head*

"In *Pennsylvania Station*, Patrick E. Horrigan tells a very moving story about the love of an older and a younger man, a pioneering gay activist in the early 1960s. In doing so, he shows that the fusion of same-sex romance and narrative realism can still work the kind of literary and emotional alchemy first practiced by legendary novelists like James Baldwin and Patricia Highsmith."
—Michael Moon, author of *Darger's Resources*

PENNSYLVANIA
STATION

PENNSYLVANIA STATION

A NOVEL

Patrick E. Horrigan

LETHE PRESS
AMHERST, MASSACHUSETTS

Published in 2018 by Lethe Press, Inc.
6 University Drive, Suite 206 / PMB #223 • Amherst, MA 01002 USA
www.lethepressbooks.com • lethepress@aol.com
ISBN: 978-1-59021-636-1 / 1-59021-636-9

Set in Garamond, Caesar, and Geometric 231.
Interior design: Alex Jeffers.
Cover art/design and interior art: Franco La Russa (aka Thion).

Cataloging-in-Publication Data on file with the Library of Congress.

FOR EDUARDO

SANDRO: Who needs beautiful things nowadays, Claudia? How long will they last? All of this was built to last for centuries. Today, ten, twenty years at the most, and then? Well… Claudia, shall we get married?

(from Michelangelo Antonioni's *L'Avventura*, 1960)

1962

CHAPTER ONE

FREDERICK BAILEY HAD TO BE CAREFUL NOT TO SEEM "TOO MUSICAL." ONLY certain people knew about his passion for musical theater. He was sometimes ashamed to admit it, even to himself, but Julie Andrews did something to him. He would never forget the first time he saw *My Fair Lady* in April of 1956. He and Jonathan bounded out of the Mark Hellinger Theater on a wave of something he rarely experienced anymore. It felt like love. The reason was Julie. He knew the moment Freddy Eynsford-Hill bumped into her, and she came tumbling downstage all in a heap, crying like a wounded animal, dressed in rags, her hair a mess, her face smudged with soot, her basket spilling out of her hands, her violets scattered across the pavement—from that moment she belonged to him. And when she opened her mouth to sing—

A uniformed usher and a matronly woman in blue stopped at his row. The usher checked the ticket and pointed a white-gloved finger in his direction. Frederick, along with the Oriental couple on the end and several others in between, stood up. He hoped the woman wasn't coming to claim the seat next to him. He braced himself for disappointment. Closer she came, pressed in front of him (he leaned back and even tightened his abdomen to avoid physical contact), then soldiered on a few seats further to his right. What a relief. He sat down again. With any luck (he checked his Timex—ten minutes till curtain) the seat would remain unclaimed.

He looked around. His eye followed the graceful curve of the proscenium arch up and over, then the billowy waves of the loge seating along the side, the wide sweep of the balcony overhead, coming back around to the proscenium. Curves, bows, arches, arabesques. Modern architecture, by contrast, with its unyielding squareness, its rectilinear severity (he thought of the boxy white-brick apartment building he'd spent most of the day rendering at the office), was impoverished for its refusal of such lovely, organic forms. His country house, he decided, if it ever got built, should have some curved element that referenced nature. Or history. Perhaps a tall window with a Gothic arch overlooking a ravine, somewhere deep in the woods. He thought of the Gothic windows of Grace Church with their flame tracery, visible from his living room.

The auditorium was steadily filling up. Most people had come with companions of one sort or another. Two men made their way towards the seats directly in front of him. Hard to know if they were… One whispered something in the other's ear as they removed their suit jackets. They laughed. He and Jon used to love going to the theater together (*Listen old man, just because I'm getting married…*). It was Jon with whom he'd seen *My Fair Lady* the first time (he stood with the telephone receiver to his ear, his entire family straining to listen from the parlor, the Christmas-tree lights flashing, the snow falling outside the dining room window). But nowadays he really didn't mind attending the theater alone, inherently social though it was—that is, until the lights went down. For then, he thought, you are free. Free to be anyone, do anything, go anywhere you please. And whether you're extroverted or introverted, married or single, normal or queer (*it's just that with Rachel…*), for those few blessed hours, you let go.

He hadn't, in fact, expected to be seated here on a Wednesday evening about to see *My Fair Lady* a second time. But he'd had a dream last night. Jon had come back to him. They were making love, and it was so real, so vivid, he awoke with a breathless sense of loss. He couldn't fall back asleep, so he got out of bed and went ahead with his morning routine. He discovered the *Times* had already been delivered. There was a notice in the entertainment section—after seven smash years on Broadway the show was closing at the end of September. He thought, why not? Revisiting an "old flame" might be just the thing to start the evening (he had vaguer thoughts of ending it at the Snake Pit, and who knew what might happen there, whom he might meet?). It might also fortify him to put on the family mantle this weekend. He chewed the edge of his nail. Pop's seventy-fifth birthday. The annual trip to Reading. He'd done it countless times before, and tomorrow, dutifully, he would do it again, though he was getting tired of the drill, tired of forced smiles and superficial conversations, tired of questions about girlfriends and why at his age he was still a bachelor (a handsome young man stood in the aisle scanning the crowd). He ran through the list of things that needed doing tomorrow before his five o'clock train (momentarily their eyes met). He still hadn't bought a birthday gift for his father—he was thinking a nice tie or a handkerchief (he held the young man's gaze, but the young man frowned and turned away). Gimbels had a decent selection, and it was right on the way—

He remembered the protest in front of Penn Station. "Action Group for Better Architecture in New York." Deborah had called this afternoon to remind him they were protesting the impending demolition of Pennsylvania Station and to encourage him to join the protest. What a nuisance! Young people and Negroes demonstrated in public, not serious, well-dressed, middle-aged professionals like himself. The truth was, he wasn't a joiner. He didn't believe in causes. And frankly, he wasn't certain the loss of Penn Station would be so tragic. A sooty, baggy, ill-kept monster of a building, a confusing mixture of styles—faux classicism, Crystal Palace ostentation (again he scanned the ornate proscenium with its heavy red curtain)—Mc-Kim, Mead, White at their excessive, pretentious, derivative worst, wasn't it? He hoped he could avoid the protest on his way into the station. How awkward it would be to run into Deborah. One thing to dodge a mere professional acquaintance, another to disappoint a friend. He really ought to make a date with her, they hadn't sat down to talk in months. If only she were accompanying him to Reading this weekend! He smiled to think how his family persisted in the fantasy of some dark lady in New York. "When are we gonna meet that Manhattan mistress of yours?" his father would invariably joke, thinking, no doubt, of Deborah, whom he'd met on one or two occasions over the years, and Frederick's comeback was always, "I'm too busy for romance, I have good friends, and anyway, Pop, you know *Architecture* is the love of my life."

"Come on now, Freddy, nice young fella like you, all alone in that big city..." his mother would begin. But he would change the subject, or counter with, "For heaven's sake, Ma, forty-eight isn't young, and—speaking of the city, did I tell you...?" He worried about his mother. Her health was declining, and the forgetfulness was rapidly getting worse. Or so he understood from his sister's letters. (More intimate laughter from the two men in front of him.) Well, he would see for himself this weekend.

He opened his *Playbill* and there on the inside cover was Jon: clean cut, handsomely dressed in white jacket and black tie, smoking a cigarette, sharing a private joke with a woman wearing a floor-length cape. Jon was a "type," and ever since their breakup (*Listen old man, Rachel and I are engaged. But nothing has to change between us. Just because I'm getting married doesn't mean we can't see each other. You and I will always... It's just that with Rachel...*), Frederick had the sensation of seeing him on the subway, in the street, on the television, in magazine ads—"Treat your taste kindly with KENT, the cigarette with the new micronite filter. Refines away rough taste." Nothing would taste so good this moment, he thought, as a cigarette.

He flipped the pages. An article on theater outside of New York. Cunard Cruise vacations—now *that* sounded appealing—"...to the Mediterranean...North Cape...the South Pacific and Far East...West Indies and South America." An ad for the original cast album of *My Fair Lady* (he knew it by heart). More cruises! "This Spring enjoy 45 delightful days aboard the magnificent S.S. Statendam. Discover a kaleidoscope of Mediterranean life. Madeira. Gibraltar. Villefranche. Piraeus. The Greek Isles of Delos and Mykonos. YOU HAVE A DATE WITH THE GREEK GODS on the Mediterranean 'Discovery Cruise.' Sailing from New York March 13, 1963." He turned the page. "If you're too young to go gray...then *don't!*" The men in front of him both had full heads of dark hair. His own hair had started going gray, he couldn't remember when. Years ago. But he didn't mind, because...

Now the lights dimmed. The conductor stood up in the pit. Frederick applauded along with the rest of the audience. Silence. The baton rose. *Zing, Zing, Zing, Zing!*—the first four sizzling notes of the overture—and the orchestra was off with "You Did It," followed by "On the Street Where You Live" and, most gloriously, "I Could Have Danced All Night." Wave upon wave of pleasure! But as soon as poor Margot Moser made her entrance as Eliza, everything fell apart. She was unobjectionable—pretty to look at, though perhaps a little too square in the face. Her voice was likewise pretty, if completely indistinguishable from a thousand other pretty voices. After countless hours listening to the original cast recording, and now seeing this other actress, he was reminded that Julie Andrews had a strength, a self-possession for all her young years (she was barely out of her teens when she took on the role), that, combined with the rich beauty of her voice, and her undeniable physical beauty, produced for Frederick something magical. Out-of-body. She also had an innate sense of comedy, which this new girl lacked. He missed Julie's grace and good humor, even when playing a girl of the streets.

He tried not to let Moser ruin the experience for him. He was happy enough, he told himself, just to be sitting here comfortably in the theater. All the more so because the seat next to him was unoccupied—room enough to cross his legs.

During intermission he stepped outside for a cigarette. Lured by the sultry air, theater patrons and passersby crowded the sidewalk. Frederick looked at the metal marquee rimmed with naked light bulbs bursting over the entrance (a recent addition to the Renaissance-style façade) screaming names, awards, critics' accolades—

A mad scuffling of shoes. A young woman fell to the pavement, several shopping bags tangled around her arm. Frederick caught a glimpse of someone running headlong up Broadway before vanishing into the crowd. He dropped his cigarette, rushed to the curb, and bent to help her up.

"He stole my purse!"

"Are you all right?" A small group of bystanders clustered around her, but only Frederick touched and spoke to her. "He got away," he said, looking up Broadway. "I can't even see him now." He lifted her to her feet but held on to keep her steady.

"He stole my purse." She began to cry.

"Are you hurt?" He noted scrape marks on her arm. He pulled the handkerchief from his pocket and wrapped it around her elbow.

"Thank you, I'm all right."

"Where are you going? Should I walk you to a pay phone or the subway?"

"No, I'll be all right." She wiped tears with the back of her hand, then held out Frederick's hanky while arranging the shopping bags on her shoulder.

"Keep it. Do you need a quarter for the subway?"

"Really, I'll be fine. I have some coins in my skirt pocket. Thank you."

"Let me walk with you."

She protested, but he insisted it was just a few steps.

"You never know when something like that can happen, do you?" he said as they walked.

"But it's such a shock when it happens."

They waited a moment until the light turned green, then crossed. When they reached the subway entrance, he asked, "Do you know where you're going?"

"Of course..." She looked at him, almost puzzled by his generosity. "You are kind."

She straightened herself, fixed a stray lock of hair, and proceeded down the stairs, holding onto the railing. Frederick watched her for a moment, then turned and headed back across the street to the pavement in front of the theater. His act of gallantry had left him feeling self-conscious. He lit another cigarette, opened his *Playbill* as if to browse through it, and remembered walking on Penn Street in downtown Reading forty years ago with his father and coming upon a man lying face-up on the sidewalk, blood trickling from his nose. He'd wanted to flee, but his father said, "No, we must stop and help him." It was nearly an hour before the ambulance carried him away, and whatever they'd planned that day (climbing the lookout atop the Pagoda or riding the dodgem cars in Carsonia Park) had to be postponed, "because," his father explained, "everyone you see—now Freddy, I want you to look around—" (Frederick raised his eyes from his *Playbill* and looked at the strangers congregating in front of the theater—a bearded man with horn-rimmed glasses, an attractive woman in pearls, two uniformed soldiers, the elderly Oriental couple from his row, a young man in white pants leaning by the entrance to the Sit 'n' Snack next door to the theater) "—every person you see is a son of God, whether he's a Catholic or not, and sometimes a man needs your help, and you've gotta be there to help him." *You've got to be there,* he repeated silently to himself, thinking it was really a *good* thing he'd be going to Reading this weekend, he might actually *enjoy* seeing his parents. And he *was,* after all, worried about his mother.

It was then he noticed the young man leaning by the entrance to the Sit 'n' Snack, adjacent to the theater, staring at him. He was small and dark. Compact. His gaze seemed mildly threatening. Frederick turned away, facing up Broadway to see waves of traffic and pedestrians coming towards him. He turned back to find the young man still leaning by the door, still staring. Now he was approaching, an indefinable smile on his lips. Frederick's heart began to pound as if this were yet another hoodlum, hot for some action (had he somehow mishandled himself with that poor woman a moment ago?), or an undercover policeman coming to inform him—

"Mind if I have a cigarette?"

It felt like a trap. Must be my sexual proclivity, he thought, written all over my face. He obliged without saying a word, afraid his voice might give him away (mustn't come across as "too musical"). The young man's smile disappeared as he accepted the cigarette and then—Frederick provided it without being asked—the light.

"Thanks. I'm Curt."

A stiff "hello" was all he dared offer. But the young man didn't ask for more, just stood his ground. He couldn't have been much taller than five feet, yet the space he occupied seemed entirely his own. Frederick turned again to look in the opposite direction. He felt uncomfortable, standing next to this attractive young man, both of them smoking in silence. After another minute he thought he might explain he had to go inside, the second act would be starting soon—but he didn't owe any kind of excuse, and why, of a sudden, did he feel as though to leave would be letting the boy down, abandoning him in some way? He decided he would extinguish his cigarette and say goodbye—no, better just to nod.

"How do you like the show?" the young man asked, picking a piece of tobacco from his tongue and flicking it away. He looked all of sixteen, but his voice was deep. He held himself with complete possession.

"Fine. I like it fine." Frederick meant to leave it at that but then added, "I've seen it before."

"You must *really* like it, then."

The sidewalk was emptying, it really was time to get back to his seat, and rather than engage further in a conversation he felt was pointless and probably dangerous, he muttered, "It's time," took a final drag on his cigarette, tossed it into the street, and turned on his heel to enter the theater, not waiting for a reply but feeling nonetheless the young man's presence behind him, worrying his abrupt departure might have been rude, wondering if he'd been unnecessarily cautious, fearing he'd let slip a golden opportunity (was it his imagination, or was this a pickup?), and as the lights went down there was a commotion in his aisle as people stood up—all other seats around him were occupied except for the one immediately to his right—a pair of tight white chinos brushed before him. It was the young man. He sat down and smiled again the same indefinable smile.

Frederick barely watched the second act. As soon as he took his seat, the young man allowed his thigh to touch Frederick's. He felt the tightness of the boy's pants and the taut muscles, the solid flesh beneath the fabric. He sat at war with himself, thinking he shouldn't indulge this kind of play (there was no doubt the boy knew what he was doing) but enjoying nonetheless the excitement, the danger—and the danger doubled the excitement. Now the young man moved his leg up and down, causing friction, and Frederick felt a pulse through his trousers and a swelling in his crotch.

Eliza was crying and cursing, asking Henry why he hadn't just left her in the gutter where he found her, for he was taking all the credit for her success at the ball, but Frederick heard and saw almost nothing as, minute by minute, the physical contact between them intensified. The young man placed his arm on the rest, allowing their arms to touch from elbow to fingertips, and caressed Frederick's little finger with his own finger. Frederick felt the hair on his hand stand up straight. Meanwhile, the young man kept moving his thigh up and down against Frederick, and Frederick gently but firmly pushed his thigh against the young man's, creating more friction, more tension.

You don't care. I know you don't care. You wouldn't care if I was dead. I'm nothing to you.

Frederick felt a shock as the young man placed his hand squarely upon his knee. He imagined his erection was visible to everyone around him, including the people on stage. But he didn't move his knee away. He did not, however, feel quite ready to place his hand on top of the boy's, though he very much wanted just now to hold his hand, to squeeze it and say, hold me close (*You and I will always…*)—but who was this brazen child to make him feel such things? If this were a trap he might find himself in serious trouble, he thought, trying to adjust his other leg to lessen the friction not just from the boy's leg pressing against his thigh, and from the boy's hand upon his knee, but from his own erection now rubbing against his inner thigh, causing acute arousal.

Just then Eliza pleaded with Henry not to hit her. The excitement was becoming unbearable, and Frederick felt he must do something to avert disaster. He gently pulled his leg out from underneath the young man's hand. But soon as he did, the young man renewed the pressure against his thigh and, simultaneously, placed his arm once again on the rest next to Frederick's arm and again began brushing Frederick's hand with his finger. Frederick pulled away again, removing his arm from the rest. He must put a stop to this, it wasn't right.

At last the cast assembled downstage and bowed. Frederick was glad to have something legitimate to do with his hands. Out of the corner of his eye, he saw the young man turn his head towards him, but Frederick maintained a steady gaze at the stage as he clapped vigorously for a performance he'd almost entirely missed. The young man clapped too, going so far as to stick two fingers into his mouth and give a whistle so coarse and piercing the woman in blue over to their right felt compelled to lean forward and shoot them a disapproving look.

The audience began vacating their seats. When Frederick gained the aisle he felt the young man on his heels. He continued moving with the crowd, trying to ignore the young man's presence. The crowd was thick and slow and Frederick felt great impatience to make his exit and start walking away from the theater, putting the whole escapade behind him. Now all he wanted was to go home, get a good night's rest (forget going to the Snake Pit), and take care of tomorrow's chores before leaving for Pennsylvania. At last he reached the sidewalk in front of the theater and started heading towards the subway.

"Hey, where you going?" The young man caught up alongside him. "I just wanted to talk. What are you doing now? I don't know your name."

Frederick stopped and turned as if to reprimand him but realized to do so would only further entangle him in a situation he now regretted. He looked at him without saying a word for one, two, three seconds, and the seconds felt like an eternity. Something inside him slipped, like falling off the edge of a cliff, and he'd wanted to kill himself only once, after the breakup with Jon (*Listen old man, just because I'm getting married doesn't mean...*), and here was something vital and fresh, something new, the boy was beautiful and he was making himself available ("YOU HAVE A DATE WITH THE GREEK GODS"), asking him what are you doing now, can we talk? He saw himself turn from the precipice, away from danger and possible death, but the boy's face held other dangers, other uncertainties, other mysteries, while in a deep, reassuring voice he was saying don't be afraid, come closer...

"I won't hurt you. I don't bite. I just wanted to talk, or at least say thanks for sharing in the theater. I enjoyed it a lot, and I thought maybe we could—"

"What did you say your name was?" He remembered full well the boy's name—Curt—but he wanted an excuse to introduce himself properly.

They exchanged names and shook hands. Curt pulled Frederick out of the way of the other theatergoers, beneath the shelter of an awning over an empty storefront next to the Sit 'n' Snack. "I'd like to see you again."

"That..." Frederick cleared his throat. "...should be possible."

Curt giggled, repeating Frederick's words, including his cough, and imitating his cautious intonation as if it were the cutest thing he'd ever heard, then said, "*Good!*"

Frederick grew tight-lipped. But the more he held back, the more intrigued he became. This boy knew his business. Knew how to handle himself. No doubt had done this kind of thing before. Frederick wanted, above all, to know how old he was, but to ask the question would introduce a note of defilement, as if he were a customer and the boy a prostitute (then the ugly thought occurred to him, what if he *is* a prostitute?).

Curt laughed at Frederick's second show of reticence, as if he were dealing with a mental incompetent.

"So? What do you wanna do?"

"I'm not free tonight, and I leave town tomorrow," Frederick said, thinking it was just as well he'd be away in Pennsylvania for the next seventy-two hours.

"When do you get back?"

"Saturday, but I'm not—"

"What about Sunday? I'm going to the beach, wanna join?" The beach felt like a trap. Not the sort of place one could leave easily if one had to. "Or afterward. How about eight or nine o'clock?"

Feeling he couldn't stall any longer, Frederick agreed. "I think I should call you to confirm in the early evening."

"Oh, that's too bad. I don't have a phone number, and I don't know if I'll be anywhere near a phone on Sunday."

"Aren't you coming home after the beach?" But he wished he hadn't asked, for he sounded like a domineering parent.

"No," Curt said with a wink and asked, instead, for Frederick's phone number.

Now was the moment of decision. Tearing off the back page of his *Playbill*—an ad for Chesterfield Kings showing a man (another Jon lookalike) and a woman, each holding a lit cigarette, facing each other across the open hood of an automobile, smiling—he pulled a pen from his breast pocket and wrote his phone number in the air over the smoking couple's heads. He proposed they meet under the arch at Washington Square, say around 8:30. He jotted that down too, folded the page in quarters and handed it to Curt.

"The arch at Washington Square, say around 8:30." Curt again imitated Frederick's exact words and intonation, this time with an adorable smile.

Frederick warily held out his hand.

Curt just looked him in the eye, ignoring the proffered hand. "I think I want to kiss you goodbye, Frederick," he said, and before Frederick could protest or make a move, Curt grabbed his shoulders and pressed his lips hard against Frederick's. He then turned and walked down Broadway towards the pulsing lights of Times Square. Frederick walked hastily in the other direction, trying not to make eye contact with anyone, fearing a hundred New Yorkers had just seen two men kiss. At the intersection, however, he looked back, hoping to see Curt still walking towards the square. But he was gone.

Frederick felt as if he'd just been rejected.

CHAPTER TWO

FREDERICK CHECKED HIS WATCH (PLENTY OF TIME BEFORE HIS FIVE O'CLOCK train) as he rode the elevator to the fifth floor men's department at Gimbels. Of course I won't meet him on Sunday, he said to himself, astonished he'd even considered it for a minute. He'd gone straight home from the theater last night and taken a shower as if to wash himself of the dirty escapade with Curt, then lay awake in bed until 2:00 AM replaying the encounter in his mind. How had he succumbed so easily, so quickly to his…? "Charms" was hardly the word. He thought of the young man's muscular thigh, the firm but gentle touch of his finger, the silky brown hair that brushed across his forehead and down over his ears, the devious but irresistible look in his eyes when he said—No! It was a sordid little game, instigated by a juvenile delinquent for purposes Frederick could only guess. Imagine the nerve, he thought as the elevator doors opened, the audacity, the reckless-ness (he chewed the flesh around the nail of his right thumb) to kiss me on a crowded street in Times Square.

He took a deep breath. Stacks of folded shirts, racks of suit coats, beds of socks, rows of shoes, trees of hats—how pleasing, he felt, the neatness and order of the cool, clean-smelling store. There was something about the smell, especially, of new men's clothing that stimulated him. He gazed down upon a table laden with neckties. Blue diamonds, red octagons, purple chevrons, green gazebos, stripes of pink, gold, black, and silver, plaids of brown, mustard, and gray, rainbow spirals and onion domes, dancing locks and keys, cartoon ducks and palm trees, cotton coats of arms, silken branching leaves and flowers, rayon bursts of coconut, lemon, mango. They ravished his senses.

"You know what you're lookin' for?" A gangly man with a gap-toothed smile appeared before him.

"A present for my father turning seventy-five. I'm thinking contemporary but not too flashy." He thought for a second. "Something to remind him…" He meant to say *of me*. "…of New York."

"Does age matter? Maybe at seventy-five he's ready for somethin' he never tried before, waddaya think?" From the table of neckties, the salesman (Will was the name on his lapel) fished up a specimen half-red, half-blue, with an atomic symbol embroidered in gold. "And see here, if you look close, a purple spiral on top of the atom."

It wasn't the tie Frederick would have chosen ("He have a sense of humor?" Will asked), but it appealed to him.

"I'll take it."

As Frederick watched him gift-wrap the tie, he felt an upsurge of excitement and hope. His father was always difficult to buy for, and he never seemed to care much for the things Frederick gave him. This time might be different. Just then he spied another customer—or was it another clerk?—sitting on a stool at the end of the counter. He seemed to be observing their interaction, with disapproval or benignity Frederick couldn't tell. But what was there to be ashamed of? He hadn't said or done anything inappropriate. Unless it was the timbre of his voice. Frederick had a perpetual fear that he *sounded* queer. Sometimes he wondered if normal men had a sixth sense about inverts. He looked the gentleman in the eye. Dangerous to do so, but it happened before he realized what he'd done ("Come again," Will said in a singsong melody, but Frederick only muttered a baritone "yes" so as not to sound too friendly). Unless as sometimes happened, he thought, taking the elevator back down to the street, the look of disapproval he suspected in the other man's face was in fact a look of camaraderie. Or even desire. Men were inscrutable that way. He remembered Curt's *Mona Lisa* smile.

Better to expect nothing, he thought, now on the sidewalk lighting a cigarette, *or the worst*, and there won't be any unpleasant surprises.

Thirty-second Street teemed with people spilling into the street against the onrushing traffic. Frederick allowed himself to be pulled along with the crowd. Delivery boys on bicycles, foreign tourists pointing with maps, men toting briefcases, women yanking children by the hand, taxis, buses, cars, trucks, whistles blowing, horns honking, obscenities shouted, all mingled together and permeated the air like the unpleasant smell of urine that met his nostrils the closer he approached Penn Station. The unbroken row of Doric columns across the façade gave it the appearance of a massive stone jail. Or a tomb. The central hexastyle portico barely projected from the line of adjacent columns, reinforcing the station's overbearing attitude of power and pomposity. Almost to relieve his eye, Frederick looked up at the Statler Hotel—one, two, three, four, he counted the flights as he scaled the building, thinking, as he always did whenever he came to this neighbor-hood, of Jon—six, seven, eight—of the room they shared that afternoon during the war. Where was he today? If they ever ran into each other, he wondered, scooting around a workman unloading cases of soda pop onto the sidewalk and hearing voices chanting, what would he say? Something about "shame"—"destroy"—the protest!

He stopped and stood like a post on the corner of Thirty-second Street and Seventh Avenue, at the foot of the Statler Hotel directly across from Penn Station, commuters swirling around him, fanning out across the av-enue, running against the light. A line of well-dressed protesters walked in a circle beneath the giant pillars. Crossing Seventh Avenue, one, two, three, four, he counted the pillars to calm his nerves—he wasn't a joiner, didn't wish to participate in any public protest, didn't care if Penn Station was torn down—nine, ten, eleven, twelve—some of his colleagues from Emerson, Root were sure to be there, not to mention Ada Louise Huxtable, Lewis Mumford, probably a dozen important people—nineteen, twenty, twenty-one, twenty-two—so many people on the sidewalk in front of the station, it was hard to tell who was part of the picket line and who was just passing by—twenty-seven, twenty-eight, twenty-nine, thirty. Neatly hand-painted signs bobbed up and down.

ACTION GROUP FOR BETTER ARCHITECTURE IN NEW YORK
PRESERVE OUR HERITAGE
PROGRESS IS QUALITY NOT NOVELTY
DON'T DEMOLISH IT! POLISH IT!
SHAME!
ANGER
Deborah emerged from the picket line.

"You made it!" She wrapped him in an embrace and kissed him, then noticed he was carrying a suitcase and asked where he was going.

"I've got a five o'clock train to Philly, I'm—"

"Oh, there's Seymour!" Having spotted her husband amid the protesters, she pulled him by the elbow down the picket line. "There's something I want to discuss with you later."

Seymour waved a hand while shaking a sign that read "BE A PENN PAL."

"Look what I found!"

"I didn't know you two were lovers! Fred, half the men at this protest are here because they used to date my wife."

"I made a few phone calls. Can I help it if I wasn't born yesterday?"

Tightening her grip on Frederick's arm, she pulled him into the picket line along with her husband. Commuters swerved around and sometimes pushed right through the line. Most seemed utterly indifferent to the protesters, even as young secretaries with clipboards and middle-aged men in pinstriped suits carrying stacks of flyers buttonholed passersby, trying to convince them to sign a petition or even just pay a minute of attention. This was the last place on earth Frederick wanted to be. He didn't believe in the cause. Didn't believe in causes, period. Then he laid eyes on someone he recognized from the firm, talking with another man as he approached. He'd seen the swarthy young man occasionally around the office (the boss's son?), though they'd never properly met.

Seymour made the introductions: "Alan Emerson, Fred Bailey, I think you two know each other. Jordan Houk, Fred Bailey."

Deborah embraced and kissed both Alan and Jordan—she seemed on intimate terms with everyone. Jordan immediately informed the group, as if resuming a prior conversation, of his latest efforts as the lawyer for AGBA-NY to persuade the City Planning Commission to withhold the necessary permit to build the new sports arena on the Penn Station site. "And they said they *were indeed* concerned with the adequacy of service rendered to the traveling public, but in the absence of some substantial reduction in service the proposal to demolish the station doesn't require the Commission's prior approval."

Seymour, Alan, and Jordan launched into an animated debate about the meaning of the words "service to the traveling public," specifically whether aesthetics and the sense of self-worth conferred by a grand port of entry such as Penn Station counted as public service. They ridiculed everyone who disagreed with them—Robert Moses, the Planning Commission, the unions.

"Obviously we need to educate the public on architectural matters," Deborah said, "but, really, how are we to do that?"

Frederick was struck by her use of the word "we." Was she so committed to her husband's work?

"All anyone seems to care about is the columns!" Seymour mentioned a number of proposals for salvaging them—a mall in Battery Park, a classical landscape in Flushing Meadows.

"But there are real reasons," Deborah said, "why Penn Station is headed for the dustbin. We can't ignore them."

This led to a debate about the architect Charles McKim's intentions, his attitudes toward cities in general ("he hated tall buildings"), the kinship between Penn Station and the great train stations of Europe ("except Penn Station was always redundant because the trains were electric from the start and never needed a lofty train shed"), the question of whether Americans were even capable of appreciating, much less maintaining and preserving, a piece of architecture that makes reference to buildings from other cultures or eras—"and what is 'modern,' anyhow?" Jordan asked rhetorically. "Modern doesn't stay modern forever. Penn Station is total architecture. Not just Greek columns here, Baths of Caracalla there, with a little bit of Brandenburg Gate thrown in for fun." (For the first time in his life Frederick realized the main entrance to Penn Station made visual reference to the Brandenburg Gate in Berlin. How could he have failed to see it?) "It makes a single, coherent argument. You move through the neoclassical spaces, you wind up in the modern glass and steel concourse. McKim is actually telling a story about the progress from the old—"

Just then a passerby interrupted: "What's all this about?"

"Don't you want to save this magnificent building?" Seymour shouted.

"What building?" came the brusque reply, and he continued on his way.

Seymour spluttered something about how *people can't even see Penn Station anymore*, but Deborah took hold of his hand to calm him down.

"It's because the Manhattan street grid doesn't encourage people to look at their surroundings," Alan offered.

"It's also because Penn Station is so rundown," Jordan said. "Just look how black and filthy it is! You ignore a building when it gets like this. Most people have no memory of how Penn Station used to look. It was pink, for God's sake, when it opened in 1910."

Now Frederick caught a glimpse of Philip Johnson crossing the picket line and coming this way.

"Philip dear!" Deborah cooed and began comparing notes with him on who was there, who was who, who'd gone AWOL ("Have you seen Jane?" "Jacobs? Yes, she's…over there somewhere"). After a couple of minutes, "Do you mind if I cut in?" Seymour said, then he and Philip exchanged words about the press conference prior to the protest.

Deborah sidled up to Frederick. "You've met Philip before, haven't you? Weren't you at that gathering at the Glass House two, three years ago?"

Frederick didn't like to be reminded—he'd been invited to a salon at Johnson's Connecticut compound, Philip made what Frederick took to be an advance, Frederick demurred (well-preserved for his age, he remembered thinking, but not my type, and anyway aren't he and David Warner together?), Philip snubbed him the rest of the evening, and he was never invited to Connecticut again.

"I don't think there's anything we can do about it," Philip was saying. "Someone's got to buy Penn Station, someone committed to saving it. Or it needs to be adapted to some other use like the Jefferson Courthouse."

"Which was just voted one of the ugliest buildings in the city," Seymour said.

"In 1880, it was voted one of the five *most beautiful* buildings in the whole United States," Philip countered. "Tastes change. What's beautiful today looks ugly tomorrow and vice versa." But he had to return to a friend on the other side of the picket line ("Call you tomorrow," Deborah said with a peck on his cheek), and the conversation carried on among the men as he made a quick retreat.

"Philip's a delight," Deborah said to Frederick, "when you can catch him. We should all get together sometime."

He checked his watch.

"Must you go?"

Now the men were laughing at a lewd joke. "But let's not get carried away," Seymour could be heard to say, "historic preservation isn't about effeminate men mooning over some antique chifforobe once owned by Aunt Esmerelda."

"Speaking of effeminate men, who's the latest Mrs. Philip Johnson?"

"Tell me about your affair in Pennsylvania," Deborah said, as if to distract him. "Remind me where your family lives?"

"Reading." But she needn't have tried—his attention was fatally focused on what the men were saying.

"I'm not familiar with it."

("You'd better watch your back, Al.")

"It's one of the railroads on the Monopoly board."

"I always called it 'reeding'!"

"It's pronounced 'redding.' Everyone makes that mistake."

("He has a penchant for younger men.")

"And what's the occasion?"

A family reunion, he said, in honor of his father's seventy-fifth birthday.

"I rarely hear you talk about your parents. Your mother—she's still living, isn't she?"

("You could end up the next Mrs. Johnson!")

A siren pierced the air as an ambulance raced down the avenue, all other traffic pulling aside to let it pass, and for several seconds Frederick saw but couldn't hear Alan, Jordan, and Seymour laughing together in dumbshow.

"What's that?"

"I said your mother is still living, isn't she?"

Yes, he said.

("I'm not *that* ambitious!" Alan said. More comradely laughter.)

"And how are they, your parents?"

"I haven't seen them in quite a while. I only know what my sister tells me. She lives in Reading and sees them often, naturally." (Now the men were talking about whether the automobile industry would put the railroads out of business.) "My father is sharp as ever. In amazing health for someone his age. Walks several miles a day in every kind of weather."

"And your mother?"

The picket line had grown steadily since Frederick's arrival, and now he and Deborah were separated from Seymour and the others by a group of newly arrived protesters. Frederick welcomed the added distance from the men.

"She's seventy-seven and slipping. Physically she's very frail. My sister tells me she gets more confused by the day."

"Listen, I forget what I did *this morning*!"

Frederick was feeling sharply uncomfortable. "I better run. Do me a favor, give my regards to Seymour and the others?"

"Of course, but—I want to make you a proposition."

He was already heading towards the entrance.

PENNSYLVANIA STATION

"Come for dinner next week!"

The words echoed in his ear as he entered the long corridor of shops leading to the waiting room. A black Cadillac DeVille sat sphinx-like on a platform as people streamed around it in both directions. Protected by a low railing, it looked like an exhibit in the dinosaur room of the Museum of Natural History—except, Frederick thought, it's the way of the future. He noticed John Ryan's Men's Shop was gone. Half the businesses in the gallery, in fact, were shuttered.

Crossing the ornate vestibule at the end of the gallery, he nearly had his eyes put out by the mushroom of fluorescent light emanating from the ticket counter in front of him. He paused atop the staircase leading down into the massive waiting room and noticed, for the first time since it was installed a few years ago, how the modern ticket counter actually had the effect of decapitating the lofty space above it. Though high as the nave of Saint Peter's Cathedral in Rome, the waiting room of Penn Station now couldn't be seen above the level of the low-slung ticket counter, so blinding was its light and so distracting its effect. The design of the counter was better suited, he thought, to the TWA terminal at Idlewild—supersonic, saw-toothed, suspended from fans of cables bolted to the Corinthian columns that flanked what had been the passage from the waiting room to the train concourse. Gracefully sweeping movement, it was clear, was what McKim's original design provided for, but movement was precisely what the space-age ticket counter now impeded as bottlenecks of commuters accumulated on either side of it.

Every other modern "convenience" added to the waiting room, Frederick now realized, looked similarly intrusive: large aluminum-framed, backlit poster boxes advertising jewelry, cigars, international travel destinations, steak dinners; plastic vitrines containing hats and shoes; stark black-and-white telephone booths; gimcrack stainless-steel kiosks and shops; come-hither cigarette and soft-drink machines—all of it giving a 42nd Street tawdriness to what had been one of the great uplifting public spaces in New York. Whatever Penn Station was, whatever it was intended to be, he thought as he watched throngs of people shoving their way to the concourse to find their gates—but the concourse, he knew, would only be more of the same—crazed crowds of people rushing in every direction amidst billboards and booths and shops and candy counters and temporary lockers and not nearly enough benches to sit upon—however noble Penn Station appeared on Charles McKim's drafting board, the reality, after fifty-some-odd years, he had to admit, was indisputably corrupt.

"*Dixie Squire, with stops in Trenton, Philadelphia, Baltimore, Washington, Richmond, and points south, ready on Track 15.*"

Anyway, he said to himself, descending the stairs, no matter what happens at home with my family, it'll be a relief to escape New York for the weekend.

And it was just as well Curt had no telephone. Sketchy little hustler, he thought. I simply won't show up.

CHAPTER THREE

FREDERICK'S FATHER WAS SEATED IN HIS FAVORITE WING CHAIR, OPENING gifts. His throne, Frederick thought, wondering why his mother never had a chair of her own in the living room. He glanced into the dining room and saw her sitting with the aunts at the table on one of those uncomfortable, straight-backed Chippendales.

"And what have we here? A framed photograph of the Banks family! Thank you, Emily dear. And Bob and Tim and Kelly."

This was met with enthusiasm and passed from hand to hand around the room, the aunts remarking how grown-up Kelly had become and how it would be her time soon to marry now that her older brother was engaged ("taken care of" was the expression they used).

Frederick stood near the back of the group gathered around his father, which suited him fine because it afforded the chance to take in the entire downstairs without being the object of anyone's attention. The furniture mostly dated from the 1920s, he noted, the last time his parents spent any money on decoration. The lace doilies on the armrests and side tables were yellow with age, though everything was neatly maintained. Hanging on the wall above the dining table was a large copy, luridly colorful, of Leonardo's *Last Supper*, made years ago by Fred Sr., a "Sunday painter," as they said in the family. On the upright piano, a myriad of photos of himself and Marge from infancy through young adulthood. The largest was a studio portrait taken in 1918 when he was three, dressed in a sailor suit, hugging a balloon. He looked like a porcelain doll, like one of Mama's ceramic Hummel figures, he thought, glancing at the china cabinet full of knickknacks.

A burst of laughter came from the staircase where his cousins' kids, all somewhere in their mid-twenties, sat like a flock of pigeons, giggling over Tim's wedding and what kind of dress the bride-to-be should wear. Thinking *they* seemed awfully young, and then trying to place them in his mind next to Curt, Frederick realized all over again the absurdity of having made a date with the boy. Even the youngest of his cousins, Philip McDevitt, who had to be at least thirty by now (Aunt Sara always called him her "Depression baby" because he came along at "just the *worst* moment possible," and she and Uncle George would laugh—Frederick envied the easy jocularity of the McDevitts as opposed to the Baileys, who were a quieter, more keep-to-themselves kind of people—in that sense he was a Bailey through and through)—even *Philip* belonged to a different generation altogether. "Depression baby"? Frederick had been born in the middle of the *Great War*! He bit the flesh of his thumb until he drew blood.

"And this is from…what is this?" Frederick's heart swelled. His father tore open the card. When he saw that it was from his son, his smile contracted ever so slightly (probably no one but Frederick noticed) and he merely nodded in his direction. He opened the package. "It's a tie," he said, holding it up for inspection. "Thank you." Frederick came forward, bent over his father and opened his arms for an embrace, but the old man, remaining seated, abruptly thrust out his right hand for a handshake.

"Unique gift idea, Fred," Chuck Parisi said, barely keeping a straight face.

"Man can always use a tie" Fred Sr. said, though Frederick couldn't tell where at that moment his sympathies lay.

"No, I *don't* think they have the same values we do."

Frederick's cousins Steve and Bill Galen, instead of watching Uncle Fritz open presents, were arguing over the Russians.

"I'm talking about *human* values. You really mean to say they don't have the same concern for life, the same instinct for self-preservation?"

"It's not the same as a concern for *life*."

"You think the Russians would rather see the whole world destroyed than negotiate with the American gov—"

"Yes! Their system is evil. They're bent on dominating the world, and if that means destroying half the world to do it, they'll do it. All this liberal egghead nonsense about human feelings and community…"

Seeing her brothers heading for their usual standoff, Emily got up from the dining table, where she'd been telling the aunts about Tim's wedding, all the while keeping her eyes and ears on "the boys," as she persisted in calling her now-middle-aged younger brothers, and entered the parlor.

"Can't we just have a nice visit for once? Does it always have to turn into a contest?"

"Aw, c'mon, Em, we're just talking."

"No one wants to hear about the Russians on Uncle Fritz's birthday."

"I don't mind hearing about the Russians on my birthday!" Fred Sr. said, the tie still in his hands, and everyone roared. The conversation proceeded in spite of Emily's attempts to make peace. The Russians led to Martin Luther King, Jr. and the Southern Christian Leadership Conference, which in turn led to Pope John and the Second Vatican Council. The recurring theme was that things in this country were steadily getting worse.

"What'll be next?" Fred Sr. was baiting his nephew Bill, the only man in the family willing to stand up for the liberal point of view. "Lady priests?"

Bill's wife Liz asked, "Would it be so bad if someday we had women priests?"

Shouts of laughter and outrage filled the room.

Thinking Emily was right—whenever Steve and Bill got together, everyone, male and female, young and old, got conscripted into their fraternal dueling match, and then there was no point in trying to engage in adult conversation, but in less than forty-eight hours, he reminded himself as he entered the dining room and saw the chair Emily had vacated, I'll be back in New York (he wasn't sure how to break off the engagement with Curt—it would be rude not to show up; on the other hand, he simply couldn't go through with it)—Frederick went to his mother and sat beside her. The aunts were talking about people they knew from fifty years ago. Clare sat staring vaguely at the centerpiece of flowers on the table.

"How are you, Mama?"

"I don't know who they're talking about."

"It's okay, once they get going about who married whom and his second cousin on his mother's side once removed, the rest of us don't have a prayer." He smiled.

"It's so good to have you home," she said. "How long can you stay?"

He'd gone over this with her upon his arrival Thursday night, and then again several times yesterday and earlier today. "Remember I told you, I must go back to New York tomorrow."

"When was the last time you were home?" she asked, as if to a stranger.

"Last summer."

"You should come more often." She put her hand over his hand and squeezed it. He was surprised by the strength of her grip. Her hand was cool and dry. Her nails were badly bitten, like his own. "Do you know that I love you?"

She'd already told him so half a dozen times today.

"Clare, you givin' your little boy a hard time?" Aunt Peggy asked, sensing tension. (Why did all the women in the family speak as if all the men were infants? he wondered.)

"He loves his mother, don't you, Freddy?"

"Sure, Ma," he said as she gave him a kiss.

"How long has it been?" She looked as if she were asking it for the first time.

"It's been a year, Mama," he said slowly and with emphasis.

"It's so good to see you. How long will you be home?"

"Mama! You keep asking me the same questions over and over!"

"Until tomorrow, dear," a voice came from behind. At what point his father had entered the dining room Frederick didn't know. "He has to go back to New York early to prepare for an important meeting on Monday." The old man joined them at the table. "So tell us, what's new? Haven't really had a chance to talk to you yet."

Flustered, all he could say at that moment was, "I'm fine. Work is fine."

"Where do you work?" his mother asked.

"I work at an architecture firm. In New York."

"You remember, Clare, he's an architect."

"I work at a firm called Emerson, Root and Sons. It's going well."

"They made you a partner yet?" his father asked.

"No."

"Is there some normal progression where you'll eventually become partner, or is it more merit-based?"

Feeling an implied criticism in the question, Frederick answered, "It's a little more complicated than that." He tried to explain it wasn't just about merit, but neither was there a routine procedure by which one was made partner, there were other factors that entered into it, and in any case he liked his current position because it allowed him to do one of the things he most enjoyed, which was—but every time Frederick tried to articulate a complete thought, his father was on to another question.

"They pay you enough? …Like your co-workers? …Your boss a good man?"

"He's—" ("Good" was hardly the word he would have used to describe Wilbur Emerson.) "—a decent boss."

"How's New York?"

"New York?"

"You live in New York now?" his mother asked.

"I've lived there since 1934. When I entered Columbia College. I've been there for twenty-six years, Mama."

"Twenty-six years! That's a long time! You must like it there." The aunts and even Fred Sr. laughed in spite of themselves. "Fritz, don't you remember the World's Fair in New York? They said in fifty years, trains will be obsolete and everyone will drive automobiles at speeds of—"

"You know the main train station in New York, Penn Station?" Frederick interrupted, hoping a little story might focus her attention. "Thursday evening as I was going to catch my train, there was a protest in front of the station. The railroad plans to tear it down, so a group of architects were protesting—"

"Is that right? D'you have a girl?"

Patience. "No, Mama, I don't."

"Why not?"

"I guess I haven't met the right person yet."

"Oh, now, a nice young fella like you? I guess it's hard to meet the right kind of girl in New York."

"I don't know about that, it's just—"

"All kinds of girls in New York," Fred. Sr. said with a mischievous twinkle.

"But not the right kind for Freddy," Clare defended her son.

"What about that woman we met the one time we came to the opera?" Fred Sr. said. "What was her name?"

"You mean Deborah?"

"I always thought you and she—"

"Pop, she's a married woman."

"I'm sure when there's a girl, we'll find out," Clare said as if to reassure him.

"Sure, Mama."

Then his father asked, "Ever hear from your friend Jonathan?"

"Jonathan…" he said tentatively as if he were trying to place the name. He needed to take his time on this one.

"Jonathan Pryce."

"Yes—I—no, I haven't."

"Used to be good friends, weren't you?"

"Yes, but…we lost touch."

"Isn't that a shame," Clare said.

Uncertain where the conversation was headed but sensing the need to stall, "What is?" he asked. The aunts seemed to hang on each word.

"That you don't talk to your friend anymore."

Everyone sat quietly. He feared they were thinking the truth and had known it forever. "Just one of those things."

"I'd like another glass of wine," Clare said.

Peggy said she'd better wait until dinner, she seemed tired.

Raising her voice, "I am *not* tired, I want another glass!"

Fred Sr. told Frederick to get her another glass but whispered, "Water it down."

Frederick went into the kitchen and asked Marge where she kept the white wine. (Forty-eight hours, he said to himself.)

"If it's for Mama, I'll take care of it."

"We need to add water."

"I know. One glass and she hardly remembers her own name. Do me a favor, will you? Check on Markie. He's up in the spare room."

Glad to have a reason to absent himself from the party, and thinking how they would all just croak if he ever came home one day with someone like—well, someone like Curt on his arm (but that wasn't reason enough to keep their appointment tomorrow night), Frederick went upstairs to his old room. It had been refurbished as a guest room but was otherwise given over to storage, old appliances, out-of-season clothing. The only remnants from the days when it was his room were his tiny bed and a painting made by his father of the Pagoda on Mount Penn. He used to love that picture. He and everyone in the family always referred to the Pagoda as "Freddy's Pagoda."

Markie was splayed on the floor surrounded by Legos. He approached the child gingerly, at first not saying a word, and Markie, accordingly, felt no need to acknowledge his uncle. Frederick sat in the old rocker and watched for several minutes, fascinated by the child's absorption. At length, he asked what he was making. Markie said it was supposed to be a castle. What kind of castle? Frederick asked. A castle for my soldiers, came the answer. And what are they going to do in the castle? Frederick asked.

"Just..." Markie seemed to mull it over. "...play by themselves." He told a convoluted story about three soldiers who ran away from battle and found a castle in the woods abandoned by the king who was killed in the war. The soldiers killed the king and destroyed half the castle, which was why it lay in pieces all over the floor, so now they had to rebuild the castle, only this time they were going to make it better. They each wanted to have their own room and their own kitchen and a big room where they could keep their weapons and then a lookout post on top where they could see the enemy whenever they were approaching.

"So you have to build the castle so the enemy can't attack."

"Yeah."

"How about if we build a strong base with sloping walls? That way, the castle won't collapse if there's an earthquake." They set about collecting all the white pieces they could find.

"And let's make a wall at the top with openings so the soldiers can drop stones down on any intruders."

"Okay!"

"And then we can put the bedrooms and the kitchens and the meeting rooms on top."

"And a lookout post on the tippy-top!"

Handling plastic bricks with his nephew felt strangely energizing after hours of conversation with the adults. He was intrigued by Markie's concentration, broken every now and then by a stream of babble about the wars and the soldiers and trucks and dinosaurs, all the while the sloping walls of the castle rose, row upon row of toy bricks, until it was time to lay the platform for the keep on top.

Markie asked what a keep was.

"That's what you call the private residence on top of the base. It's called the castle keep. It means a safe place to live. It keeps you safe." Frederick looked at the child and wondered what it would be like to have someone like Markie to take care of—to love and keep safe—all his life.

The sound of applause could be heard from downstairs. Frederick checked his watch and was surprised to see that he'd been with Markie for almost half an hour. Aunt Theresa was playing the piano. He used to love when she performed for the family.

"Wanna come downstairs with me?"

Markie said no as if he only half heard his uncle's words.

Frederick said he'd call him when it was time for dinner, and Markie gave no reply.

In the parlor Theresa was showing the young people how she used to play piano for the silent movies.

"The lovers," she said, and played a sentimental air with loads of arpeggios and trills. Her large hands moved easily up and down the keyboard. As she played she turned her head to her audience to explain what happened next.

"Then in comes the villain!" Slashing minor chords interrupted the lyrical melody.

"Shock!" Two sharp dissonant chords, and her hands flew up from the keys, tracing an arc through the air, and fell to her lap.

"What to do? Where to go? We must run!" A galloping series of chords as the lovers fled the villain, first on horseback, then a speeding train.

"But the train hits a broken rail on the viaduct and goes tumbling over the edge!" Her fingers slid down the scales from the top of the keyboard to the bottom.

"Where are the lovers? Did they survive? Are they dead?"

Then the sweet, sentimental melody.

"The lovers! They were safe in the station the whole time, while the *villain* plunged off the viaduct with the train. And they lived happily ever after! The end!" A final flourish with chords pounded out at opposite ends of the keyboard. The entire house erupted in wild hoots and applause.

"Play the lovers again!" someone shouted.

"No more lovers," Marge said, wiping her hands on her apron as she entered the parlor, "we're eating in fifteen minutes. Fred, where's Markie?" He assured her he was fine, playing upstairs with his Lego set, and then she asked him to start the exodus to the dining table.

When everyone was assembled, Chuck Parisi clinked his glass and stood up. "Aunt Hilda has asked me to say grace," he announced, and Frederick felt a twinge of jealousy. "Bless us, oh Lord…" Chuck began, and to Frederick's surprise the entire family immediately joined in, "…and these Thy gifts which we are about to receive from Thy bounty through Christ our Lord, Amen."

"Here's to Uncle Fritz," Sally said, and everyone raised a glass. A dozen "happy birthday's" bubbled up from all corners of the table.

"And thanks for bringing Freddy home," Aunt Barb said to shouts of "Hear, hear!" and "Cheers!" all around. "Your parents are so happy to see you," she whispered in his ear as the family dove into the meal. "Your mother misses you a lot. You know that, don't you, honey?" He looked at Clare. There she sat between Peggy (boasting how she could eat, talk on the telephone, and watch the Andy Williams program simultaneously) and Chuck (doing his best, derisive impression of President Kennedy), eating small bites of food and sipping her wine from a glass that trembled in her hand. He felt a tidal wave of sorrow for her. She was feeble. Alone. He should have made a point of sitting next to her to help her through the meal.

"I do, Aunt Barb."

He thought of how his father tended to her needs every morning, noon, and night ("You've gotta be there to help"). There the old man sat in silence on the other side of his sisters, who were talking about their parents, and how they found Grandmother in the bathtub the morning after she'd had her stroke.

He looked down to the opposite end of the table at his sister. She, too, sat quietly in the midst of an animated conversation among Sally, Liz, and Catherine. They were talking about movie stars. Occasionally Marge would nod or make a one-word reply, but mostly she kept to herself. He wondered if it was exhaustion from all the preparation. But no, he thought, she's been sullen since she arrived.

And so there you have it. The Frederick Bailey Sr. family. Disjoint, at odds and ends, none of us particularly enjoying ourselves, each of us ultimately withdrawn and unhappy (he wanted to bite his nail but thought, Not in front of the family).

Now Marge was gone from the table. Frederick asked Sally where she went.

"Outside to…" She mimed the act of smoking a cigarette.

He discreetly absented himself and found his sister alone in the backyard, sitting on a discarded lawn chair.

She gave him a cigarette and lit it for him. She apologized there wasn't another chair, but he said he didn't mind, he'd sit on the ground.

"How are you?" he asked.

"I'm fine, but tired. I think I wasn't quite ready for this party."

"You've done a lot."

"Mom can't do anything. You see what it's like to be with her? She needs constant attention."

"It must be a huge burden on you."

"And Pop's not getting any younger, is he? One of these days I'm gonna find them unconscious with the gas turned on, or God forbid—" She burst into tears. Frederick got up to put his arm around her.

"It's okay, I'm sure they're not—"

"I'm pregnant." She turned her face away from him.

He shook her gently as if to cheer her up. "Well, that's wonderful!"

"It's terrible. I don't think I love Chuck anymore."

He was stunned. So he wasn't the only one in the family whose loves were painful and broken. "Did something happen?"

"No, I just don't love him anymore. I married him because he fought in the war and was handsome and funny, but he's not so handsome anymore and everyone *else* seems to think he's a laugh riot. All I see is a former high school football star who doesn't have any idea what I feel."

"How is he with Markie?"

"Markie, thank God, is in his own world half the time. Chuck's not a terrible father. He loves Markie, I guess. I'm not sure what love means." She looked at her brother now. Her eyes were full of tears. "I used to admire him. I respected him. I don't anymore, and that breaks my heart because…I'm afraid it's really over between us."

"Have you thought about what you want to do?"

"I don't want this baby. I know it sounds crazy, but I have to make a decision. I'm nearly one month pregnant."

Frederick was silent. Never had his sister confided in him like this about her own life, her own decisions.

"Is there something I can do?" he asked, not expecting she'd have an answer.

"You could be more a part of this family. You're never here. You live completely for yourself."

"I think we both live the lives we want to live," he said, suddenly defensive.

"Yes, we know, architecture is the love of your life!"

Now he was indignant. "My life is more than just architecture." It was the first time he'd heard himself say it.

"I don't know anything about your life." She gave him a confrontational look and his blood went cold. Was she about to…? "I write to you, I keep you informed about what's happening here, and…I guess I always hope you'll respond or, I don't know, share something in return." But rather than give him a chance to do so now, she put out her cigarette in the grass and stood up. "I'm sorry for saying this. Don't hate me and stay away another whole year. I have to help get dessert."

She turned and went inside.

Frederick sat in the back yard a few minutes longer as the kitchen filled with people and plates and silver clinking. He saw Marge through the kitchen window starting to rinse the dirty dishes. He bit the nail on his right index finger. Was it true he only lived for himself? He thought of Curt and their conversation in front of the theater two nights ago and their date tomorrow night in Washington Square Park. His family had so little notion of what his life consisted of. What he cared about. What he wanted. Perhaps he *would* meet Curt, if only to say he didn't think it was a good idea, their seeing more of each other.

He went back into the house. The aunts remained at the table, and his mother sat distracted as they now recounted stories about their childhood, about Fritz and how he was the apple of everyone's eye. What a beautiful child he was. How spoiled he was. What a fancy dresser he was. They laughed to think how they spoiled their precious baby brother.

Philip carried the cake into the dining room, having already started singing "Happy Birthday" from the kitchen. Little by little, the rest of the family picked up the song. Fred Sr. blew at the candles weakly and a chorus of "Oh!" came up from the table.

"Make a wish!"

"It's too late, the candles are out."

A crush of people moved from behind Fred Sr. to take their seats, including Frederick, who decided there was no harm in having one drink or a meal with Curt, but he would see that it went no further—no sex, no second date, he would be firm about that, when suddenly a chair toppled over and Clare fell to the floor face-first, her wine glass flying from her hand and shattering clear across the kitchen. There was a collective shout as everyone heard the crash.

"Help! Fritz!" Clare cried.

George and Tim dove towards her.

"I'm dying!"

Frederick advanced towards her as well, but Chuck pushed through from the kitchen and thrust out his arm to bar the way, telling Frederick and the others to stand back, don't touch her. He knelt down and gently placed his hands on either side of her head. "It's all right, Mama," he said, "it's just a bump, you're gonna be all right."

"No, I'm not! Fritz!"

"He's right here," Chuck said.

"I'm here, Clare," Fred Sr. said but couldn't get near her for all the people crowding around.

"Where's Fritz? I'm dying!"

Frederick watched the room rearrange itself, watched his brother-in-law turn his mother over onto her back, saying, Mama, it's all right, you're gonna be all right. Tears rolled down her cheeks.

"Fritz!" she called again. Then softer, "I'm dying."

Frederick looked out the dining room window. He heard his mother's voice. Freddy, telephone for you. *Nothing has to change between us. You and I will always... It's just that with Rachel...*

"I'm dying," she whimpered.

"It's okay, Mama," Chuck said. He called her "Mama" and he wasn't even her real son. And his wife was planning to abort his child.

"We just want to sit you up. Someone get some ice. Everything's gonna be fine."

Frederick looked at his mother sitting on the floor with blood on her face.

"I'm dying."

He would have to take a later train to New York tomorrow, he couldn't leave his mother like this. He bit the hangnail on his index finger. The question was, could he still make it to Washington Square Park by 8:30?

CHAPTER FOUR

FREDERICK DIDN'T LIKE TO THINK HE'D CHOSEN CURT, A PERFECT STRANGER, over his own mother. Really, he thought, walking down University Place towards Washington Square Park, he'd done everything he could for her. Hadn't he? She'd bruised her head, so they rushed to the emergency room at St. Joe's where they waited an hour, Frederick holding the ice pack to her forehead, reassuring her, Don't be afraid, it's only a bump on the head, the doctor just needs to check to make sure nothing else is wrong. It turned out to be a fractured rib, nothing more. For the next couple of weeks it was going to hurt when she breathed, the doctor explained, but the real danger was, to compensate, she might take short, shallow breaths, and then her lungs could become infected. Her homework for the next month was to breathe deeply through a breathalyzer every twenty minutes. The bump on her forehead would take care of itself, but, he warned, it'll get worse before it gets better. Her face would turn black and blue.

"I'll just tell people Fritz beats me." Clare smiled, gripping Frederick's hand on one side of the bed and his father's hand on the other. "If it hadn't been for these two fellas, my husband and my son, Freddy—he lives in New York—"

"Mrs. Bailey, try not to talk," the doctor said, smiling at Frederick. "Just rest. We want you to stay here overnight."

By the time Frederick got into bed it was well past midnight. But he was wide awake at five, oddly exhilarated. I'm going home, he said to himself, as if he were a teenager off to the big city for the first time.

"But don't worry, I'm staying in Reading," Marge assured her mother as they checked her out of the hospital. Then on a sour note, directed more at Frederick than Clare, "I'm not going anywhere."

The rest of the morning was spent getting Clare settled back home and teaching her to use the breathalyzer. His father had wanted his help with some household chores, but Frederick said those would have to wait until the next time he came to Reading, for if he took the evening train he'd get home too late and (this was a lie) he had some things to prepare for tomorrow's meeting, papers to consult, which he'd left at home—he was sorry, but he had to make that one o'clock train.

But he had done, more or less, everything he could. And Curt wasn't a perfect stranger. They had exchanged words. Curt had gone out of his way, in fact, to solicit him ("solicit"—the specter of prostitution again). He could find a stranger for sex if that was all he wanted, but now, passing beneath the arch and searching for some place to sit, he felt, somebody wants me, I have something to look forward to, and he thought of Curt's extraordinarily beautiful face, and the childlike way he stood smoking his cigarette, then the way he followed him like a panther back to the seats, and after the performance how he pursued him, asked his name, made a date to see him again. Frederick held close the memory of those delicate moves, like the first gambits in a game of chess.

He checked his watch. Nine o'clock already. Washington Square was filled with locals enjoying the warm evening air. Kids played in the fountain, throwing a football from one end to the other. He kept thinking, That ball's gonna hit me in a minute. Balls seemed to have a mind of their own whenever he was near, and he always felt particularly foolish whenever one came his way, for if he should attempt to return it, he was certain, even small children can see I'm queer. Was that all he was now? A silly old queer waiting for his piece of action? Maybe it was all an elaborate ploy to get him home, take advantage of him. He'd heard of things like that, queers getting rolled or arrested in "Chicken and Bulls" stings, and it always frightened him (he remembered the incident with his friend Raymond, who'd taken a hustler to a hotel room, when suddenly the hustler turned on him, made him strip down to his shorts, tied him up with his own necktie, emptied his wallet, slapped his face, held a knife to his throat and said, If you tell anyone, say anything—and Ray couldn't complain to the hotel staff or go to the police for fear of exposure).

He had gotten to the park twenty minutes early. In fact he *wanted* to get here early—certainly to be here when Curt arrived—to show he was a dignified man, this was not some sordid, secretive assignation. To all the world it should look…like what? Uncle and nephew? Father and son? It needn't look inappropriate or sexual. Cordial—teacher and student, perhaps (this was the heart of the New York University campus, after all).

He looked at Two Fifth Avenue, the building that had secured his place at Emerson, Root. Every time he looked at it, he felt differently. The "compromise design"—setting the tower back from the park and maintaining, at the base, the low roof line along the park's northern edge—and then his idea to salvage the granite portico with the Corinthian columns from 14 Washington Square North and incorporate it into the new, modern structure ("a paste-up job," Seymour joked at first, then became his strongest defender to the rest of the team)—at first he was exceedingly proud of the design. It was good design, not slavishly beholden to those who would stop all building and development in the city (the Rhinelander Houses—what, really, was their historical importance? Just the dwellings of another wealthy New York family, Seymour said, and he was right; if George Washington never slept there, what was the point of preserving the building?). At the same time, the Municipal Arts people were also right—tall buildings *did* detract from the beauty of the park, the perimeter buildings *should* be kept low, there *should* be plenty of light and air. So the solution was, do both. Build the tower, but set it back from the park, and in place of the old Rhinelander homes, create a modernized version of similar proportions as a base for the tower. But now, as he looked at that portion along the northern edge of the square, he was bothered by the horizontal picture windows and the metal balconies. The modern addition now seemed not a violation, exactly, of some historic buildings, but…what? *Not* such good design after all? Whereas, looking at the still-intact row houses on the other side of the avenue along the park, he realized (thinking of the Royal Crescent in Bath) there had been an attempt at something different here, once upon a time. There are so few examples of coherent urban planning in New York we've forgotten even to want it anymore. We don't know *how* to want it.

It was a peculiar idea, he thought, looking through the arch and wondering from which direction Curt was likely to come (9:15 now)—"Not knowing how to want." Times changed, whole peoples forgot, but here was the disturbing thing: We lose touch with our values, time goes by, we change, and we don't even notice the change.

He heard someone call his name.

Trotting across Fifth Avenue with her dog came Deborah. As she passed beneath the arch, she let go of the leash and the dog made a beeline for Frederick's lap.

"Waverly, get down. Sorry, Fred. Bad dog!"

He panicked. What if Curt comes while she's here, what will I say? What will *he* say? What if he kisses me?

"What a wonderful coincidence! How was your weekend in Pennsylvania?"

Not wanting to prolong their visit, but at the same time wishing he could pour out all his insecurities about spending time with his family, and then the news about his sister's pregnancy, her marital crisis, not to mention his mother's accident, he merely said it was okay.

"Just okay? Waverly, heel!"

"What kind is he?" He reached down and petted the dog, but thought, No, the idea is to find a way to break this up.

"Terrier." But she was intent on hearing details about his weekend. "You seemed a little worried at the protest."

He reassured her the weekend was fine.

As he wasn't taking her lead on the subject, she proceeded, instead, to fill him in on developments since Thursday. She described the denouement of the protest and the article that ran next day in the *Times*. It leaned heavily, she said, on the human-interest side. "They mentioned the Lingrens and their little girl in the stroller. They were carrying a sign that said 'Don't Let Them Destroy My Heritage.' A few other names—Philip Johnson, of course, Charles Hughes, Norval White, Aline Saarinen. They mentioned Seymour's sign, 'Be A Penn Pal'!" She'd joined the contingent that went to New York International that night to meet the mayor's plane. He was coming back from vacation in Europe, and—"Actually it was quite exciting! We stood there en masse as he came off the plane, and then Norval approached him, and we sort of inched along behind him. We had the reporter for the *Times* there—" (He kept looking over her shoulder. No sign of Curt. He would have to do something quickly.) AGBANY staged the whole thing, she said. They'd prepared a letter asking Wagner to make a commitment to historic preservation, and Norval handed him the letter. Frederick grew more and more agitated as she continued. "He was respectful, though he looked a little crumpled from his trip."

"Well, that's great," Frederick said, knowing he sounded detached. She must be wondering what's wrong with me, he thought, why I seem so cool. He hated being in this position.

"I'd love it if you came to the next meeting of the Municipal Arts Society. We're taking a list of about three hundred buildings and Alan Burnham is developing it into a book. He's with the AIA, but it seems AIA is more on board with this now because of the protest. There was a lot of tension between AIA and AGBANY at first, but now I think everyone sees that AGBANY gets results. I'm going to help with the editing, and I'm sure they'd love your input. We have historians, but we need someone who knows architecture. Seymour won't do it, and I wondered—I was hoping to speak to you about it at the protest, but since you're here, what do you think? Come to the next meeting and talk to Alan with me. I'll tell him I've spoken with you and you're interested." He looked at her. His heart was pounding. "Assuming you're interested, I mean."

"Yes, yes, tell him."

"Good! We won't tell Seymour, this will be our secret."

But all he heard was the word "secret."

"It's later than I thought." Indeed, it was now 9:30 PM. Was he actually getting stood up? "I'm on my way to meet a friend for a drink."

"Oh, I'm sorry, I assumed you were just out enjoying the evening."

"No, it's all right, I—I didn't realize the time."

"Which way are you going? I'll walk you."

"No—no—I'm—where were *you* headed?"

"I usually walk him once around the square, right, Waverly?"

They proceeded over to Broadway, all the while Deborah filled him in on the *Times* editorial she had reason to believe would appear next week about the Penn Station protest. The AGBANY people had close ties with Ada Louise Huxtable at the *Times*, who was a great champion of the cause of historic preservation. She'd been told Huxtable would be writing an editorial in support of the protest.

"That's good," he said, but raged inside as he approached Broadway, his back to the square.

"She calls AGBANY 'the local counterpart to Britain's Anti-Uglies.' Any idea what she's referring to?"

It took effort to stay focused on the conversation. Anti-Uglies. A group of architecture students in Britain, as he recalled, who protested—something or other. "But that's all I know."

"Oh, then that must be it." Here was the subway entrance.

"Frederick, I'm so glad I ran into you. And this really does mean you have to come over for dinner. It's been too long. I'll speak with Seymour and we'll pick a date."

"Okay, and which way do you go now?"

"Oh, probably down Broadway. You want to walk down Broadway, baby?" But Waverly was barking at another dog across the street. "It's always good to see you, Fred."

"And you," he returned.

They kissed and said their goodbyes, and Frederick, feeling a complete fool, descended the stairs to the subway, waited two minutes, then raced back up, back to the square, but his bench was now occupied, and no sign of Curt anywhere. Now it was nearly 10:00 PM. He found another bench on the opposite side of the arch. He sat down and looked at the arch, with Two Fifth Avenue beyond it. He hated the sight of it and began to chew the nail on his pinky finger. Another bland apartment tower, another historic building razed to dust, a lazy design solution to appease everyone but please no one. The building was a failure, the Row had been violated, great nineteenth-century architecture had been sacrificed for mediocre modern architecture, and *goddamn* this kid for not showing up on time! He really had hoped to spend the night with him, or at least take him to bed for an hour or two, feel his touch. He wanted more than anything else right now to be held close.

Darkness had fallen. The park was still crowded with kids and couples and teenagers playing music. Every now and then a football came perilously close to his head. One time he caught it and said angrily, Watch what you're doing, you almost hit me in the head, and the kids said Sorry, but out of the corner of his eye he saw one of them laughing and poking his friend, and he knew they were laughing at the foolish old queer sitting on the bench on this hot Sunday night in August.

When he got up to leave, it was past 11:00 PM. On his way out of the park, he saw two young women sitting on the edge of the fountain, each with her ear to a transistor radio held between them, weeping. As he passed, he overheard the news: Marilyn Monroe was dead.

CHAPTER FIVE

CURT STARED AT THE HORIZON BECAUSE HE COULDN'T STAND TO LOOK AT Collin another minute. His body was drained but he couldn't sleep. Collin, on the other hand, could sleep through anything. He was actually snoring. The beach was very crowded now, kids playing all around them. The sun was at its peak. He'd been awake since 5:00 AM when Collin got up to go to the bathroom. He came back to bed and they embraced and then kissed. Collin liked having sex first thing in the morning, so Curt hoped this would be the morning. Collin hadn't fucked him since the night they met, and it was driving him crazy. They did everything else, sometimes several times a day, but he wouldn't fuck. He couldn't fall back to sleep. He lay there waiting for Collin to wake up, and then he did wake up but stayed in bed, going in and out of sleep, for another two hours, and all that time Curt lay there hoping Collin would fuck him, wondering when the right time would be to say something but not wanting to ask for it, feeling he shouldn't have to ask for it.

He didn't know why he put up with Collin. He wasn't so great. Okay, he was cute, in good shape. And yeah, he had a nice dick. But all this crap about being a "singer-dancer"? C'mon, he was a lousy chorus boy. He'd only been living in New York for one month but already he'd met more attractive, more interesting, more successful men than he ever met in Chicago.

Like the guy he met on Wednesday night at the theater—the handsome older man with the graying temples and the sexy lips and the dark blue eyes—the one who helped that girl who got mugged. Frederick. They were supposed to meet tonight. Washington Square Park, underneath the arch or something. But for some reason, Collin had a grip on him. New York was so big and crazy, it was nice to have someone there for you, a shoulder to cry on, and he'd been crying a lot lately. He'd been saving up to move to New York ever since he heard from his shrink about the Mattachine Society and how there were more homos in New York than any other place in the world. Ballet classes were fun, but he wasn't working too hard. He was still learning his way around, getting a feel for the different neighborhoods, and where to meet men. He'd heard the 34th Street Y was "simpatico," so that's where he was living for now, but he wanted to get out, there were too many lowlifes there. And yeah, the shower room was a gas, but after the incident last night (a bunch of greasers chased him from the subway shouting "faggot"—he could have sworn one of them had cruised him on the train) he knew he had to get out, find a better place. But that would mean finding a better-paying job. Well, he already knew he wasn't gonna last at Aldo's. Fucking mafia. And the snooty customers, especially the homos. "Where's my salad!" "This lettuce tastes like it has detergent on it!" You want Roquefort, Italian, or gasoline? Fucking faggots. And the worst part of it was, they only complained to *him* because they knew he was a sister. They would never say anything to the straight waiters or the manager. They'd eat shredded newspaper with dressing poured on top before standing up to the real enemy.

He walked to the water's edge and watched two women, a little farther out, laughing and talking. Both of them were dressed in tight, skimpy bikinis. As fashion trends were going, pretty soon women would be free to go topless and people would think it normal. Whereas men—he turned to look at the refreshment stand up on the boardwalk and saw two cops stationed near the entrance to the public toilets nearby—men had to cover their briefs with a towel on the boardwalk. He knew the ordinance was aimed at gay men and no one else. Riis Park was notorious for homos, the cops and the locals knew that, and so they set rules to make it hard as possible for "undesirables" to come and have a good time. He watched as a group of teenage faggots paraded past the cops to the men's bathroom, sashaying and flipping their towels like skirts, putting on a show for the cops, acting like silly queens. He returned his gaze to the two women in front of him. Women were lucky, in a way. The whole society seemed to accept the idea that a woman's body was something to be looked at, enjoyed, a thing of beauty. But men's bodies were supposed to be cold, hard slabs. Totally nonsexual. Their boxers and briefs were supposed to conceal their erogenous zones, like they had no front packages and no rear ends—exactly the parts of the body that were most sexual. Oh sure, men could walk around without their shirts on and that was normal. And he wasn't complaining! He could spend hours just watching men go by, all kinds of men, young, old, even the fat ones—men's bodies fascinated him. Especially mature men's bodies. He never tired of looking at them. But no one thought men's chests or arms or legs were "sexy"—well, straight men didn't—and how typical of straight men, to flaunt their bodies any way they wanted because something hadn't occurred to them (that other men might find them attractive). But as soon as a gay guy puts on a bikini, as soon as his shorts are too short, his pants too tight, he's a faggot and told to cover up, wipe off the makeup, walk tall, chest out, get tough, lower your voice, don't cross your legs like a girl, don't look at your nails that way, don't check your heels that way. Jesus! The whole thing was a fucking straitjacket. And it was the same in New York as anywhere else. Shit, the boys at Chicago Junior School were braver than most queers he saw in New York. They used to go around holding hands, everyone talked about who was going with who, they slept in each other's beds, jerked each other off, kissed and hugged and had pet names for each other (Go-Cart, Shrimpy), and yes, Mr. Kilburn called them faggot and made everyone sign a statement saying they didn't engage in any "inappropriate behavior." But he refused and said so to Mr. Kilburn's face, and the goddamned thing was, he didn't get punished for it! As if the most outrageous thing you could do to someone like Kilburn was just tell the truth plain and simple, without anger or attitude. Yes, I have sex with boys. So what? And Kilburn did nothing. That was when he knew there was something special about him. Something truly fearless. Where it came from he didn't know. But sometimes it made him just want to go off like a rocket.

Of course by the time of his confrontation with Kilburn, everyone thought he was trouble, and they knew he would raise hell if they interfered with him. And things kept right on as before. But Chicago Junior was a world unto itself, way the hell out in the country, with its own rules and customs, and none of the housemothers and administrators could do much to change things. And it was kid stuff, at least that's what all the adults thought. Let them kiss and hold hands and choke the chicken. What harm can it do? As soon as they grow up and go out into the world and meet girls, all that sissy stuff will vanish. But for Curt it was real. More real than anything he'd ever known or felt in his entire life. And it made him angry to see how disrespected by society it was. How dare anyone call him faggot, tell him how to dress, how to carry himself? What fucking right did they have? He turned back to see if Collin was still sleeping. There he was, flat on his back. Fucking asshole.

He was thirsty and hot. Maybe a Coke would fix him up. But as soon as he thought of going to the refreshment stand, he remembered he'd have to put on his towel. But he didn't feel like wearing a towel. It was so hot, and he liked the way he looked in his bikini. He liked the way men stared at him in his trunks. He knew he had a cute body. He knew he looked younger than his age. And the boardwalk was packed with men. He wanted to walk up and down the boardwalk and soak in the attention and flirt and maybe ask someone for a cigarette and talk and flirt some more and who knows where it could lead? And why should he capitulate to some blue-nosed rule about proper attire? Look at all those women on the boardwalk wearing next to nothing at all!

He headed towards the refreshment stand. The cops were watching him. Let them watch. He would walk right past them, go straight up to the counter, order his Coke, and fuck 'em if they didn't like it. He wouldn't be rude, he wouldn't be provocative. Wouldn't camp it up. Just go about his business, like he was entitled to, just like anyone else.

"What the hell you think you're doin'?" one of the cops said to him. He stood with folded, muscular arms. A pair of aviators obscured his face.

Curt halted. "Going to the soda stand."

"Not like that you're not."

The words lit a match inside him. "Not like what?"

"You can't walk on the boards without a towel."

Curt shrugged, walked past him, and stood in line at the counter.

"Hey, pussy, did you hear me?"

Curt looked over his shoulder with contempt. "What did you call me?"

"I called you pussy!"

"Leave me alone!"

The cop moved fast, grabbing him hard by the arm.

"Let go of me, scumbag!"

"Take him back," the other cop said with dispatch, and his partner yanked Curt around back of the refreshment stand to a shed with a radio and a file cabinet. He shoved him against the wall. Curt heard the door slam and the click of a lock. The room smelled like body odor.

"What's your name?"

"Curt Watson."

"Address."

"I live at the 34th Street Y. So what?"

The cop stepped within inches of him. He took off his glasses, revealing dark brown eyes. He spoke softly. "Lot of homos live there, don't they?"

Curt said nothing.

Raising his voice: "Don't they?"

Still nothing.

"Answer me, faggot!"

Curt wiped the cop's spittle from his face. "Go fuck yourself!"

The cop raised his backhand and swung it with all his might at Curt's mouth.

Stars burst in the sky, then everything went black.

1963

CHAPTER SIX

La Gioconda's indefinable smile has been the object of countless explanatory attempts, though its mystery has never been solved. According to Vasari, Leonardo's contemporary, the smile results from the fact that Leonardo "retained musicians who played and sang and continually jested in order to avoid that melancholy which painters are used to give their portraits." Sir Kenneth Clark has compared it with the smile of the Gothic statuary of Rheims. Marcel Brion sees *La Gioconda* as "the last great religious painting."

"I always preferred Walter Pater's view," Sam whispered into Frederick's ear. "He says she's a vampire, a deep-sea diver, a seller of shawls in a Middle Eastern bazaar... "

Frederick chuckled. Sam was one of his oldest friends, and he couldn't think of anyone he'd rather suffer through this experience with. They'd stood in line this frigid February morning a full two and a half hours just to get into the museum when it opened at ten, and then it took another hour to get close to the painting itself, which hung in the Medieval Sculpture Hall against a red velvet curtain in front of the massive Spanish Renaissance choir screen. Two guards from the Louvre were stationed on either side of it, and a pair of US Secret Service men stood at opposite ends of the velvet rope, urging people to keep moving. A reverential hush descended upon the crowd and filled the chapel-like room. Whatever fatigue he might have felt, by the time Frederick stood before the *Mona Lisa* its undeniable spell had begun to work upon him. Unlike Sam, who muttered catty remarks about the painting's over-inflated reputation and was preoccupied with its monetary value ("according to the *Times* it isn't even insured because it's priceless"), Frederick stood awestruck, letting sink in the reality that this was no reproduction but the real thing.

"Oh, that's interesting," Sam said, reading the information panel to their right. "It was hidden in a chateau in southwest France during the war."

A peal of sharp laughter broke the general quiet of the room. Frederick turned to see what the commotion was about. There was Curt. His blood ran cold. Curt looked at him with unblinking expressionless eyes. Then he smiled. Frederick responded in kind, but his smile quickly contracted as the memory of being stood up in Washington Square Park six months ago came rushing back as if it were yesterday.

"Someone you know?"

"No. Sort of."

"That kid with the blue scarf?" Sam was intrigued.

"Please keep moving," the guard said, and Frederick and Sam were forced to step aside as eager spectators crowded the space they had just occupied. Frederick turned back again and Curt was still looking at him, even as his companions, another young man and a girl, continued to share some joke.

"He's certainly got his eye on you."

"It's nothing. I'll tell you later."

"You want to speak to him?"

"I can't make up my mind."

Frederick looked a third time, as Curt began maneuvering through the crowd.

"Looks like he's made up your mind for you."

"Frederick!" Curt said with the sunniest of smiles.

"Hi," he returned, not knowing whether to show joy or hurt. He felt both. His heart was pounding. "Sam this is Curt. This is my friend Sam."

"You remembered my name."

"How do you *do*?" Sam said with more emphasis, Frederick felt, than was entirely necessary.

"Excuse me, please!" and "keep moving" came from several directions as they realized they'd created a traffic jam where people were trying to head toward the exit. Sam took both of their arms and ushered them off to the side near the wall where there were fewer people.

"It's good to see you!"

"Yes," Frederick said, struggling to contain his nervousness. "And you."

Now Curt's friends arrived, a young man whom Frederick quickly dismissed as too effeminate and a rather masculine though sweet-faced young woman.

"Collin and Bev. This is Frederick and—what is your name again?"

"Sam," he said with a light laugh, acknowledging the mild absurdity of the situation.

They both murmured Hi, but Collin was impatient to leave.

"I'm gonna blow my stack if I have to stay here another minute," he said, showing no interest in polite conversation.

"I hardly got to see it because this lady kept pushing me," Bev added. "I was expecting something huge."

Sam laughed. "So many things in life are like that." The kids didn't respond to the joke. "They should be distributing free souvenir posters for all the trouble we went to."

"What did *you* think?" Curt asked Frederick.

"I think it's…fascinating," he said, and Curt nodded in agreement, looking seriously into his eyes and making Frederick confused, all of a sudden, about what it was they were really talking about.

"I'm gonna split," Collin said to Bev, as if reacting to what Frederick had just said.

"Oh phooey, all right," she replied.

They agreed to convene near the information booth in the lobby in fifteen minutes.

Bev said "Nice to meet you" while Collin started heading towards the exit, tossing off "Fifteen minutes" with his back already turned.

Sam tried to make an exit himself. "I have to find the rest room."

"I'll go with you."

"I'm a big boy, I can go myself. Shall I meet you at the information booth in fifteen minutes?" Frederick glared at him. "I'll take that as a yes. Curt, it was a pleasure." And he was gone.

"This is so incredible! I can't believe I've run into you. That time we were supposed to meet in Washington Square Park—"

"I waited."

"I am so sorry, Frederick. I was at the beach that day and the craziest thing happened."

Trying to maintain his dignity, he said, "You don't need to explain anything." But he wanted an explanation.

"I swear it wasn't intentional." He described the incident at the beach, the dress code on the boardwalk, how the cops provoked him and beat him up. "Then they booked me and threw me in jail for the night. I could only make one phone call, so I called Collin because he was the only person I knew who I could ask to bail me out. I wanted to call you but I didn't think it was right."

"Were you hurt?"

"Hell yeah! They broke a tooth, I got a split lip and a black eye."

"I'm sorry." But Frederick couldn't resist. "And the next day, or whenever you got out of jail, you didn't think to call and explain?"

"I lost your number. I felt so bad but there was nothing I could do."

He didn't know how much of it to believe. The story didn't sound implausible, but he wasn't ready to forgive just yet.

"I want to make it up to you. I have a feeling about you. I haven't forgotten what happened when we sat next to each other in the theater, have you?"

"No, I haven't forgotten," he said, and the words were truer than Curt could know.

"So what'll it be?"

"How old are you?"

Curt laughed heartily, and his laugh brought forth all his beauty. "I'm twenty."

"Are you in school?"

"I'll tell you about it when we meet." He gently touched Frederick's hand. "I believe in coincidences, and our meeting like this is a sign. We were meant to find each other again. Don't you feel that?"

"I'm not that kind of believer."

"Oh well, if you don't want to see me again…"

Frederick saw Sam approaching from the lobby. He caught Sam's eye, and Sam waved but kept his distance, seeing that Frederick and the boy were still talking. He held up his wrist, pointed to his watch, and mouthed the words, I'm leaving. Curt half turned but didn't acknowledge Sam's presence. Looking again at Frederick, he wore a sly, almost confrontational expression on his face, as if to say, I dare you.

"I do," Frederick confessed. "I do want to see you again."

"What about tonight?"

Frederick had planned to spend the evening at home working. But this couldn't wait.

"Let's not meet in public so, in case I'm late, you won't be left—"

Frederick protested.

"No, I'm just saying—"

"Seriously, if you're not interested—"

"I'm interested, okay? Jeez!" Curt gave an exasperated laugh. "How about if I come to your place? You live alone?"

"Yes. Where do you live?" He asked only because it started to feel as if he were giving everything and getting nothing. In fact, a part of him didn't want to know anything about the boy.

"I live on 29th Street with Collin. It's no good, I can't bring anybody there."

"Why not?"

"That's something else I'll explain tonight. What time, seven o'clock?"

Frederick agreed, producing a pen, and Curt wrote the address and phone number on the palm of his hand. "This way I can't lose it."

"What if you sweat?"

"I'm always cool, can't you tell? I'm also crazy!" Frederick didn't have time to think about the statement before Curt hugged him. "Don't worry, I'm not gonna kiss you. You'll have to wait till tonight."

"I'm glad we ran into each other," Frederick said unbidden.

"*Are* you?" Curt said with a broad smile and a wink. He made a motion to leave.

"What's your number?" Frederick asked, as if waking from a dream.

"Sorry, can't give it to you. Collin would go bananas." Frederick frowned. "I'll explain *everything* tonight!" And he departed, this time without a smile or a wink or anything really, Frederick felt, that might have put a cordial period to the rude, astonishing coincidence of their meeting again. He turned to look at the *Mona Lisa* once more but all he could see were the backs of other people's heads.

FREDERICK SIPPED HIS SCOTCH ON THE ROCKS AND TRIED TO FOCUS ON THE task at hand. He chewed the nail of his middle finger. Here he was again, waiting for Curt. It was nearly 7:00 PM. If he was anything of a gentleman, he thought, he'd arrive early as a show of respect to prove he's serious. But— "gentleman"! It was absurd even to measure him against such an ideal.

A sonata for solo violin by Bach played on the hi-fi. He always found baroque music particularly suited to drawing and writing. Presently he was going over the entry for the Brokaw Residence. *Northeast corner Fifth Avenue and East 79th Street. This little castle on its corner site is one of the few remaining town houses which could boast such splendid isolation. Romanesque in many of its details, this mansion is basically of French Renaissance inspiration in its fenestration and roof lines. The marble interiors clove to the Romanesque revival and were some of the finest and most original work of this style.* With prodding from Deborah, he'd taken over the job of revising the entries when the Municipal Art Society's president, Harmon Goldstone, playfully joked at the last annual meeting that, given Alan Burnham's scholarly pace, the New York Landmarks book should be ready for publication by the end of 1998. It was an odd experience, describing these buildings from bygone eras. He felt as though he were adopting a tone, a vocabulary that wasn't exactly his own (the marble interiors "clove"?). What amused him, however, was how easily he could slip into boosterism ("some of the finest and most original work of this style"), never mind he'd always found the Brokaw house rather squat and pudgy.

But where was Curt? It was now past seven. His stomach hurt. He lit a cigarette and refilled his glass. The telephone rang.

"Hello."

"It's Sam."

His heart sank. He mustn't tie up the phone in case Curt was trying to reach him. It was unthinkable he could pull this again. Sam wanted to debrief after their trip to the Met this morning. He was full of questions about the fetching lad they ran into. But Frederick didn't feel comfortable telling him the whole story. Had the shoe been on the other foot, Sam would have bragged that so young and attractive a man had approached him, asked for a date, their dalliance during *My Fair Lady* (he would have had a field day with that), but Frederick felt there was something unsavory about Curt, about the way he'd already let Curt walk all over him—the kiss on Broadway, the degrading scene in Washington Square Park, now Curt and his friends (he wondered if Curt and Collin were lovers).

"I was worried about you. Something didn't smell right. He's awfully cute, but you seemed taken aback."

True enough. So he went through the story, only omitting certain details lest the intensity of his involvement should provoke a lecture. He let slip Curt's age.

"Ha! In the mood for some chicken, are you?"

Frederick bristled. "I wouldn't put it quite like that."

"I know you wouldn't, you're too genteel. When's he due to arrive?"

"He *was* due fifteen minutes ago."

"Lock the door! Or go out. Tell the doorman if he comes, you're not in."

"I know that's what I should do."

"Frederick, be careful. I wouldn't have given him a second chance. I don't care if he *was* arrested, you really want to get mixed up with a kid who flirts with danger like that? And then the silly thing loses your phone number! Oh no, not me, doesn't matter how cute he is."

What Frederick wanted to say, but couldn't, was that he felt nearly powerless to change the course of events. And wasn't sure he would if he could. "Sam, I really ought to go."

"Let me know what happens."

He lit another cigarette and poured himself another Scotch. He tried to continue his revisions but found it hard to concentrate.

The phone rang.

"Fred, this is Deborah." She wanted to talk over the revisions for the book. She'd been relegated to the Bronx and wanted Fred to promise he'd accompany her when it was time to do the site measurements. "Wayne Andrews and Ken Dunshee are supposed to join me, but I'd rather have you. I'm sure if I said you and I were gonna do it ourselves, Burnham would give us the go-ahead."

"But I've got all these Manhattan buildings, plus a few in Brooklyn."

"I can help you with those. I can't do the drawings, that's your department, but I can do the text."

It wasn't the revisions, however, that Deborah really wanted to discuss. Alan had just informed her he was adding an index that would break down the entire list of buildings according to four categories—"Are you ready for this?" she laughed—"structures of national importance, structures of local or regional importance, structures of importance designated for preservation, and structures of note filed for ready reference."

Frederick wasn't sure which ruffled him more, Deborah's inopportune phone call or Burnham's eleventh-hour expansion of the project. "And who's gonna make those determinations?"

"We are! And that's not all. He also wants, next to each building, a code to special features. He gave me the list: community interest, historical interest, stained glass, metalwork—well, it just goes on and on."

He said he wasn't averse to doing the work, but it did cause something of a problem, what with his busy schedule at Emerson, Root.

"Say we'll do it together. You're the only person on the committee I really enjoy, and doing it with you makes it worthwhile for me."

She was hard to refuse. He looked at his watch. Seven-thirty.

The intercom rang.

"Would you hold just a second?" He buzzed downstairs.

"Mr. Bailey." It was Milton the doorman. "I found some dry cleaning here for you. Should I send it up?"

Almost angrily, he said, "Oh, I don't care. All right. It doesn't matter, I can get it tomorrow."

"I'm happy to send Bernie up with it."

Why was Milton bothering with dry cleaning at seven-thirty on a Sunday night? Out of patience but not wanting to show it, he agreed to have it sent up. "Deborah, I'm sorry. Listen, I should go. I…" He was about to concoct a lie but realized he needn't. "I'm expecting a visitor and have to do something in the kitchen."

"Okay, I'll phone you tomorrow after work. When's a good time?" That partly depended on Curt, should he ever arrive. He said *he* would phone *her*.

"I'm really glad we're doing this together."

His bladder was about to burst. And now he felt a bowel movement coming on. Absolutely the wrong time for that. Not with Curt due any minute. But what was he thinking? That time was past. It was now close to 7:45 PM. Forty-five minutes late! Frederick wanted to break something. Punch someone. The doorbell rang. Could it be?—but they would have buzzed—still it might… No, it was the dry cleaning. "Thanks Bernie," he said. He took the dry cleaning to the bedroom and hurled it onto the bed.

The phone rang. Must be Curt! "Hello!"

"You sound angry."

It was Marge. "No, I'm sorry. I've been a little frustrated this evening."

"What's wrong?"

"Nothing. I don't want to talk about it."

"Sounds serious."

"It's not. I'm having trouble with some work…" He saw the papers for the New York Landmarks book lying on the couch. "I've been asked to help write a book about buildings in New York that should be designated landmarks." She was listening. "And they've just asked me to do…" But the more he said, the more he realized he'd have to explain, and this was the opposite of what he wanted right now. "They've asked me to do something in addition to what they originally asked me to do."

"Oh."

He wasn't making much sense.

"It's nothing. Sometimes I overreact."

"Well, I was just calling. I'm alone tonight." She started to cry.

"What's happening?"

"It's Chuck. He's left."

He asked when.

"We had a fight—I guess it was Wednesday night. He hit me."

"How badly?"

"He smacked me on the cheek."

"Marge, I'm sorry."

"I told him to go. And…" She was weeping without inhibition now and had a hard time getting the words out. "Now I feel sick. And this is the first time since Wednesday I feel really alone." She sobbed into the receiver.

"Margie, I'm so sorry." He'd caught a glimpse of this new sharing side of her at their father's birthday party, but now she really seemed to need him. "Why don't you call your friend Dorothy?"

"I shouldn't have called you?"

"No, I mean, maybe Dorothy can—I thought—"

"I just feel alone for the first time. I know it was the right thing to do. And with the baby coming, I think now is the time to do this. Really end it."

He worried she wasn't thinking clearly. She was seven months pregnant, depressed, overwhelmed by the work of raising Markie and looking after their parents. Separation did not seem the thing to do now.

"I'm sorry, I shouldn't be burdening you with this."

"It's okay," he said.

"I'll be fine. I'll go over to Dot's tomorrow. I just need to get through tonight. I'm sorry."

"I said it's okay."

"Tell me about you." He froze. "When we saw each other last summer, you said something I haven't forgotten. You said I never ask about your life." His guard went up. "So I'm asking."

"Asking what?"

"Is there someone in your life?" He felt terrified, as if she were ready to confront his secret at last.

"What do you mean?"

"Is there anyone important? I don't mean friends, I mean romantically. You never talk about…a girlfriend or…anyone important."

"No, Marge. There's…no girlfriend." He thought about his usual remark when such questions arose ("Architecture is the love of my life"). "I am very content. I'm fine."

"I wasn't asking if you're fine," she said irritably, "I'm asking if there is a special person. In your life."

He thought of Curt. It was going on 8:15. "No," he said firmly. "There is no one." He fell silent for a moment. Then, "Well, I was just about to go to bed and I'm extremely tired, I've had a long day, and I…" He had this awful habit lately of starting a lie before he'd thought it out clearly. It was bound to get him in trouble one day. "I have a bit of a headache."

"I just wanted to say one other thing." He saw the second hand on the clock in the dining room. "I wanted to ask you if you could come to Reading for a couple of days when I have the baby. I'm afraid Mama and Pop might need something, and I won't be able to do anything for a couple of weeks. I don't expect you to take off that much time, obviously, but just for a few days when I'm in the hospital having the baby. I could also use some extra help with Markie."

"Yes, of course."

"Thank you."

"Let me call you this week."

He hung up the phone, put his head between his legs, and fought back tears. No one had ever done this to him before. How could it be happening two times in a row? He turned to the manuscript. *PENNSYLVANIA STATION (OUTER CONCOURSE) Seventh and Eighth Avenues between West 31st and West 33rd Streets. This great concourse of steel and glass is one of the few reminders we have of a once practical and expressive design for railroad architecture. The precedent for such an enclosure is found in the train sheds which were located over the tracks in many of the older terminals. Here, in this great station, it was particularly well suited to its use as a pedestrian concourse, giving a wonderful sense of openness and light.* He read over the blurb once more and added a final sentence. *It may soon be demolished to make way for a remodeled station.*

Around 11:00 PM, the buzzer rang. Frederick was half asleep on the couch, surrounded by papers and photographs of New York landmarks. He answered drowsily.

"Mr. Bailey, Curt here to see you."

He was a rumpled mess. He needed to brush his teeth. He tore into the bathroom and rinsed his mouth. He splashed cold water on his face. The doorbell rang. He opened the door and there stood Curt. He entered without saying a word, dropped his shoulder bag on the floor, put his arms around Frederick, and rested his head on his shoulder. They stood silently in each other's arms for a minute. As the seconds wore on, Frederick became increasingly uncomfortable. How long did he intend to stand here just hugging him without speaking? At last he turned his face up to Frederick's.

"All I can say is, it's good to be here."

Frederick took his coat and invited him into the living room. He decided to tread lightly, not ask too many questions, and above all not reproach him. He was here. That was all that mattered for the moment. "Want something to drink?"

"Yes. What are you having?"

"I wasn't having anything, I was asleep." (Reproachful?)

"Oh, sorry."

"I think I'll have some brandy."

"Make it two."

They broached conversation delicately. Curt, for his part, seemed contrite, as if he knew he'd done the very thing Frederick dreaded he would do.

"Did something happen to you?" Frederick asked with a touch of parental concern in his voice.

"I promised I'd explain everything."

"You don't have to explain everything, and it's too late for that anyway. Are you okay?"

"Yeah, I'm fine."

It was odd, the way they were talking. It seemed to Frederick they'd known each other a long time. As if they'd already seen and touched something essential in each other. "Collin is my boyfriend and we had a fight when he found out I was coming over to see you. He threatened to kick me out. So I left and went over to Bev's apartment. She's my best friend. She was the girl with us at the museum this morning." Suddenly his tone changed from remorseful to breezy. "Hey, wasn't that wild? All those people there to see that little painting!"

Frederick wondered whether to extract more information or make small talk. Curt's five o'clock shadow made him look like a ragamuffin. His hair was a mess. In a way he looked more attractive than ever. "It never leaves

France, so this is a unique occasion." He knew he sounded like some PR man for the museum.

"So I started to fall asleep at Bev's and then I woke up and I thought, I should call Frederick, but I was afraid it was too late or you wouldn't want to talk to me, so I decided what the heck, I'll just go there and if he tells me to fuck off, okay. He has every right. *I'd* tell me to fuck off if I were me!" He burst out laughing and spilled his brandy.

Frederick jumped up to get napkins from the kitchen. When he returned, Curt was draining the glass.

"Sorry, Frederick. You must think I'm an ass. This is a nice place you have here. Can I spend the night? I'm sorry, I'm an ass."

Frederick was patting the brandy stains on the carpet. Everything was coming apart.

"*Do* you think I'm an ass?"

"I don't know—are you high?"

Curt got a little indignant, though he turned his indignation into a flirtation. "You think I'm high?"

"I don't know." Frederick stood up.

"You don't know? Can I have another glass?" He burst out laughing again. "I'm sorry. I told you I'm crazy, didn't I?"

"You did," Frederick said as he filled both glasses. He sat down next to Curt on the couch.

"I am crazy. I'm crazy for *you* because you're such a nice man. You open the door for me at eleven o'clock at night and you don't tell me to fuck off even though I'm four hours late and spill brandy all over your expensive furniture. Why are you such a nice man?"

Frederick liked hearing he was a nice man, even if he suspected he was being made fun of. "I don't know," he said.

"You don't know much, do you, Frederick?" Curt set his glass on the coffee table and leapt into his lap. Their mouths were together. Curt's kisses were voluptuous and hard, tasting of brandy and cigarettes. His stubble scraped against Frederick's face and filled his eyes with tears. He squeezed Frederick's hips between his thighs and thrust his pelvis into his abdomen. Frederick grabbed hold of his ankles and pulled him even closer, trying to restrain his thrusting for fear he would knock over the table, which only made him buck harder. He now felt the full size of this young man's body. It seemed he held his entire body in his hands.

Curt tore off his t-shirt and tried tugging at the buttons on Frederick's shirt, but Frederick stayed his hand and quickly undressed himself. He buried his face in Curt's chest—his skin was smooth and salty, his nipples large and sweet—and Curt ran his fingers through Frederick's hair and pulled on his ears. He went for Frederick's belt buckle.

"We'd better do this in the bedroom."

"Where's that?"

They rose from the couch. Frederick took his hand and led him down the hallway. In the bedroom they hurriedly shed their shoes and socks, their slacks and briefs. Curt pushed him hard onto the bed and jumped on top. Though small in stature, Curt was tough and strong like a wrestler. They made love without breathing, hungrily exploring each other's bodies, kissing and sucking with blackout intensity.

When Curt said "I have to fuck you," Frederick didn't demur for fear of breaking the spell, though he preferred to be on top. Curt spit into his hand, stroked his cock, and entered, all the while thrusting his tongue into Frederick's mouth and biting his lips. Frederick was in pain but continued to say nothing. Curt reached up and gripped the headboard as he thrust harder. He looked Frederick in the eyes and smiled with what appeared to be sheer amazement. "Frederick," he said, and Frederick expected some sort of declaration (he'd begun searching for words himself), when a few seconds later Curt said, "I'm gonna come," and raising his voice, "I'm gonna come!" and Frederick worried Mrs. Reilly next door might overhear. Curt pulled out and came onto his chest, letting out a long angry shout as if peeling off a Band-Aid. Then he rolled over onto his back and grunted.

Frederick looked up at the ceiling and felt his racing heart slow down to its normal beat. He didn't reach orgasm that night. No matter how attracted he might be, it took him weeks to feel comfortable enough to ejaculate in another's presence. And he was relieved that, rather than pressure him or make him feel awkward, Curt didn't seem to care one way or another.

CHAPTER SEVEN

FREDERICK SLEPT POORLY THAT NIGHT. HE FELT A DULL PAIN IN HIS GROIN from not having ejaculated, on top of which he lay in a state of confusion, half the time, as to whether he was awake or dozing. Curt, meanwhile, was dead asleep, almost as soon as he'd climaxed. Frederick cradled him in his arms, smelled his hair and scalp, caressed his shoulders (letting a finger rest in the cavity of the scar on his upper arm), his biceps and forearms, his hips and buttocks, his thighs and calves, felt the firm flesh, the light dusting of hair, wanted to have sex with him all over again, envied his steady breathing, his stillness. Sometime after 4:00 AM (he remembered looking at the clock and wondering how on earth he was going to get through today) he must have gone under, for when the alarm sounded—by accident he'd set it an hour late—he woke with a shock. He switched it off and checked to see that Curt, who merely turned over on his stomach and pulled the blankets up around his neck, remained undisturbed.

He slipped out of bed. Quietly but with dispatch, he gathered his clothing for the day (he had a meeting first thing) and dressed in the bathroom after the briefest of showers. In the kitchen he started to write a note for Curt, inviting him to help himself to anything in the refrigerator—sorry they didn't have a chance to talk this morning or even say goodbye—but he didn't like to use the word goodbye, for he was determined now he wouldn't lose track of him. This time it had to be different. But how? He was essentially in the same position he'd been in since the day they met: Curt pulled all the strings, Frederick had no way of contacting him, the ball was entirely in Curt's court. But there was no time to puzzle over all this now, he was going to be late for the meeting as it is. He tore up the note and, on a fresh piece of paper, simply wrote, "Curt, I hope to see you when I get home" and, after a split-second scruple, left his number at work "in case of emergency." He thought of signing off with something affection-ate. "Love" would be too strong, though improbably it was what he felt, "sincerely" too formal, "cheers" too cheery. He settled on an enigmatic "L, Frederick," which never in his life had he written, but now, it seemed, was the time for new things, more daring things. "I dare you" Curt had seemed to say to him, and Frederick felt the only way to play this young man's game is to do the dare. "L, Frederick" it was.

He wondered if Curt might call him at the office at some point during the day. He even stayed in for lunch in case he should. He preferred to be there at his drafting table ready to answer rather than have the secretary take a message. He staggered through the afternoon, made minimal advances on the drawings due midweek, had a brief conversation with Deborah about the New York Landmarks book, and left the office uncharacteristically, promptly at five.

Tired though he was, and dozing over his biography of the architect Charles McKim on the subway, he revived once above ground. He walked home with a spring in his step, hoping Curt would be there to receive him. Of course, he had to remind himself there was a good chance Curt would be gone by the time he arrived. And not hearing from Curt all day did strike him as foreboding.

When he opened the door to his apartment, everything was still. He tip-toed through the entrance hallway and heard the tick of the Swiss clock in the living room. All the lights were out. He cased the apartment for evidence Curt had been there—in the bedroom, the bed was left unmade. He looked in the bathroom for signs of any grooming products Curt may have used. In the medicine chest, he noted his pain killers and sleeping pills—none of the bottles were disturbed. In the kitchen, there was his note, now turned over with some words scribbled on the back. The handwriting was so sloppy it took him a minute to decipher: "*couldn't stay will call*" No punctuation, no personal pronoun, no object, no salutation, no "L." The message was astonishingly cold, given what they'd shared the night before. At least he said he'd call, Frederick thought.

Still wearing his overcoat, he slumped into his easy chair in the living room, dropped his briefcase to the floor, and looked out the window at the spire of Grace Church, lit up in the dark. When had Curt awoken? Did he take a shower? (Has my bar of soap caressed his body—the intimate crevice between his legs, the caves under his arms, across his chest...? Frederick felt himself going erect and shifted uncomfortably.) How long had he spent in the apartment? He couldn't very well ask Milton—it would sound sordid, and possibly send up an alarm signal that would only complicate matters for him, for he felt his personal life was already too much on display.

The point was to get things back to normal as much as possible, though there was nothing normal about any of this. He felt a curious mixture of contentment (he'd spent one of the most heavenly nights of his life) but also anxiety. What *had* Curt done in the apartment while he was away? Like a detective come across a scrawl in the killer's hand, a key to the mystery, the *Mona Lisa*'s smile (Leonardo's priceless portrait seemed far away from him now), he looked on the table and saw the exhibition brochure he'd purchased with a stain from Curt's brandy glass right across Lisa's face, then the stain on the sofa, and on the carpet. Frantically he stood up, threw off his coat, and began searching the apartment for his valuables. The portrait of Granny—his passport—his mother's rosary—his father's cufflinks—money he kept stashed in a drawer in the kitchen—the mask he'd brought back from Mexico City—the mask from Venice... He stopped and looked out the window and noticed one of the lights on the spire of Grace Church was out, leaving it half in shadow. How long, he wondered, before someone re-placed it? Grace Church was one of those buildings, according to Burnham and his team, that should be preserved "at any cost."

What price was he willing to pay for Curt? Was he worth a dime? Sam would have dropped him the minute he got stood up. But Frederick had let things go much further. And here he was again, waiting, wondering. "Couldn't stay, will call." The words were so clipped, so drained of promise, of care, concern. But he'd had him. His mouth was still swollen from their rough, passionate lovemaking. He almost wished the scars would never heal.

But Frederick's scars did heal, and it was over two weeks before Curt phoned again. In the meantime, he had plenty of time to sort things out. He was deeply attracted to Curt, perhaps more than anyone he'd ever met, including Jon. He recognized it as an obsession and accepted the fact. He also knew it wasn't just a sexual obsession. There was a boldness about Curt that both appalled and thrilled him. He seemed to cut like a blade through all the nonsense of the world. How much Frederick wanted to see Curt again, however, depended on the day and his mood. He clung to the memory of their night together and he taught himself to believe, even if he didn't really believe, that if he never saw Curt again it would have been enough. Other days he was hungry. When he felt a sexual urge, he wanted Curt to satisfy it. He noticed one beneficial thing: he no longer pined after men on the street. And he stopped going to the bars. It was as if he and Curt had gotten married in his mind. He was committed to Curt. He wasn't "skirt chasing," as Sam liked to call it, anymore. That was a relief, because he could now focus with full attention on work. And that wasn't all: one day while starting a new drawing, he unrolled a fresh sheet of paper on his drafting board and pinned it at the four corners. He picked through the mug of drawing implements on his side table and chose a dark green pencil. Holding it between his fingers, he examined the point to see if it needed sharpening when he noticed something extraordinary: his fingernails had grown back. The white tip of each nail had increased by what must have been an eighth of an inch. And he'd had no idea. He had actually stopped biting his nails.

Deborah, meanwhile, had asked him to divide the list of New York landmarks into groups according to their historic and aesthetic importance, and the task became a curiously absorbing one. He spent weekends at the Public Library doing research on buildings designed by McKim, Mead, and White, including the library at Columbia University, the arch at Washington Square, and of course Penn Station, trying to determine the key features that made them worthy of preservation. He was especially fascinated, though in some ways disappointed, to learn more about Penn Station, in one sense little more than a giant granite gazebo, a dispensable architectural folly atop the network of underground, underwater tracks that bound Manhattan Island to the continent; the Tenderloin district once inhabited by Negroes, evacuated by force, along with the tenements, bars, nightclubs, and brothels torn down to make way for the station; McKim's attempts to ennoble the business of train travel by creating lofty, dignified spaces through which one should promenade, never rush, a progression of spaces from the long Seventh Avenue arcade to the grand waiting room and then onto the dazzling glass and steel concourse—a sequence meant to be experienced, he realized, primarily by persons *leaving* the city, not arriving. It was a philosophy completely at odds with the tempo of modern times and with the city that epitomized it. No point, he knew, wishing things had turned out differently (for it was official—the station was set for demolition starting in October). The world turned, time moved forward, never backward.

Then one evening in the middle of March while reading his biography of McKim (he was in the middle of McKim's speech to the Royal Institute of British Architects wherein he bemoaned the wanton destruction of good architecture in America for commercial purposes—buildings inspired by the great British architect Christopher Wren, buildings whose destruction was deplorable not only "in the loss of historic monuments, but for the lessons they invariably teach of sound proportion, simplicity, and good manners"), he was jolted by the ring of the telephone.

"How are you?" came the low, scruffy, youthful voice.

"Hello. I'm—miss you." The grammatical upset was only one sign of letting go. Frederick knew to be with Curt in any sense meant to let go of all kinds of standards, to let down all kinds of barriers, to let him in whenever the opportunity arose.

"I want to see you, are you free tomorrow night?"

Frederick had a date with Sam and his companion, Ed, but he could cancel it. He would never tell Curt, of course. And he'd learned by now to expect the unexpected. First of all, to anticipate the possibility Curt might not come at all. No point in letting it anger him. He would need a Plan B. For now his biography of McKim kept him company, and if Curt failed to arrive he could spend the rest of the night reading. Frederick suggested dinner at Luchow's near Union Square—he got the distinct impression Curt didn't want to be bothered by details, just choose a time and place—but they should meet at the apartment, he insisted. Right, Curt remembered, "We don't want to run the risk of leaving Frederick out in the cold again," and he laughed.

This time Curt was only forty minutes late. They embraced, as before standing in each other's arms silently, not kissing, not caressing yet, just holding each other, as if there was a mutual understanding that now this was their ritual. But desire welled up and they began to kiss and Frederick could see, within a matter of seconds—

"I think we shouldn't." Curt pulled away. He walked uninvited into the living room and sat on the couch. "Sit down," he said, as if it were his home rather than Frederick's. "I don't think we should have sex right now."

Frederick didn't agree, but he was just as fascinated to see what Curt was up to this time. It was, at least, one way of getting to know the elusive boy.

"Whatever you want."

"Is that what *you* want?"

"Of course I want to make love to you, but I don't want to force you."

"Good, I don't want you to force me either."

"So, since you *don't* want to have sex, what *do* you want?"

Curt scratched the top of his head like a monkey, then broke out in a bright smile. "Food!"

Frederick laughed. "What are we waiting for?"

They decided to go to Luchow's as planned. Frederick asked what he was hungry for.

"A thick, juicy steak with potatoes and carrots and green beans," and the list went absurdly long.

"Sounds like you haven't had a proper meal in days."

On the way to the restaurant, Frederick tried to get some sense of Curt's home life. He wanted to know about the arrangement with Collin. But Curt didn't want to discuss Collin. Something had happened between them. Frederick spoke to him as if it was mutually understood that Collin was an obstacle to be surmounted.

At the entrance to Luchow's, Curt halted. "Collin was in the room when I was talking to you last night and he heard me say the name of the restaurant. He might already be in there waiting for us."

"What would he do if he saw us together?"

"He's the jealous type. He could make a scene in front of everyone."

Frederick said they would go somewhere else then.

"Can't we just go back to your place? He doesn't want me to see other people. The problem is, he won't give me what *I* want."

Frederick didn't understand. But here on the sidewalk in front of Luchow's wasn't the place to be having this discussion.

"He says he loves me but then he won't have sex with me."

Frederick had to ask: "So that's why you come to me?"

"No, it's not only that. I mean, yeah, it's partly that." And he reached out and gently stroked the palm of Frederick's hand with his middle finger. "I know you don't like it when I touch you in public."

Frederick was aroused. "I think we should cook dinner at home."

They went to the supermarket and walked the aisles and laughed at their own impulses—Oh, let's have ribs, you know how to cook ribs? And salad.

What do you like on your salad? Curt piled so many vegetables into the basket it would be enough to feed an army. And let's get some wine! Red or white? Or how about champagne? They enjoyed the ordinariness of shopping for ingredients to make dinner. Dessert! We forgot dessert! They stopped at a bakery. I want—Curt scanned the case—this and that and that and one of those! You'll get a tummy ache, Frederick said.

"Then you'll have to nurse me back to health."

Frederick liked how that sounded, partly because it suggested Curt would be staying longer this time.

The clerk behind the counter glared at them as they playfully talked about what to buy. "Have you decided?"

"Yes, we'll take" this and this and one of these, Curt said, grinning.

Out on the street, they laughed to think they might have been mistaken for father and son.

"Do you think I look like you?"

Frederick appraised him. "Not at all."

"Well, it depends on who my mother is. You ever have sex with a woman?"

The question made Frederick suddenly uncomfortable, partly because he didn't want anyone in their vicinity to overhear the conversation, partly because he didn't want to admit that intimacy had ever existed or could ever exist again with anyone besides Curt.

"Why do you ask?"

"Why not ask?"

"Well, the answer is no, actually, I haven't. Have you?"

"Oh, yeah."

"And?"

"And what?"

"How was it?"

"You'll have to try it yourself." Then, as if not satisfied with own his smart-alecky answer, he added, "It was okay, sort of. I can see myself with a woman someday." Was Curt toying with him—testing to see how much he wanted him, to discover how far he could be pushed before declaring his devotion? But Frederick thought it best to hold back from pursuing the dialogue any further. Besides, they were entering the building and people he knew were all around.

As Frederick prepared dinner, Curt sat on a stool at the counter drinking wine, getting drunk, and teasing Frederick about his cooking, about being a good housewife, about being a good parent. "Do you want a child?"

Another question that made Frederick's back go up, at least when it came from someone he had feelings for. It seemed they were getting to know each other from the wrong end of the telescope. He, too, was getting drunk.

"No. I think it's a little late in life for me to start thinking about raising a child."

"Oh," Curt said as if showing sorrow for someone who was hurt, "how come? Children are so cute."

"You're cute, most children are not."

"But I'm a child, aren't I?"

"Are you?"

"Compared to you."

"Do you usually get involved with older men? How old is Collin?"

"Twenty-seven."

"I rest my case."

"I like older men."

"Lucky me."

The idea that someone as young and beautiful as Curt could find him attractive was flattering in the extreme. Curt admitted young guys might be better looking than old guys ("Old?" Frederick thought), but he was turned on by something else in mature men, which he didn't bother to explain. Frederick might have pressed him, but every topic of conversation got derailed either because of the wine, or the business of preparing dinner, or some flip remark of Curt's, or the way he kept changing the subject, affirming the notion, which Curt now seemed the first to embrace, that he was queer, crazy, confused, a child, bent, in need of a good whipping. "Will you give me a good whipping someday?" Curt asked with a wicked smile.

That "someday" sent a shiver through Frederick's body. Now they were sitting down to table. Frederick brought out a pair of candles and lit them. It was the most nonsensical conversation he'd ever had.

"Do you want a good whipping?"

Curt was kittenish. "Maybe. But..." From Frederick, he started to explain, though he was drunk, and had lost, apparently, his appetite, he wanted something more. "Not that I don't ever want to have sex with you again," and now Frederick began to wonder if this was Curt's way of shifting the terms of their affair away from sex towards something more platonic.

"What *do* you want, then?" It was the second time he'd asked Curt the question this evening.

"A man I can trust," Curt answered without missing a beat. "A man I can look up to. Travel with, go shopping with, dancing, the theater—remember?" He kicked off a sneaker, bit his lip, and nuzzled his foot between Frederick's legs. Frederick reached down and held his foot in his hand.

"Why did you come to me that night at the theater?"

"Honestly? I saw you rush over to that girl who got mugged at intermission. The way you helped her. You seemed safe." It wasn't the answer Frederick expected. "I didn't really have a ticket to that show, y'know." It would never have occurred to him. "I snuck in during intermission. I do it all the time. I followed you in and saw the empty seat next to you and went for it. I'm glad I did."

Frederick was touched to think Curt was drawn to his goodness.

"Don't get me wrong, I like the theater, I just don't like money!" he said pulling his foot away. He told him about his former job at Aldo's Restaurant, his tense relations with the management, his hatred of the mafia, but especially the snotty gay clientele. "I can spot those faggots a mile away." Frederick suddenly wondered if, in Curt's eyes, he himself was one of "those faggots." But he felt sympathy for the boy, and the job did sound humiliating. He hated to think of Curt being humiliated, even as, it seemed clear, Curt was perfectly capable of humiliating others. Frederick suspected it was his defense, the way he survived in a hostile world.

"I'm sorry you had to go through that."

"Yeah, queers are the worst. The worst! I mean, I love having sex with them, but I've never been able to be friends with a homo. The guys I mean. All they want is to take care of themselves, they don't give a shit about anyone else."

"Who are you talking about?"

"After I got arrested, I went to a meeting of the Mattachine Society, ever hear of it?" Frederick was aware of the group—Sam and Ed had gone to an occasional meeting, had once encouraged him to join, but they weren't regular members and they knew it was hopeless to enlist him in the cause. In any case he never thought seriously that homosexuals could organize, say, the way Negroes did, into unions and groups. The idea of speaking about one's hurts and wrongs—fit for the analyst's couch, perhaps, but not for the public square. "And they were mostly guys in their forties and fifties and I felt really out of place. No one let me talk, and when I did they said, Well, you shouldn't have been parading around the boardwalk without a towel! Those fuckers, can you believe it? I was the one who got fucking beat up by the cops and thrown in jail, and they're blaming me! I think they were just jealous 'cause I was the only good looking person in the whole room."

Frederick was made uncomfortable by the turn in Curt's speech. Now it seemed the problem with the Mattachine Society wasn't so much their ideas about homosexual rights or how to advocate for better treatment of homosexuals but the fact they were middle-aged men. He tried not to take everything Curt said personally—tried to think about the real issue that had galvanized him—but his feelings of vulnerability about his age and appearance, and his real desire for intimacy, played havoc with his ability to think clearly. His senses were blurring. He'd had far too much wine.

He got up from the table and brewed a pot of strong coffee. Curt refused, but Frederick drank. He felt his faculties coming back into focus. It was late. Curt was tired and stretched out on the couch next to him, laying his head in his lap. Frederick stroked his hair.

"That feels nice. You're a nice man, Frederick. I've never met a nice homosexual like you."

Frederick reached for a volume of Whitman lying on the side table.

"Shall I read to you?"

"No one ever read to me before."

"Your mother didn't read to you as a child?"

"My mother sent me to boarding school. My father left when I was four, and she always had some loser boyfriend living with us at home. Then she married my stepfather, who was abusive and a drunk. She never had time for me."

Frederick wanted to make up for everything Curt was missing in his life. "Do you like Walt Whitman?"

"I don't know, he's…who is he?"

"An American poet."

"Yeah, I think we had to read him in school, but I never did the reading."

Frederick opened the volume to the Calamus poems. He read how the poet's name was celebrated in the city, but it wasn't a happy night, I caroused and laughed but was unhappy inside, until I left the city and came to the shore and wandered alone over the beach, undressing, laughing in the cool waters, and saw the sun rise, and thought with joy how my dear friend, my lover, was on his way to see me, and each breath tasted sweeter, all the day my food nourished me, and then at evening came my friend, and that night while all was still I heard the waters roll continually up the shores, whispering to congratulate me, for the one I love lay sleeping by me under cover in the cool night, in the stillness in the autumn moonbeams his face was inclined toward me, and his arm lay lightly around my breast.

"*And that night I was happy.*"

"Did you make that up?"

"No, that was Whitman. 1860."

"Wow, that's… I can't believe a man wrote that in the 1800s. They sure didn't teach us that in school."

"Incredible, but it's true. I get a lot of pleasure from Whitman. A lot of comfort."

"Read me another."

Frederick read poem after poem, of two boys together clinging, one the other never leaving, elbows stretching, fingers clutching, eating, drinking, sleeping, loving; of two men in a barroom, content, happy in being together, speaking little, perhaps not a word; of other men in other lands yearning, thoughtful, how we should be brethren and lovers if only we could know each other; how I bequeath myself to the dirt to grow from the grass I love. (Curt's eyelids were closing and opening. Frederick stroked his head.) *If you want me again look for me under your boot-soles. You will hardly know who I am or what I mean, but I shall be good health to you nevertheless.*

He read of the person drawn toward me, of the warning, be careful, I am surely far different from what you suppose. Do you think you will find in me your ideal? Do you think it so easy to have me become your lover? Do you think I am trusty and faithful? Do you see no further than this façade, this smooth and tolerant manner of me? Do you suppose yourself advancing on real ground toward a real heroic man? *Have you no thought O dreamer that I may be all maya, illusion?*

And he read of two simple men on a pier in the midst of a crowd, saying goodbye to each other, how the one to remain hung on the other's neck and passionately kissed him, how the other pressed him to remain in his arms.

Curt was asleep, his breathing steady. Frederick looked at the young man in his lap and petted his hair and bent to kiss his cheek. He hadn't felt this tenderness toward another person in such a long time. Not since Jon. He gave no thought to the possibility it may be all maya, illusion.

CHAPTER EIGHT

FREDERICK'S TRIP TO READING IN APRIL WAS DIFFERENT FROM HIS VISIT THE previous summer. If in August he'd felt his usual ambivalence about family gatherings, plus sheer impatience to get back to New York to meet Curt, now the following spring when Marge had her baby (it was a girl, she named it Clare, after their mother) he felt separate from his family for another reason. Now he was insulated by love. Love was a narcotic, and he was heavily under the influence. He felt no wish to tell anyone, share anything about the change that had occurred in his life (not that he ever could, of course), but the change was real and he knew it. He arrived on Good Friday, the day Marge went into labor. Her friend Dorothy waited for her at the hospital while Frederick took his parents to church. Even the gloomy Good Friday service, with its self-hating Reproaches and histrionic veneration of the cross, couldn't darken his mood. Instead he let his eyes lovingly trace the eccentric Moorish molding above the gothic windows, and he lost himself in strangely blissful contemplation of the circular window above the high altar, a stained-glass copy of Botticelli's *Madonna del Magnificat*. He marveled, even in this second-hand version, at the delicacy of Mary's hand as she dipped her quill into the inkwell proffered by one of the gaggle of boy angels surrounding her, as the Christ child's plump hand straddled his mother's forearm and the page of the book in which she composed her canticle (*Magnificat anima mea Dominum, My soul doth magnify the Lord*).

Everything he did—the visit to the hospital to see Marge and the new baby, making dinner for his parents and Markie, attending Mass on Easter Sunday morning, visiting the aunts in the afternoon, and then taking the train back to New York Sunday night—happened as if behind bullet-proof glass. Nothing anyone said or failed to say could touch him, for he carried something inside him (the thought amused and appalled him) almost as if *he* were pregnant (*My soul doth magnify the Lord because He that is mighty hath done great things to me*). Even Marge's newly straitened circumstances—Chuck was gone and she would have to start earning money once she was on her feet—didn't faze him. Because of her condition he had less opportunity to speak to her than to anyone that weekend. Dorothy filled him in on the details of where things stood with Chuck (her biggest fear wasn't that Marge was now alone but that she might take him back after what he'd done to her), Marge and the baby slept most of the weekend, and since it was a cesarean section she would have to stay in the hospital longer than expected. Dot could look after Markie, and one of the Galen kids, Ann or Joan, could help out if Mama and Pop needed anything in an emergency. So he returned to New York in good conscience: everything was more or less under control, and he'd been there when Marge needed him. Best of all, there'd been no opportunity for Marge to pursue her line of questioning about a "special someone" in his life.

Meanwhile, the basic facts of his relationship with Curt had not changed. Curt continued to live with Collin. They had not clearly broken up. Frederick had no way of contacting him. They did, however, see each other more regularly now, two or three times a week. Curt made the phone call when Collin wasn't around, they arranged to meet at Frederick's apartment, and though Curt was chronically late (one night Frederick prepared Curt's favorite dish—veal parmesan—but by the time he arrived the food was cold; another night they were supposed to meet for a performance of *Who's Afraid of Virginia Woolf?* but Curt was late and wasn't admitted until twenty minutes into the first act; still another night Frederick had long abandoned hope of his arrival and gone to bed, only to be awoken by the sound of the front door opening—Curt now had his own key—and then the smell of alcohol and cigarettes as he stumbled into bed)—on all such occasions, Frederick forgave. He found within himself surprising reserves of patience. Things important to him now took their place a notch lower in the scale of what he cared most about. Really, he cared about one thing only—one person—and that was Curt. For it was apparent that Curt needed him. Frederick didn't mind that Curt, as so often seemed the case, phoned him when there'd been a fight with Collin. Sometimes he would arrive past midnight, stand at the door with his arms held out for an embrace, and fall sobbing into Frederick's arms. Frederick would lead him to the couch, and they would sit and talk about what had happened—often it was Collin threatening to kick him out, and then where would he go, he had almost no money. He never went so far as to outright ask Frederick if he could move in with him, though Frederick figured it would come to that before summer was out. He did a lot of listening when Curt was like this. He didn't feel jealous, or hardly at all, because he knew at the end of the crying jag, Curt would dry his tears, and then change the subject, start laughing and teasing, and pretty soon teasing would turn to lovemaking.

One night toward the end of April Frederick couldn't resist asking Curt the question that increasingly hovered over all their interactions, both sexual and non-sexual. "Are you in love with Collin?"

"I don't know. Maybe. I think so. But I love you too."

The words "I love you" had not yet been spoken either by Curt or Frederick, and in a sense they still hadn't been spoken, for this was something less than a full-throated declaration. Nonetheless Frederick received Curt's statement with calculated benignity. He hardly raised an eyebrow, as if to do so would frighten the timid creature back into its cave.

"What do you want from him?"

"To leave me alone, or…" It was rather difficult to understand what Curt now tried putting into words—something to do with Collin loving him like he used to—loving him fully—which somehow didn't, to his mind, preclude being with Frederick, and then the issue slid almost imperceptibly from fidelity (or monogamy or the opposite of monogamy, it was hard to tell which) to physical appearances. It didn't matter, he started to say, if Collin was younger than Frederick and good looking—"*You're* good looking too, that's not what I'm saying—I mean—what I really want is to not be like this."

"Like what?"

"Like *this*: I just come to your apartment, we talk a little, we eat, we have sex, I leave, then we don't talk for a couple of days, then I call and we meet and we have sex and we eat…" Frederick was puzzled, for the arrangement had seemed until now to suit Curt perfectly, and hard as it was to admit, it had always seemed that Curt didn't much care what toll it took on Frederick. "It's not that I wish things were different between us. It's not about *us*. It's about me. I want me to be different. I want to be a different person. Sometimes I hate myself. The way I am."

Frederick was bewildered. He asked him what he hated about himself.

"I don't do anything important. Look at you, you're an architect. You've made a career for yourself. You can walk through the city and say, I built that, I designed that. A building is real. What have I done? I ran away from home and worked in a restaurant and now I'm a grocery clerk and it's all shit. My life is shit."

Frederick was disturbed to hear Curt had such a low opinion of himself, but even more disturbing was the suggestion that he, Frederick, seemed to make so little difference in his life. Curt's very presence in his life had put an extra layer of protection between him and the world, but Curt had seemed to grow more vulnerable, more depressed, more angry since the day they met. But what inspired his anger seemed to change from day to day. Sometimes it was Collin, other times his job. Then it was his mother, who rarely called or wrote or came to see him and never asked him to visit her in Chicago—for she knew Curt and his stepfather couldn't be in the same room together. Or his father, whom he never heard from but once a year, and then it was just a Hallmark card on his birthday. "At least he remembers my birthday, piece of shit."

Sometimes it was politics. By early May, the news from Birmingham, Alabama, was all he could talk about. He was exhilarated when the television news showed scenes of police using attack dogs and fire hoses turned on full strength to repel the Negro student protesters. He was especially excited, he said, by the fact that the protesters were students, and he noted their seeming hilarity at times, until things turned violent.

"They have nothing to lose and they're putting their whole lives on the line for what they believe in, for what's right," Curt said.

To Frederick, the turmoil was horrifying but remote. He thanked God he lived in New York and not the south. When he read in the *Times* that the national director of the Congress of Racial Equality had sent a telegram to President Kennedy urging Federal action to restore civil rights in Alabama, adding that "Alabama now rivals the racist police state of South Africa," Frederick was glad to be an architect, glad to be an artist, to be doing something that made a contribution to society that would outlast this hideous civil war overtaking the nation.

"It makes me want to throw bricks at the cops, motherfuckers!" Curt said.

Startled, Frederick put down the newspaper. "Are you all right?"

"No, I'm not all right. What kind of country do we live in?" He reminded Frederick of the incident last summer at Riis Park, of being beaten and thrown in jail. "What happened to me was—is like—it's like what's happening to the Negroes in Alabama!" The comparison struck Frederick as grotesque.

"That was an isolated incident. It was terrible, what happened to you, but this involves thousands of people. Whole sectors of society are marshaled against Negroes. This isn't a question of what they can wear in public, it's about being prevented from using public restrooms, pools, theaters" (he ticked off the items on his fingers), "department store dressing rooms, libraries, motels."

The clarity and vehemence of Frederick's argument made Curt furious.

"Whose side are you on?"

Frederick frowned. "I'm not on any side. There are no sides. I'm saying these are two unrelated situations."

"I disagree."

"I don't think we have the right to just…" He wanted to say something about homosexuals behaving any way they liked in public. An image of Curt kissing him on Broadway the night they met flashed in his head.

"The right to just what?"

"I don't want to get into an argument with you about this. We're not talking about homosexuals. We're talking about Negroes. And we're agreed what's happening in Alabama is terrible, okay?"

Curt wasn't mollified, but he didn't pursue the issue any further for the time being. But neither did he forget the argument in the days to come, and when an open letter by Martin Luther King, Jr. written from the Birmingham city jail was published two weeks later in the *New York Post*, Curt brought up the subject again. He trailed Frederick around the apartment as Frederick got ready for work.

"Listen to this: 'One has a moral responsibility to disobey unjust laws. I would agree with St. Augustine that "an unjust law is no law at all."'"

"And I would say the kind of law St. Augustine had in mind was not a law prohibiting men from flaunting their bikini bathing suits on the coast of Carthage."

Curt read on, ignoring Frederick's sarcasm. "'To put it in the terms of St. Thomas Aquinas: An unjust law is a human law that is not rooted in eternal law and natural law. Any law that uplifts human personality is just. Any law that degrades human personality is unjust. All segregation statutes are unjust because segregation distorts the soul and damages the personality.'"

"You're saying the law you broke is an unjust law that means to distort your soul and damage your personality? That wearing your bikini on the boardwalk is an expression of your personality, of your very soul?"

"Why are you such a bitch about this?"

"Because I think you can't compare the two things. You can't compare the treatment of Negroes in society and the treatment of homosexuals in society."

"Why not?"

A thought crossed Frederick's mind quicker than lightning: homosexuals don't demonstrate, they don't scream and cry out about injustice, they keep it to themselves, they are finer than Negroes. But what he said was, "Martin Luther King is talking about the morality of law. Nothing homosexuals do as homosexuals is considered moral under any jurisdiction, in any religious framework. It's completely outside the pale, and no interpretation of religion, no twisting of the law can save you from that fact. You want to talk about natural law? My God, what homosexuals do goes against nature in every sense of the word!"

"I can't believe you're saying this."

"All I'm saying is, the idea of civil rights doesn't make any sense when applied to homosexuals. You can't have a bill of homosexual civil rights."

Curt refused to drop the issue. "Listen to this: 'I have almost reached the regrettable conclusion that the Negro's great stumbling block in his stride toward freedom is not the white citizen's councilor or the Ku Klux Klanner, but the white moderate'" (stabbing the newspaper over the words "white moderate," he now followed Frederick into the bathroom, continuing to read aloud) "'who is more devoted to "order" than to justice; who prefers a negative peace which is the absence of tension'" ("Excuse me" Frederick had to interrupt—Curt was standing in his way at the sink) "'to a positive peace which is the presence of justice; who constantly says, "I agree with you in the goal you seek, but I cannot agree with your methods of direct action—"'"

"You think *I'm* the real enemy?"

"I completely understand what King is saying."

"So do I, and it has nothing to do with us." But Frederick saw the need to change his tack (if only because he was late for work). He was usually ready to concede anything to Curt. This was the odd exception, but he was afraid it could turn into something bigger, more divisive (politics had a way of doing that—he'd seen it happen between himself and his own father, first over the New Deal, then the House Un-American Activities Committee, now President Kennedy). "I hate to think of what happened to you that day," he said taking Curt in his arms, "I wish I could have saved you from that."

"How could you have saved me?"

He wanted to say, I would have insisted you put your towel on, but he knew that would only antagonize him. "I would have said, 'He's my son, and we had no idea about the ordinance. It won't happen again.'"

"So you would have lied and capitulated to the cops."

"I would have protected you and prevented you from getting into an argument with someone bigger and stronger than you. Yes, I would have capitulated. I don't think a law like that is worth laying down your life for, but *you* are worth laying down my life for." He felt butterflies in his stomach. He couldn't unsay it and didn't want to.

"You're saying you'd die for me?"

"Let's not scare ourselves with wild what-if stories. I love you." Now he'd said it, and without qualification. "Do you know that?"

"I guess I do now," still with a trace of anger in his voice.

"I love you and I want you to be happy and safe." He kissed him on the forehead.

Curt only said "Thank you" and embraced him, but the embrace turned sexual (making Frederick late for work after all), and the disagreement was put aside.

BY THE END OF JULY, CURT COULD TALK OF LITTLE BESIDES THE MARCH on Washington. There was to be a massive Negro demonstration "for jobs and freedom," as the press was putting it, and Curt, Bev, and her girlfriend, Kay, were taking the train to DC to join in. The Sunday before the march, the *Times* ran an interview with five prominent Negro leaders including Martin Luther King, Jr. Frederick read it with uncharacteristic absorption. He was especially intrigued, though at times "repelled" might have been the truer word, by the gnomic remarks of the writer James Baldwin, who, alone among the interviewees, felt almost no progress had been made towards achieving a free country, who repeatedly questioned the meaning of ordinary words like "equality" and "goal" before expressing, what seemed to Frederick at any rate, a tortured, even counterproductive point of view. For the first time in his life, Frederick thought seriously about the intricacies of the racial controversy: What exactly *is* meant by equality? How can it be achieved? How much progress has been made towards it? When will we attain it? And how does one eradicate racial bias in the thinking of white people? The answers were cloudy and unsettling. "One probably does not eradicate racial bias in the thinking of any people," Baldwin said, though "more people would be free to do right if we could establish in this country a moral climate in which the individual mind was less penalized and the popular mind less adored" (Frederick did think there was wisdom in that).

He mentioned the article to Curt the next day and, as they discussed it (Curt hadn't read it but, to Frederick's amazement, managed to cover more or less all the important points), decided he needed to join the March too. For Frederick had read the article in the *Times* through Curt's eyes and, in so doing, gained enormously both in his sensitivity to the issues and in his imagined intimacy with Curt. Going to Washington seemed as much a "pledge" to Curt as it did to the cause of Negro equality. In fact the two things became fused in his mind, so that whenever he read or saw anything on the television relating to the civil rights struggles of Negroes, he thought of Curt. But it wasn't because he thought, as Curt habitually did, that the struggles of Negroes were parallel or perpendicular or whatever geometrical figure best described Negro rights relative to homosexual rights. Frederick still wasn't convinced homosexuals *had* or *deserved* any rights per se. Curt put two and two together and came up with five, and that was a mistake. No, Frederick was going to Washington because he didn't want to miss what promised to be such a momentous day in the life of the nation *and in the life of Curt*. If anything, showing his interest in the cause of Negro equality was a way of apologizing to Curt for their disagreement over the cause of homosexual equality and even, subliminally, of distracting Curt from that latter cause. He was willing to take whatever risk participation in the March entailed, for the risk of not participating, he concluded, was greater: the risk that Curt would outgrow him and become, in a short space of time, a stranger to him.

The train to Washington was packed to the brim. Their party—Frederick and Curt, Bev and Kay, and, at the last minute, Sam and Ed—were not able to sit together but divided into couples. That meant Frederick and Curt had each other to themselves for the entire four-hour journey. Curt slept most of the way, sometimes with his head on Frederick's shoulder. At first the gesture made him uncomfortable, but at one point, going through a tunnel, Frederick caught sight of their reflection in the train window—an older man reading, a younger man asleep on his shoulder—and the pietà seemed right, not queer. Neither the train conductors nor anyone sitting around them seemed bothered by their physical intimacy. Curt looked winsome this morning with his uncombed, freshly washed hair and his loose-fitting black and white striped t-shirt, almost like a pajama top. Then they were surrounded by Negroes, and while at other times that might have made Frederick uncomfortable, he felt today was a day unlike any other day. Everyone was headed to the March this morning. Penn Station was choked by armies of people at 5:00 AM. Yet there was a palpable air of festivity about the station mixed with solemn purpose. He thought of that day during the war, after hours of waiting in despair, thinking his train would never make it, when Jon appeared seemingly out of nowhere…and they raced across the street to the Statler Hotel and…Frederick fell asleep, never knowing that his head rested on top of Curt's, his cheek touching Curt's hair, breathing in the boy's aroma.

They were woken up by Kay, who'd come to tell them they were due to arrive any minute.

"You two look cute."

"God, I'm wasted," Curt said. "What time is it?"

"Almost 10:15."

"Where's Bev?"

"She's in her seat. We switched places with these two guys so we could sit across from Sam and Ed. Sam's funny."

"Never go on a long journey without Sam," Frederick said.

"He told us about the time you kicked your neighbor's dog out of the elevator."

"What?!" Curt perked up.

Nothing was sacred today, Frederick thought. "You'll have to hear my side of the story sometime. Whatever he told you, it's sure to be full of puffery. I didn't kick the dog."

Kay laughed. "He says he'll help us hand out flyers next week," she told Curt and explained to Frederick they were trying to drum up new members for the Mattachine Society. Sam, apparently, had promised to pitch in.

He'd thought Sam had a rather jaundiced opinion of Curt and his friends, but maybe everyone was changing. "Well, good, so if you all get arrested Sam can talk your way out of it."

The concourse at Union Station was filled beyond capacity, but Frederick didn't feel confined. Human traffic flowed freely through the station, and he and his companions were carried almost effortlessly out of doors within minutes. As the dense crowd fanned out across the traffic circle in the direction of Constitution Avenue and the National Mall, he stopped, letting the others go on ahead, to inspect the shapely Beaux Arts façade with its three triumphal arches. A smaller depot than Penn, it nevertheless put its more ostentatious New York cousin to shame, so in keeping, he thought, turning away from the station, with the monumental grandeur of the Capitol building itself, which he could see now gleaming white through the trees, just up the hill. The problem, he was convinced (catching up with the others), is New York itself. When money is the driving force, as opposed, say, to government or the maintaining of our physical surroundings (he'd forgotten what a verdant city Washington was!), then nothing is sacrosanct, not even the finest architecture.

In every direction, around every corner, people filled the sidewalks and streets, singing and shouting, wearing buttons and hats, waving signs and banners:

WE DEMAND AN END TO BIAS *NOW*
WE DEMAND DECENT HOUSING *NOW*
WE DEMAND VOTING RIGHTS *NOW*
WE DEMAND JOBS FOR ALL *NOW*
CIVIL RIGHTS PLUS FULL EMPLOYMENT EQUALS FREEDOM
NO U.S. DOUGH TO HELP JIM CROW GROW

Already, muffled echoes of speeches and songs could be heard from the podium at the base of the Washington Monument where the March was set to begin. People had come from all over the country. Near them was a group of teenagers from California, a church choir from Georgia, a contingent of senior citizens from Iowa. Journalists and TV cameras were everywhere. Curt had brought along his transistor radio, so their progress along Constitution Avenue was marked, block upon block, by "Walk Like a Man," "It's My Party," "He's So Fine."

Spotting a couple of androgynous Negro women—or was it a woman and a man?—Bev and Kay began testing their powers of telling who was queer and who wasn't. They agreed it was harder to tell with women than with men, which they attributed to the greater *freedom* women had to express themselves in public but also (Frederick, Curt, Sam and Ed to a man struggled to grasp the girls' logic) to women's relative powerlessness. This prompted a debate about sex discrimination—Bev had been reading the new book by Betty Friedan and argued that in 1963 it was as morally indefensible as racial discrimination. Curt, meanwhile, was keeping his eyes on the police, watching their faces, their hands and feet, the way they stood, the way they interacted with each other, looking for signs of jitters, or disrespect, noticing in particular the occasional Negro cop and wondering what went through his mind on a day like this. Remarkably, no disturbances were seen, no confrontations between marchers and cops.

The March was supposed to kick off from the Monument at 11:30, but already the crowd had a mind of its own and, well before that time, was surging toward the rally site in front of the Lincoln Memorial. There seemed no beginning, no end, no shape to the movement. It was everywhere and time and space were suspended beneath the blazing sun and the overwhelming power of so many thousands of people.

Eventually, as they neared the Lincoln Memorial, they heard voices of singers—Odetta, Joan Baez, Josh White—"*Ain't nobody gonna stop me, nobody gonna keep me from marchin' down freedom's road!*" When finally they reached the east side of the reflecting pool, Curt grabbed Frederick's arm in one hand and Sam's in the other, as Ed, Bev, and Kay followed, saying, "I need water." They managed to insinuate themselves through the crowd and decided to go no farther. They saw nothing but bodies from here to the Lincoln Memorial, and it was clear there was no hope of getting any closer. Amid the swaying and shifting and gently pushing crowd, a space along the edge of the water opened up, and pushing others aside, the six of them sat down. Curt took off his shoes and socks and waded into the pool. The girls followed, while Frederick, Sam, and Ed watched with amusement and some envy.

"He's very cute," Ed said. But Frederick was numb to conversation, so overwhelmed by the scene, the heat, and the strangeness of his party of companions to reply with anything more substantive than a bemused "Yes." He watched as Curt and the girls kicked water at each other along with a score of other teenagers and young people who took their cue and plunged in after them.

Then the speeches began. Curt came out of the water and sat along the edge, squeezing himself in between Sam and Frederick. Under cover of the crush of bodies, he held Frederick's hand tight, as if everything that had happened so far, everything he had done and said today, were summed up in that strong handgrip. Words echoed fitfully through the air amid the murmur of two hundred thousand souls. We are the advance guard of a massive moral revolution for jobs and freedom...Our ancestors were transformed from human personalities into private property...The sanctity of private property takes second place to the sanctity of the human being...Get in and stay in the streets of every city, every village and hamlet of this nation until true freedom comes, until the revolution of 1776 is complete, and with every phrase of every speech Curt squeezed Frederick's hand as if recording his assent.

But they were all growing weary. They had spent hours on the train, hours walking the streets and the Mall, the sun was hot, they were hungry and thirsty. Then Mahalia Jackson took the microphone and the crowd came alive! She sang how the Lord *brought her, taught her, kept her, never left her,* and Frederick envied her and everyone in the crowd who clapped and sang along and knew the words, envied their faith, their conviction in a personal relationship to God, their certainty they were not alone, and he marveled that a people so downtrodden, so disrespected, so demoralized could find within themselves the strength, the physical and spiritual stamina, to praise and sing and give thanks.

At last Martin Luther King, Jr. rose to the podium and spoke of the Negro, how he lives on a lonely island of poverty in the midst of a vast ocean of material prosperity (this was greeted by a roar from the crowd), how they've come to Washington to cash a check that will give us the riches of freedom and the security of justice, and he reminded them of the fierce urgency of now, that 1963 is not an end but a beginning. They would meet physical force with soul force. The marvelous new militancy, he said, which has engulfed the Negro community must not lead us to a distrust of all white people, for many of our white brothers, as evidenced by their presence here today, have come to realize that their destiny is tied up with *our* destiny, that their freedom is inextricably bound to *our* freedom. The crowd cheered. But our children, he said, are stripped of their selfhood and robbed of their dignity. He commended his people for their creative suffering and urged them to go back to Mississippi, back to Alabama, back to South Carolina, back to Georgia, back to Louisiana, back to the slums and ghettos of the northern cities, knowing the situation can and will be changed. For he had a dream, he said, and conjured before their eyes in the blazing sun and the suffocating heat a panorama of the American landscape, the prodigious hilltops of new Hampshire, the mighty mountains of New York, the heightening Alleghenies of Pennsylvania, the snow-capped Rockies of Colorado, the curvaceous slopes of California, leading them higher and higher until the final words of his speech were drowned in a pandemonium of rejoicing. Curt let go of Frederick's hand to clap and raise his voice along with everyone else. Frederick turned to look at him and saw tears rolling down his face.

Now A. Philip Randolph bid them stand and pledge to continue the struggle: "I affirm my complete personal commitment for the struggle for jobs and freedom," they repeated after him, "I pledge that I will not relax until victory is won." Curt said the words and believed he was making a promise to himself and his future, and Frederick said the words but felt someone else, *another* Frederick, was the one now speaking, for he wasn't a joiner, didn't believe in causes, though in his heart of hearts he admired those who did, and they said, "I pledge to carry the message of the March to my friends and neighbors back home and to arouse them to an equal commitment," but mostly the pledge he made was a pledge to Curt, as if, before these hundreds of thousands of people, he stood up and declared his commitment to him, "and I will pledge my heart and my mind and my body," he said, "unequivocally and without regard to personal sacrifice." While Curt continued cheering the end of the rally and the proclamation of his hopes and dreams, Frederick stood silent, content, happy to be here with Curt, but most of all happy that the pledge, the promise of commitment to the cause, and now the March itself, had come to an end.

CHAPTER NINE

NO CLEAR DECISION WAS MADE THAT CURT SHOULD MOVE IN WITH FRED-erick. It happened bit by bit as Curt left articles of clothing behind in his apartment, bought a bookshelf secondhand and delivered it there because it was too big for Collin's place. The day after the March on Washington, Curt returned home with Frederick and stayed through Labor Day. That weekend he asked Frederick to drive him to Collin's because he knew Collin would be at the Jersey shore with friends. They loaded up Frederick's car with the remainder of Curt's things (a suitcase full of clothes, a stained blanket, a coffee percolator, a small television), and that was that.

For Curt, moving in with Frederick had more to do with avoiding Collin than choosing Frederick. Ever since their reunion at the Metropolitan Museum back in February, Collin had been making some kind of scene every other night. If there was one thing Curt couldn't stand, it was men trying to possess him. Plus Collin was aggressive and hot-headed, and on the Tuesday before the March he threatened to kick Curt's teeth in for lying about where he'd been the previous weekend—Curt said he'd spent it with Bev and Kay, but Collin knew he'd been with Frederick. That was the last straw. Curt cried and cried in Frederick's lap as he described the indignity of being threatened with physical violence by someone you love. "What have I done to deserve—?"

Frederick interrupted to ask why he hadn't mentioned the incident on Tuesday night when it happened—and why he said nothing about it all day Wednesday—they'd spent the whole day together in Washington, it hadn't come up once in conversation, and honestly Curt had shown no signs—as, for example, his sister had when her husband slapped her—of having been traumatized by the altercation. And one more thing: why, after six months of "dating" (though the word was totally inadequate to describe the chaotic intensity, not to mention the irregularity, of their encounters during that time)—after sharing so much, why did Curt persist in speaking of Collin as if he were still the most important man in his life? Frederick was genuinely sorry to think of him ever being abused by someone he loved, but he simply didn't understand what transpired between the two of them. Still it was he who finally said, "Would it make you feel better if we just gathered the rest of your things and you stayed here?" "Stayed" was the operative word. He didn't say "live" or "move in." It was characterized as a temporary move to protect Curt.

"But is he in love with you?" Sam asked upon hearing the news Curt had moved in.

"I don't know. Does he need to love me? Now, I mean? Love takes time."

"Sweetheart, this is 1963, not 1863. What are you getting out of it? I think I know what *he's* getting out of it." Frederick rolled his eyes dismissively. "I think he's taking advantage of your good nature. You have a beautiful apartment in a reputable neighborhood, a good job, a car. He's—what? Nineteen? Twenty? Barely holding down a job as a salad boy in a—"

"He's twenty-one, and he quit—"

"Twenty-one is he? How long has he been twenty-one?"

"What does it matter? The point is, he quit the restaurant job because he didn't like the way his boss was treating him, and then he—"

"So he's unemployed?"

"No, now he's working at an advertising agency."

"Resourceful boy! How did he land that job?"

"He works in the mail room and spends half the day on a bicycle making deliveries."

"You didn't answer my question."

Frederick almost hated to admit it. "I knew someone at the firm and was able to pull a few strings."

"So he can thank you for his job now too. Sounds like a good deal to me."

"Sam, I think you're wrong about him," and Frederick launched into a litany of the charming, heart-warming, touching moments that filled his days—waking up with Curt in his arms, making breakfast for the two of them first thing in the morning, having someone to come home to, "just knowing he's there next to me when I'm working at home, we don't have to say a word. And he's unpredictable. He's fun and funny. We take road trips, we go to the theater, to the movies. We go for walks at ten o'clock at night. We ignite each other in bed. I'm sorry if it shocks you."

"It doesn't shock me. I just…I guess I can only say what I've been saying from the beginning, which is—"

"I know, but if I *had* been careful, he wouldn't be in my life."

"You're right."

It was inevitable they would learn new things about each other, their families and backgrounds. The story of the events leading up to Curt's dramatic decision to run away from home and come to New York, not knowing a soul and with nothing but the clothes on his back and a wad of cash in his pocket, grew longer and oddly entangled. Turned out it wasn't just his irresponsible mother and hated stepfather he was trying to escape. There had been, or so he said, *another* series of incidents. He was out one evening with Frank, a man in his thirties he'd been dating for a few weeks. Curt was sixteen at the time.

"Wait just a minute. How did a sixteen-year-old boy meet a—how old did you say he was?"

Curt got up from his side of the table, put his arms around Frederick's shoulders, and kissed the freckles on the back of his neck. "I don't know exactly. Thirty-five or something."

"A thirty-five-or-something-year-old man."

There was a diner, he explained, frequented by queers in the Lakeview neighborhood of Chicago, and Curt and some of his friends used to go there after school. They would sit in the booths while the older men walked the aisle, supposedly on their way to and from the rest room, cruising the boys in the booths. Curt caught the eye of one such man—Frank was his name—and they left the diner together and went driving in Frank's yellow convertible.

"It was the most amazing car I'd ever been in. God! And with the top down! We drove to Evanston and then out of the city, and we ended up in this farm area. We must have driven two hours. I didn't know where he was taking me."

"And you weren't scared?"

"Nothing scares me, you must know that by now."

They made love in the back seat of the car. Curt was usually the one to get fucked, but something about this guy—his good looks, his attentiveness—he was almost like a gentleman from another era—"it just made me want to flip him over on his belly and fuck the bejesus out of him," which was exactly what he did, and he came inside of him, and it was the first time *that* ever happened. He fell in love right then and there. They started seeing a lot of each other, and one evening they were walking in downtown Chicago. There was a curfew for anyone under seventeen, and suddenly a couple of cops pulled up, got out of the car, and started asking questions. They accused Curt of soliciting sex for money and Frank of child molestation. They arrested Frank, tried him, and put him in jail on a five-year sentence, but Curt's mother pleaded with the judge to let Curt off if he promised to see a psychiatrist for six months.

"And brother, did I ever! Actually he wasn't so bad. He told me I needed to start dating guys my own age and learn how not to get caught. I think he was queer too. Actually, I think he wanted to fuck me. He was the first person who ever told me about the Mattachine Society. He said I should channel my anger and energy into activism. That's when I started saving up to move to New York."

Sometimes when telling this story, Curt mentioned the romantic letters he received from Frank and indicated, had Frank not gone to jail, he might never have left Chicago. Along the same lines he spoke of New York as a place he came to eagerly at first but then stayed in reluctantly, a place that disappointed him and made life ten times more difficult—and more expensive—than it should be. Frederick wanted to say, but if you'd never come to New York you'd never have met me, but he couldn't, for it implied they were "together," a "couple" in a way they clearly were not.

And yet Curt seemed content as the days and weeks went by, and this came as a relief to Frederick, who'd grown weary of the constant drama of their life together. More and more he wanted normalcy, tranquility—mainly so he could do his work—with Curt, if not quite in the background of the picture, then at most one stable element of the composition. He did, however, want to be known by Curt, which meant sometimes telling him about his own life, his past, his family. Curt was particularly curious about the war and what kind of men he knew in the army, whether he'd "had something" with any of them. Eventually Frederick told him about

Jonathan, though he didn't mention his name (something sacred about that, Frederick felt, best kept to himself). Curt could sense this was someone important, though Frederick was careful not to reveal too much. He was twenty-eight, his friend several years younger, they met during basic training in January of '43. They remained close after the war. They never lived together but saw each other weekends in New York or Boston. They spoke on the telephone regularly, spent holidays together—well, as many as possible—"until Christmas of 1959. I was in Reading, he couldn't make it. And he announced he was engaged."

"Good for him!"

"What do you mean?"

"I mean, what a motherfucker! He gets to have a wife and kids and respectability, and he has you for the good stuff. He doesn't give up a thing."

"I told him I couldn't see him anymore."

"Why?" Curt asked, as if it were the last thing Frederick should have done.

Why? Frederick had never analyzed his decision to cut off contact with Jon. It had always seemed the obvious thing to do. He'd been so wounded by his announcement, so humiliated by the thought of his being intimate with another person—worse, with a woman, as if his choice to marry Rachel was an implicit rejection of Frederick's nature—of the nature of their love—and Frederick had always thought it *was* love, real, true love, the one thing in his life that redeemed the sorry, sordid truth about who, about *what* he was. Jon's love made him clean, made him beautiful. Now he was taking it all away. He had no choice but to turn away from him forever.

Frederick changed the subject—it obviously wasn't the sort of thing he could discuss with Curt, not yet, perhaps not ever—and felt mildly offended that Curt didn't object to his doing so, as if "the love of Frederick's life" (though he deliberately didn't characterize it that way) was a topic of only middling interest to him. Tell me or don't tell me, Curt seemed to say, it's not something I really need to know. It certainly lacked the flair of Curt's story about Frank.

"Oh, and I forgot the best part. When we were out in the cornfield, after we'd had sex, Frank started the car to drive back to town, and we got stuck in the mud. So he walked about a mile to the nearest gas station, and he came back in a truck with these two gas station attendants, and they looked at me and—you should have seen their faces. Oh god, it was crazy. It's like we were Martians. But they pulled us out of the mud and we got back to

Chicago around midnight and my stepfather was waiting up for me and we had another one of our shouting matches."

But Frederick resented that Curt had so blithely moved on from the subject of Jon. It was something he grew more and more to dislike about the boy. He didn't seem to know how to listen. His attention was so easily diverted. Sometimes Frederick would be talking and Curt, in a surreal shift of frame, would interrupt to say something completely unrelated.

"And so I came up with the idea to incorporate one of the porticos from the Rhinelander Houses into the façade of the new building, and—"

"Fuck, I was supposed to call Kay tonight! We're supposed to meet some people from the Mattachine Society. We want to get out and *do* something, we're sick of just sitting at these meetings and listening to people pour out their hearts about how difficult it was to be a fairy back in the old days—"

"Excuse me, you just changed the subject as if you weren't paying attention or didn't give a shit about anything I said."

"I was listening," he said and went on to recount nearly verbatim Frederick's description of the buildings on the corner of Fifth Avenue and Washington Square North and how his firm got the commission to do an apartment tower on the site and his idea to take one of the doorways from the old building and use it in the new one. "There, see? I heard every word you said."

"Then why did you interrupt?"

"Sometimes I don't want to hear a lecture."

"*You* asked *me* about the New York Landmarks book and how I became interested in historic preservation and I was answering your question. I thought we were having a conversation."

"Well, it doesn't always feel like a conversation. I'm sorry to be so blunt, but it's the truth."

"There are plenty of people for whom this kind of conversation would be perfectly normal, perfectly pleasant." He said it as much to reassure himself as he did to inform Curt.

"Good for them. I'm only talking about myself."

"Well that's nothing new," he said, and walked out of the room.

Sex often settled disagreements, but only temporarily. Sooner or later conflict would flare up again. Increasingly it revolved around what Frederick perceived as Curt's general disregard for the feelings of other people. One night he overheard Curt say something over the telephone about "the old man." After Curt hung up, Frederick said, "Is that what I am?"

"I wasn't referring to your age, Frederick. It was a term of endearment. I meant my sweetheart, my honey. You always suspect the worst about me. You *are* older than me, you can't deny it."

"I'm not denying it. But it feels disrespectful if you're calling me 'the old man' to your friends."

"I just told you it's a term of endearment, it's not disrespect."

But Frederick couldn't be sure. It seemed as if, ever since the March on Washington, something in Curt had come undone. The day had electrified him, but for most of September he didn't know what to do with his energy. Some nights when he felt restless, he and his friends would ride the subway and cause trouble. Wearing tight pants, costume jewelry, eyeliner and mascara (Curt became an expert at painting "doe eyes"), they would go "wrecking," as they called it, on the subway. For the price of a fifteen-cent token, they could have a long night of dangerous fun. They did chorus-line kicks and sang songs and made outrageous passes at well-dressed, buttoned-down men.

"Hey, pussycat, buy me a cup of coffee?"

When the object of their desire made a threatening move, they would run wildly through the car, jump off the first opportunity, laugh, howl, scream how they made a fool of that asshole and wasn't it funny to see his face, "I almost thought I was gonna pee in my pants!" Sometimes they would acquire an extra teammate—a young kid or a stray adolescent—who was dazzled by the older boys' bravado and sense of style. Curt always felt especially protective of these waifs. He was good at making people notice him, even of being afraid of him, and he liked the rare feeling of being older and wiser, of having someone look up to him.

One night they were out wrecking and started singing irreverent lyrics to the tune of "Howdy Doody": "*We are the Village queens, we always wear blue jeans, we wear our hair in curls, because we think we're girls!*" Curt wore a boa he'd picked up at a Salvation Army shop, and as they exited the train he dragged the boa around the neck of one grimacing old lady. To his surprise, she followed him off the train and proceeded to reprimand him and his friends, telling them they were a disgrace, they should be ashamed, "Why don't you act like young men instead of a bunch of fairies? What do you accomplish…" But they couldn't hear the rest of her tirade because they were already above ground at Sheridan Square. After another hour of dancing and carrying on in the Village, Curt decided he'd had enough and would just go home.

PENNSYLVANIA STATION

The next morning, Frederick was riding the elevator when his downstairs neighbor, Mrs. Bradshaw, got on. She lit up with tightly controlled anger. "Last night I was taking the subway, and that young man I see you with came onto the car with several other hoodlums and they terrorized the passengers with their insulting songs and gestures. He humiliated me in front of everyone on the car by tying a scarf around my neck! I don't know what your relationship to him is and, frankly, I don't want to know. But if I ever see him act that way again or if he ever shows me so much as an ounce of disrespect, I tell you, Mr. Bailey, I'll report the two of you to the board and you'll be kicked out of this building so fast you won't know what hit you."

They had exited the elevator midway through her speech and she concluded it as Frederick stood with his back up against the mail chute. Even as other residents came by to drop envelopes in the slot, she kept on with her accusations, not lowering her voice, not caring who heard her incriminating words.

"I've no idea what you're talking about, but if you have something to say you should speak to the young man himself. I am not his father."

"Then may I ask, what are you to him?" Frederick turned to stone. "You have nothing to say to that, do you? People like you disgust me. Good day."

That night after work, Frederick confronted Curt. He reiterated Mrs. Bradshaw's words and added his own stern warning.

"Why are you speaking to me this way? You sound like my stepfather!" He headed for the door, but Frederick grabbed him by the arm and yanked him back.

"Are you mad?" he shouted.

Curt pushed him away with force. "What the fuck are you doing?"

"Listen to me! You live with me. People know me at the grocer and the shoe shine, at the newsstand and the dry cleaner and the restaurants. The staff of this building and all the neighbors know me. And they see you with me."

"So? What do you expect me to do about it?"

"I expect you to act with decorum, for God's sake. She threatened to report me to the board and have me kicked out—both of us kicked out. Do I need to start laying down rules of conduct with you?"

"Oh, fuck your rules of conduct. And fuck that old lady. Yes, I go out occasionally and have fun with my friends, and if some people can't take a joke, screw them. Screw all of them."

"But I have a reputation."

"You knew what you were getting yourself into when you met me."

"What are you talking about, 'getting myself into'?"

"You can't control what I do and say."

"I'm not trying to control you, but there are other people's feelings to consider. You don't change society by just willing it. You'll never change people's minds by being disrespectful and vulgar and—"

"I'm not gonna listen to this crap anymore. You live your life from one lie to the next." Again he headed for the door.

"Don't you dare walk out on me."

"Or what? What are you gonna do? You nellie, cocktail-sipping fruit."

Ah yes, Frederick thought. You think so, too. It was almost cleansing to hear him say the words. "Is that how you see me?"

"When you get all prissy about what other people think, yes." He turned and opened the door.

"Where are you going?" The question was both a threat and a plea.

"Out."

Curt let the door slam shut behind him.

Frederick went into the living room, poured himself a drink, and lit a cigarette. He had to think. *Think.* What indeed had he gotten himself into? Discretion wasn't the same thing as dishonesty. His life was not, as Curt had said, a series of lies. Perhaps he was too young to understand. What would it take to get it through his head? The obvious solution would be to get rid of him. *Especially* if he thought of him with such contempt. Kick him out, notify the front desk, change the phone number. He took a long drag on his cigarette. But could he seriously imagine doing it? He never liked Mrs. Bradshaw anyway. What right did the old battle-ax have to speak to him like that? It was one thing for Curt to hurl insults, he was a kid, and he was speaking in the heat of the moment. He almost admired him for what he'd done to the old woman. There was something powerful about his lawlessness. But did he really think of him as a…what did he say? A disgusting old piece of fruit? Again, he was a kid, and kids nowadays were vulgar and outspoken. They hardly knew any better. And Curt had missed out on the kind of love and guidance—the proper parenting—that would have softened his edges. No, the thing to do would be to sit down with him and have a rational discussion about what it meant to be homosexual in a world hostile to homosexuals. He would have that conversation with Curt when he came back.

But when would he come back?

Here he was again, in his old, familiar place. Waiting.

THE WEST SIDE DISCUSSION GROUP MEETINGS OF THE NEW YORK MATTACHINE Society were held once a month in the basement of Freedom House across the street from the New York Public Library. It was, ironically, *Frederick's* idea to accompany Curt to the October meeting. For when Curt came back the next day—all he said was he'd been to Collin's and Collin was an asshole—Frederick was so relieved to have him back, and, frankly, so relieved to hear him speak ill of Collin in the bargain, he decided to hold off on that serious conversation about being homosexual in a hostile world, decided not to push for ground rules about what to say and what not to say to others about their relationship, including what terms to use when referring to each other (he still didn't like hearing Curt refer to him as "the old man," and he didn't believe Curt's line that it was a term of endearment, but all of that could wait). So eager was he, in fact, to set things right between them, he actually admitted he probably had some things to learn about the homophile movement, and though he wasn't saying he wanted to make any drastic *personal* changes, he admitted he was curious and, more importantly, it was a group and a movement important to Curt. For his part, Curt was on his best behavior the night of the meeting, for he hoped it would make Frederick see things differently, make him understand that times were changing and he could change with them, a little bit, a lot maybe, and it would be all right.

They entered the building and explained to the woman at the desk they were here for the meeting of the Mattachine Society. Noting her expression, how she didn't break her mask of professionalism, merely indicated the way to the basement, they went downstairs and hoped for a moment together this might be the beginning of a new chapter in the story of their lives.

Bev and Kay greeted them. Curt then introduced Frederick to several of his other friends. Frederick was struck by the fact, which should never have come as a surprise, that Curt's friends in the Society were all of his own generation. They formed a bloc, and they sat together. Curt, however, feeling he shouldn't segregate himself from the older men, if only for tonight, stayed by Frederick's side.

Upon taking their seats, Frederick recognized the man to his right as the proprietor of the antique shop on Fourth Avenue—he passed the shop regularly on his way to and from the 14th Street subway. The man introduced himself as Harold Wolsky. Though Frederick wasn't sure he liked the idea of seeing anyone he recognized here, they quickly fell into an easy, familiar exchange, finding much in common on the subject of work. Frederick mentioned his contribution to the soon-to-be-published book on New York Landmarks.

"There must be a law to protect old buildings in New York," Harold said with quiet conviction, and he went on to explain his belief in a fundamental psychic need for some assurance of permanence and continuity. "I believe that a living, historic city gives us a sense of security and well-being that only comes from something that's been around longer than we have."

"You seem to have given this a lot of thought."

"To me it's common sense. The past speaks to me. I hear voices from the past. I believe the past is very much alive." Frederick noticed how often he began his sentences with the words "I believe." "Historic preservation goes beyond buildings. That's why I got into the antiques business. To me it involves saving smaller things, objects, documents, even non-tangible things like family stories. I was always attracted to old things and old people. I was very close to my grandmother. I loved listening to her stories. I felt more at home in her company than in the company of my peers." Frederick was almost embarrassed to admit to himself, much less to Harold, the same was true of him. "I kept meticulous photo albums and scrap books. In high school, I became the family photographer. I saw myself as the family documentarian, and I'd take pictures at reunions, weddings, funerals. I came from a large family in St. Louis. We're very close. Or, we were close until they found out about my tendencies, you know, that I'm 'enchanted.' One of my neighbors found some magazines in the trash I'd thrown out, and—I was stupid, I should have put them in a wrapper or burned them, I guess—and he came to me and said, 'St. Louis is not and never can be enchanted.'" Harold laughed with exasperation. "This was 1923, I was twenty years old."

Frederick was uncomfortable with the turn to sexual matters in the conversation and didn't like to be reminded of Mrs. Bradshaw's recent threat. He had been content to reminisce with Harold about childhood, about their shared love of beautiful objects.

"Well, I've always loved walking among ruins," he began, and felt the illogic of his words given where Harold ended up. "As a child, I drew elevations and floor plans of houses and made-up houses. I was always building things, apartment towers, villages, stage sets." But in deference to Harold's confession about being, as it really seemed to Frederick, hounded out of St. Louis because of his deviant nature and feeling suddenly and genuinely sorry for him, he added, "…and doll houses."

"Oh, you should come to the store sometime and see the doll houses I have. Some Victorians. They're really splendid."

"I'd like to," Frederick said, not without sincerity.

"Looks like you made a new friend," Curt whispered in his ear.

"I know him from the neighborhood."

"Mmm," Curt said, seeming to encourage the possibility of intimacy between them.

The guest speaker was a psychoanalyst named Richard Robertiello. A longtime member of New York Mattachine, whom Curt identified with scare quotes only as "Jim" ("I know he doesn't use his real name, he's a total queen," he whispered), gave the introduction: "I want to welcome Dr. Robertiello. A native of New York City where he practices psychiatry and psychoanalysis, he is married and has two children, a girl of seventeen and a boy of twelve. His BA was acquired at Harvard and his MD at the Columbia University College of Physicians and Surgeons. In addition to his private practice, he is chief psychiatrist of the Long Island Consultation Center. He is best known as the author of *Voyage From Lesbos: The Psychoanalysis of a Female Homosexual*, the first complete report of the psychoanalysis of a lesbian ever published. His mentor, Dr. William Silverberg…" ("Just when you thought it couldn't get any worse" Curt muttered—but Frederick found himself intrigued by the guest speaker's credentials) "…in his introduction to the book, praised Dr. Robertiello's 'sensitivity to what his patient was experiencing; his alertness to clues as to her unconscious assumptions; his willingness to persevere as she now advanced towards self-understanding and change, now retreated from it…" ("I'm dead. Wake me up in the next life.") "…and, above all, his unfailing good will throughout all these vicissitudes.' But let me not say more about him. You'll see for yourself. Dr. Robertiello."

"Thank you, thank you, Jim, for that generous introduction—too generous, I should say. I am very happy to be here, and I commend all of you for your bravery. Coming to this meeting must not have been easy, but you are showing great courage and responsibility in making the effort. And I really just want to help you in any way I can. Now, I consider myself a friend to the homosexual, but I am the kind of friend that gives hard-headed advice, not the kind that tells you what you want to hear just to make you feel good.

And the first thing I must say as your friend is that homosexuality is an emotional disturbance, a character defense, in which the patient does not recognize he is sick. His is a crippled psychology, a second-rate substitute for reality, a flight from life. Now, as your friend I say you deserve better in your life. Homosexuality deserves no encouragement, no glamorization, no rationalization, no fake status as a minority group, no sophistic argumentation about 'differences in taste.' Homosexuality is—and I say this with the authority of the best scientific research behind me—a sickness. But what I've really come here to say to you tonight is that you deserve fairness, compassion, understanding, and, when possible, treatment."

Quiet murmurs from the audience had been intermittent from his opening remarks, and now the murmur was rising and continuous. Frederick didn't entirely disagree with the doctor's "diagnosis" of homosexuality, but hearing it talked about publicly put him on edge—as it did others, apparently, in the room.

"I know there is considerable controversy about curing homosexuality, and tonight I don't want to talk about aversion therapy or any of the other therapies we've suggested for turning the patient towards an embrace of normal feelings. Tonight I want to talk about Alcoholics Anonymous." A woman in the audience gasped. "You see, I view homosexuality, much like alcoholism, as an addiction, an illness susceptible to, if not a cure, then to being well managed, and the way of managing I want to tell you about follows the approach taken by AA."

Now an eruption of widespread discontent came from the audience. Frederick was miffed. It started to look like Dr. Robertiello wasn't going to be given much chance to elaborate his theory, which, quite frankly, Frederick found intriguing.

"The alcoholic is disturbed, but he is not expelled from the society of man. Even the psychopath and the criminally insane can benefit from compassionate treatment, from efforts to get them back into the mainstream of life. I am glad to be living in a more tolerant society when—"

A man stood up, disregarding Jim's attempts to use Robert's Rules of Order to control the group. "If homosexuals are sick, it's because of people like you!"

A woman in a black cap shouted, "I don't see the NAACP and CORE worrying about which chromosome produces black skin, or the possibility of bleaching the Negro!" There was a surge of applause. "I don't see the Anti-

Defamation League trying to eradicate anti-Semitism by converting Jews to Christians. *Why* we are who we are is totally irrelevant."

"Please don't misunderstand me. When I speak about the pathology of the homosexual, I do not mean to blame the individual. But I believe that the entire homophile movement is going to stand or fall on this question of whether homosexuality is a sickness. There is no avoiding it."

Jim had lost control of the group. They shouted their objections and counter-objections, and soon they aimed their remarks exclusively at each other, Robertiello himself becoming irrelevant to the debate. Frederick shrank from the proceedings while Curt followed each successive volley of the discussion as if eagerly waiting his turn to enter the ring.

"Why do we persist in having people like this address us?" the woman in the black cap spoke again. "There are reputable doctors and therapists who have different views. Evelyn Hooker, Wardell Pomeroy, George Rundquist, Donal Macnamara." Applause followed each name as she said it. "Let's have one of *them* give a talk."

Jim asked, "But doesn't a professional psychologist have every right to disapprove of homosexual practice?"

"His so-called professionalism is part of the problem," she cried, "not the solution. Why are we so afraid to speak about homosexuality from *our* perspective? We invite these quacks to our meetings, and they come here and they compare us to rapists and child molesters and exhibitionists and psychopaths, and they tell us we're neurotic and need to get cured. A deviant sexuality does not necessarily mean pathology."

"That's right," one of the younger members said. "I'm sick of this genteel, debating-society approach where we present all sides of the question impartially. Our opponents will do a fully adequate job of presenting their views and will not return us the favor of presenting ours. We gain nothing by presenting their views and only provide the enemy with ammunition to be used against us."

Frederick felt offended by this talk of enemies and opponents, ammunition and fighting back. He sat frozen as the arguments escalated and people raised their voices, not really listening to each other, as it seemed to him, nor reflecting seriously on anything anyone said. One grandstanding speech seemed to inspire the next.

"Only recognized experts," Robertiello said, "can effectively influence public opinion. You won't be given a hearing if you pooh-pooh the acknowledged authorities."

A round man wearing a red bow tie shouted, "Acknowledged authorities! Don't make me laugh." (Frederick thought his tie made him look like an overgrown schoolboy.) "The literature of the mental health profession is brimming with poor research and non-representative samplings. Unless someone shows me valid evidence to the contrary, I say that homosexuality is not a pathology in any sense but merely a preference no different in kind from heterosexuality."

"You mean to tell me that homosexuals are not sick?" Jim said. "What about lesbians who wear pants and keep their hair short? What about bar-hoppers, stereotypical behavior, heterosexual marriages of convenience? We lack credibility. We *need* allies like Dr. Robertiello."

"I take the stand," the man in the bow tie said, "that not only is homosexuality not immoral, but that homosexual acts engaged in by consenting adults are right, good, and desirable, both for the individual participants and for the society in which we live!"

This produced cries of foul and yeas from all directions. The meeting was in total disarray with people speaking over each other, laughter, and multiple, separate conversations going on simultaneously.

Now Bev, the youngest in the group, stood up and spoke. A hush attended her speech: "I'm an activist. I've read nearly seventy-five books in the New York Mattachine library, and I'm fed up with readings and discussions on the subject of homosexuality. We have to move away from the respectability of debate and into the arena of social activism. We should be taking an unequivocal stand on the medical establishment's sickness theory. We should be out there picketing on behalf of homosexuals' rights. Any homosexual who would come to you for treatment, Dr. Robertiello, would *have* to be a psychopath!" The audience cheered. Frederick, however, sat motionless. There was logic to what she was saying, he thought, but it was a cold logic that ignored the complexities of the way people actually lived. Who was he kidding to think he could sail through this meeting unscathed?—for that matter, to think his relationship with a young person like Curt could ever really work? "Our movement has three options. Social service, information and education, and civil rights-direct action. It's time that social service and education take a back seat to civil rights-direct action. The prejudiced mind is not penetrated by information and is not educable. We have to take action, that's all there is to it!"

Curt leapt to his feet and embraced Bev. The moderator's only option now was to put a semblance of civility on the close of the meeting. He thanked Robertiello, having to raise his voice above the din, and said something about healthy debate and questions that won't be answered overnight, but already people were milling about, engaged in conversations, some no longer having anything to do with homosexuality, the medical profession, or the movement.

Frederick began to gather his things, and as he did so Harold slipped his card into his hand. "Come say hello at the shop sometime. I assure you this has never happened before at a Mattachine meeting, not like this." He laughed and touched Frederick's arm. "Good night."

Frederick said goodnight and hoped Curt, too, would be ready to leave. But he was huddled with his friends, including Bev and Kay, absorbed in a fast and focused exchange. Frederick longed to be anywhere but here. Most of all, he felt Bev and the other younger members hadn't considered one important thing. To march, picket, and protest for the civil rights of homosexuals, as Negroes had been doing for their people, meant the exposure of one's homosexuality to the harsh light of public scrutiny. His generation had always placed a high premium on the separation between one's public and private life. What Bev and Curt and the more liberal members of the Society were now saying was the antithesis of that. Frederick was, he reminded himself, a fundamentally private person. His professionalism and its tangible results, he believed, should be the sole basis on which history judged his contribution to society. Not what he did in his bedroom. Whether his sexual tendencies were to be labeled sick or not—and all right, maybe there *were* two sides to the issue—but *publicizing* those tendencies? (He thought of the AGBANY demonstration in front of Penn Station.) Picketing—protesting—advocating on behalf of one's homosexual tendencies *in public*? That was unthinkable.

He looked at Curt, mixing among his young friends. From now on, he thought, to avoid Harold's shop I'll walk up Broadway instead of Fourth Avenue when I take the subway at 14th Street. He wished he hadn't given him his real name.

CHAPTER TEN

A FEW DAYS AFTER THE MATTACHINE SOCIETY MEETING, FREDERICK'S FATHER telephoned when Frederick happened to be out, and Curt picked up. He said Frederick wasn't in and would give him the message, but then forgot. A week later, a letter arrived with some news of home. Clare was getting ever more forgetful, and then something happened Fritz had been dreading: "Your mother entered the room and said, 'Where is my husband?' I said, 'Clare, I'm your husband. I'm right here. It's me, Fritz.' She looked at me as if she wasn't sure who I was. She replied, 'But where is the man of the house?' In a minute she came to her senses and was reassured I was who I said I was. I've not been able to get this out of my mind." The postscript seemed to carry the letter's true import: "A young man answered the telephone when I called last week. Didn't say who he was. Said he'd give you the message. Don't know if you ever received it." Frederick replied, acknowledging the news of his mother but hastening to lay to rest what he feared were his father's growing suspicions. "The young man you spoke with is Curt Watson, the son of my friend Sandy, just moved here from Chicago. He's camping out in my living room while he gets on his feet. Looking for a job and an apartment in New York City isn't easy for a Midwestern kid fresh out of college with few contacts."

More disturbing, because closer to home, were those instances where someone from the building came into the apartment and found Curt there and, no doubt, jumped to all kinds of awful conclusions. There was a leak in the bedroom. Curt had heard the sound of running water coming from somewhere in the ceiling, and then they noticed drops of water accumulating on the ceiling right over the bed. One of the building handymen, Dimitri, came to assess the situation. Frederick told Curt to just wait in the living room while he sorted things out in the bedroom with Dimitri. Curt immediately understood that Frederick was trying to downplay the obvious fact that the bedroom—but not just the bedroom, *the bed itself*—was shared by two men. Frederick tidied up the room and put away Curt's things to make it look like only one person slept there, going so far as to leave a single pillow on the bed, even though, in all the years he lived alone, the bed was piled with numerous pillows. Curt thought him ridiculous and told him so. Not now, Frederick whispered as Dimitri poked around at the ceiling in the bedroom. Curt barged in and insisted on telling his side of the story, how he was woken in the middle of the night on—he turned to Frederick—when was it? Wednesday, I believe (he said), almost going out of his way to make Dimitri understand they shared the bed.

"Sometimes he watches the apartment for me when I'm out of town on business," Frederick said.

"And it was such an unnecessary lie," Curt protested after Dimitri had gone.

"I don't want Dimitri Pupek to know about our private life, do you understand?"

"Who gives a shit about him? He doesn't care whether we live together or sleep together."

"I see how people smirk when they know they're in the presence of a homosexual. It's nobody's business."

"But there's nothing wrong with it. You always act like we're doing something illegal or immoral."

"For your information, what we do is precisely that—illegal and immoral, and more importantly, scorned and condemned by the run of humanity."

"So if the majority says something is wrong, even if it's a prejudiced viewpoint, the majority must be right? You know, Frederick, sometimes I think you—"

"Leave me to my conscience and my God, and please stop trying to interfere with the way I live my life."

"Maybe you should live alone, then, because I can't keep up your charade."

There was Curt's trump card. He knew Frederick wasn't willing to give him up and didn't want to live alone. But keeping Curt meant having to renegotiate just about every aspect of daily life. And Curt was becoming more and more difficult to negotiate with, for the message he'd gotten from the October Mattachine Society meeting was: Run fast against the opposition. The more they oppose you, the more right you are.

In the following days, wild ideas came to him: What if, every time some homosexual was beaten by a heterosexual or by the police, homosexuals went out "wrecking," but this time not to ruffle the sensitivities of perhaps well-meaning heterosexuals but actually to bash one, anyone, chosen at random, woman or man? "Well, let's make it a man, women do tend to be physically weaker than men, don't they?" (This provoked a prolonged debate with "the girls," as Curt sometimes called Bev and Kay—"And that's another thing," Kay insisted, laughingly, "*don't* call us 'girls'!" He said he was only kidding—didn't mean it—what's the big deal?—he spit out half a dozen inadequate responses—the truth was, he'd never much thought about it—"Whatever you say," he finally gave in, but felt they were being unnecessarily touchy.) Another idea was to give homosexuals a deadline—say, January 1, 1970—by which time they must publicly declare their sexual orientation or else an ad would be run in the paper with their names, and he could hardly get the words out because they were all screaming with laughter at the outrageousness and the brilliance of the idea.

"The point is, we need more people like us."

"But how do we find them?"

Membership in the New York Mattachine was pitifully small compared to SDS or SNCC, and they believed if younger, more open-minded homosexuals joined the organization, new ideas, new methods of doing things would lead the way. They would see a breakthrough in consciousness about the rights of homosexuals the way the nation—the entire world—was now riveted on the civil rights struggles of the Negro.

"Look what happened after the church bombing in Birmingham and those little girls were killed. Imagine if something like that happened to homosexuals!" As Curt said it he felt the strange mixture of horror and delight that seemed the constant lining of his thoughts and emotions nowadays.

"Well, in fact, that kind of thing happens all the time," Bev said. "Homosexuals are beaten and killed and harassed every day, everywhere, all over the world. But no one cares. That's the difference."

Informal meetings and conversations with older members of Mattachine proved dispiriting to Curt and his friends. George, the editor of the newsletter, for one, feared that any "unmonitored" outreach, as he called it, would lead to an inundation with beatniks, dungareed radicals, and other professional nonconformists. Exactly the kind of people who would prevent Mattachine specifically and homosexuals in general from gaining a decent reputation and, ultimately, acceptance. Any membership drive should be conducted, he argued, with the intention of attracting people with a certain degree of reasonable conformity. That word "reasonable" set off endless debate (what was "reasonable" in the eyes of heterosexuals? for example—if they had their way, every last queer would be put in a concentration camp, Curt insisted, provoking utter disdain from George). The elder members disapproved of affected mannerisms, special shops for homo tastes and styles, sleazy underground bars that catered to an exclusively homosexual clientele—the whole "subculture" idea, which, to their way of thinking, only separated homosexuals from the mainstream and reinforced differences between people that simply didn't exist.

Clearly, Curt and his friends would have to experiment on their own. Their first idea was to try to bring in fifty new people for the November meeting. They made flyers advertising the meeting and went all over the Village stuffing the mailboxes of apartments in which two men or two women were listed as occupants. When Curt told Frederick what he'd done, Frederick exploded.

"How could you!"

"What's wrong with it? We need to get the word out about the Mattachine Society."

"Do you realize how that might affect people? Imagine a homosexual who is discreet about his private life getting a flyer like that in his mailbox. What is he going to think? Is he going to think, Oh wonderful, an organization of homosexuals, I think I'll go to the next meeting, or will he be afraid someone has found out about him, and now his private life is public knowledge, and now he has to live in fear for his home and his job and—"

"Why do you always see the negative?"

"I see the practical. This could easily be taken as a witch hunt. Haven't you ever heard of something called 'entrapment'? Christ, do you even know who Joseph McCarthy was? The House Un-American Activities Committee?"

Curt admitted, after cooling off, that Frederick had a point, though he also felt a handful of people adversely affected by his action was a price worth paying for the greater good of liberating the homosexual. He felt their next attempt at outreach, however, should be done face to face. He organized his friends into teams of two, one male, one female. The idea was to go out in the evening and hand out leaflets to passersby. They would approach anyone and everyone who seemed at all sympathetic, heterosexual or homosexual—for that had become a new bone of contention: should homosexual rights concern the homosexual only, or did the heterosexual have some kind of stake in homosexual welfare?

They met one rainy evening in Washington Square Park. Curt was thrilled to see everyone in the group looking to him for guidance. He had never before been in so responsible a position. To his surprise, he found himself counseling moderation. "Be composed and polite when you speak to people. And remember, we're doing this in boy-girl teams because we don't want folks to look at us and immediately start thinking of guy-on-guy sex or two girls sucking titties." Everyone laughed. "If anyone insults you, don't react aggressively, and don't talk back. Make sure you personally hand each of your leaflets to a person, don't dump them in a shop or at a bar, okay? Let's meet back here in two hours."

Curt and Bev were a team. They stationed themselves on the corner of Seventh Avenue and 12th Street near the subway entrance and, more importantly, near one of the busiest cruising grounds in the Village, Greenwich Avenue. Most passersby were nonplussed.

"Good evening. Please take a leaflet for the Mattachine Society. Support the rights of homosexuals."

A harried-looking middle-aged woman wearing a trench coat and rubbers, with a scarf around her head, stopped to read the entire leaflet. Curt and Bev braced themselves for a stream of invective. "I don't know anything about homosexuals," she said, "but your cause has to be good if you're willing to stand outside in such terrible weather!" With that, she turned and went down the steps into the subway.

Curt and Bev floated on air all the way back to the park.

The more Curt became involved in organizing his friends outside the confines of the Mattachine Society—and, more importantly, the more he felt flush with his own effectiveness as an organizer and as a person, the more Frederick became moody, anxious, paranoid even. He saw how excited Curt became when engaged in homophile activism, and apart from their philosophical differences it gave him some pain to realize that activism was a way for Curt to really mate with people. What is it, he wondered, that keeps *us* together? And did he even want to stay together with Curt? For there were occasional flickerings of doubt that Curt was worthy of his love. He had begun to notice something in the boy that, more than his chronic lateness, flamboyance, inconsistency, and vulgarity, diminished his affection: Curt's tendency, as he perceived it, to treat people instrumentally. He noticed it in activists generally. The tendency revealed itself the more overtly political his views and actions became. Friends were becoming "bodies" he could corral or not to show up at a particular time and place for a particular action (handing out leaflets advertising the next Mattachine meeting, protesting police harassment in the Village). Someone he met for the first time he would invariably describe in terms of their political views, their "stand" on this or that issue, their skin color, and social class. It all went a long way, Frederick thought, towards reducing people to abstractions and body parts, sanding down a person's individuality, and whether or not they were kind, intelligent, thoughtful, interesting—"Interesting!" Curt ridiculed one time. "What the hell does that mean? 'Interesting' isn't a quality any two people can agree upon. What interests you may not interest me."

"Yes, and most likely *will* not."

"Whatever turns you on," he said dismissively. "The concept is just so…" And Frederick could have predicted the word to follow: "…bourgeois."

"Well, darling, I apologize if I'm hopelessly bourgeois. If you have a problem with that…" But he couldn't finish the sentence, because, more and more, the end point of all their arguments seemed to be that they shouldn't stay together, shouldn't live together, should never have come together in the first place, and that was something, in varying degrees depending on the heat of the argument, neither one of them was willing to admit, at least not openly to the other.

It was now the end of October, a little more than a year since they'd met and just shy of two months since they'd started living together. Frederick was especially conscious of time's passage because it was in August of last year that he attended the protest in front of Penn Station. He'd met Curt the night before at the theater, gone home for his father's birthday that weekend, and returned to the city in a restless mood. That was how this whole crazy affair began. He'd felt hypocritical marching in that picket line, for it seemed an exercise in futility. Either the station wouldn't be torn down or it would, and in either case nothing a handful of architects, city planners, and (he was thinking of Deborah) their well-meaning wives said or did would have much impact. The only thing a protest of that sort was sure to do was inspire derision ("Fey young men and middle-aged ladies in floppy hats and tennis shoes"—the kind of thing people said about "historic preservationists," as they were now calling themselves). As a favor to Deborah, he'd helped in the production of *New York Landmarks*, and tonight the book was being launched at the Museum of the City of New York. It was a rainy Monday morning. Deborah telephoned first thing.

"Freddy, dear, can you leave the office early this afternoon? Demolition is starting at Penn Station, and some of the AGBANY gang are going to protest."

"Protesting isn't—"

"Before you say anything, let me explain, it won't be a big, vocal demonstration. It's going to be a small, dignified, silent protest. We'll wear black arm bands and just stand with signs that read 'Shame.' The idea is to get some media attention, that's all."

"Deborah—"

"Don't decide now. Call me at noon. We can meet in the lobby of the Statler and then go have a drink afterward and drown our sorrows."

He was about to hang up when an image of the Parthenon in ruins flickered in his mind. He saw the rain coming down. The spire of Grace Church was dull and gray. "Have you heard anything about the idea to save the columns?" he asked.

"Oh, the Pratt students' proposal? They wanted to reuse them in Flushing Meadows or something, I don't know. But it's coming down, every last brick. This is going to be a wake."

Frederick found it hard to concentrate at work that day. He was drawing the elevation of a commercial office tower and kept thinking how much better it would look with Greek pediments and Roman arches. He must be losing his mind. At 11:45, he closed the door to his office and poured himself a Scotch. Earlier than was his custom, but it was an awful day, inside and out. He thought of Ishmael and all those rainy Novembers, the coffin warehouses and funeral processions, with Melville's hero, young in years but old in spirit, pulling up the rear. Maybe, like Ishmael, now was the time to push out to sea. He thought of the war, the midnight train to Camp Hulen, that night in the Pullman car, Jon's body, the letters full of passion, the stolen weekends, Thanksgiving of '43, the tryst at the Statler Hotel, and wasn't there something wonderful, something romantic about those years, even though the world was coming apart at the seams, and every day might be the last day of their lives, which made it, somehow, the best, every one of them, the best they had ever lived. But there was nothing like that now, nothing to compare. And would he want to go back, turn back the clock, be that young man again, if it were possible?

"Mr. Bailey, Deborah Silverstein on the line for you."

"Tell her I'll call her right back, I'm in the middle of something."

He was in the middle of everything. Middle age. Middle and muddle and muddy shoes and rain, rain pouring down. Who wanted to stand outside in the rain with signs dripping and smeared? "Shame." Shame on you, me, shame on all of us. How incredibly pathetic. But he remembered Curt's triumphant night in the Village, handing out leaflets in the rain, and he came home dripping wet and was sick in bed with a cold for a week. Frederick was happy to nurse him back to health, feed him, cheer him up, tell him everything would be all right. He loved taking care of Curt in those moments. When Curt fell ill, he was more pliable, more tender. He remembered rubbing his belly, and then he got an erection and Frederick began stroking him, and they made love, and Curt was hot with fever and sniffling from cold and Frederick didn't care if he caught it. Funny, he thought, I never *did* catch that cold.

But what was he going to do about this afternoon? Penn Station was coming down at last. It was inconceivable such an enormous building, which had occupied that spot his entire lifetime, should come down. But it wasn't such a long time after all. The life of a building could not, in that sense, be compared to the life of a man. The building would only have been (he made a quick calculation) fifty-three years old. In the life of buildings, that was nothing. That was infancy. A baby wouldn't even have cut its first tooth. He thought of little Clare. Marge had called the other day to say she'd started teething and was driving her mad.

And to think she might have had an abortion.

But what about this afternoon? If no one bore witness to the wanton destruction of landmarks like Penn Station, we as a society were saying, in effect, murder is okay.

Murder?

He dialed Deborah's number. The line was ringing. He hung up the telephone. There had been a photo in the paper of the AGBANY protest last year. AGBANY, small, ineffectual as it was, did have the ear of the *Times*. It garnered press. Did he want to risk ending up with his picture on the front page, exposed, one of the losing team?

He dialed again. He would make some excuse. In any case, he would see her tonight at the book party.

But this was history in the making, and shouldn't he be part of it?

But his contribution to history was his work, and that would outlast any passing act he performed on a given day.

But life wasn't just about monuments and paintings hung in museums. It was also about living, breathing, perishable, flesh-and-blood people. The things we do, here and now. In the moment.

But he was human, too. And it was human to hide, be afraid, crawl into the dark where it was safe and warm and no one could see him.

Once again he hung up the phone.

Was he going mad? Of course he would go! What was a few extra hours out of his afternoon, to take his stand, make his mark in the world, not someday in the future but here and now, to ensure that buildings survived—not Penn Station, but *other* buildings, maybe even his own, for wasn't the sad story of Penn Station all the evidence anyone needed that nothing lasted forever, there would never be an American Parthenon, it would have been torn down many times over by now…?

He dialed the number. He saw the rain coming down like tears. He hated wakes and funerals. He hadn't even attended his own grandmother's funeral (the one person in all his life whose love was unconditional), and he knew his family never understood why, but he needed to keep his grief to himself—not to hide it but cherish it, keep it from being disseminated into some larger, public, corporate grief that no longer bore the stamp of his own personality, his individuality, his particular relationship to the beloved… Deborah answered.

"I have a meeting at one," he lied. "It just came up. I can't get out of it. I'm sorry."

"You'll be at the book party tonight, won't you?" she asked. He heard the frustration in her voice.

Of course, he promised.

And he did go to the party, and congratulatory speeches were made. He went through the motions, but something had happened to him today. He felt bereft. The book, everyone acclaimed, was beautiful, "The kind of thing any cultured New Yorker will want on his coffee table," the president of the Municipal Art Society, Harmon Goldstone, said, patting him on the back.

"But the symbolism of it was revolting." Deborah was describing the demolition ceremony at Penn Station earlier in the day. One of the giant stone eagles had been removed from the 33rd Street façade and lowered to the street as the chairman of the Madison Square Garden Corporation, the vice president of the Pennsylvania Railroad, the president of the Long Island Railroad, and other officials looked on with lip-smacking satisfaction. "The sight of Felt, Jones, and Goodfellow in their hard hats, posing next to the eagle like it was some big fish they'd just bagged off the coast of—"

"Honey, aren't you over-dramatizing just a bit?" Seymour asked, eliciting snickers from the other men standing by the bar. Frederick felt a tug at his sleeve. It was Curt.

"I've just been talking with Alan Emerson." Keep telling everyone he's a distant cousin, Frederick reminded himself, and felt he was standing an inch too close, as if they were a couple, like Deborah and Seymour. He was starting to get his stories mixed up. Hadn't he told someone a few minutes ago Curt was the friend of a friend, a promising architecture student? Someone was bound to catch him in his lies if they hadn't already.

"Do you think he's a sister?"

"Excuse me?"

"Alan. Do you think—"

"I think you should stick to superficial topics like the weather."

"You want me to leave?"

"No, but can't you just be a wallflower for once?"

"Never!" he said with an air of sunny defiance and went off in search of more hors d'oeuvres.

"…and then finish the Landmarks bill," Seymour was saying, "and put it under the Mayor's nose, and make sure he gets it passed. That'll take more than black arm bands and street theatre."

But Deborah was preoccupied with the eagle. "I almost think the entire ceremony was directed against *us*. Against AGBANY. I'm telling you, they were gloating over it, like it was King Kong brought back from Africa."

"Yeah, but remember what King Kong did when he finally woke from his stupor. He ran amok, terrorizing the citizens of New York!"

"Uh huh, and then dead on the sidewalk. The End."

"Look," Seymour said, "we knew how unlikely it would be to save Penn Station without the force of law, especially with a project the size of a new Madison Square Garden in the offing, with all the money the city stands to make from it. At this point the civic groups are heavily invested in working *with* Wagner. What they really want is a landmarks law, so they're not willing to rock the boat. If that means sacrificing Penn Station to get a place at the decision-making table, they're willing to do it."

"You just reduce the whole thing to cold-hearted politics."

"Sweetheart, that's exactly what this is. Everything is politics. And I don't care if you're talking about the Negroes or old buildings." Deborah seemed unconvinced. "We have to move beyond guerilla warfare. Singing 'We Shall Overcome' on a picket line is loads of fun, but now we're talking about government. The responsibilities of government. That's politics."

"God, who was that bore you were talking to at the party?" Curt asked late that night as they were settling into bed.

"You mean Seymour? He works at Emerson, Root. I've known him since Columbia. He's married to Deborah."

"Oh, *that* was Deborah! She's nice. I was talking with her for a while."

"You really made the rounds, didn't you?"

"I like parties. And I can talk to almost anyone."

"You seemed to be talking to Al Emerson for a long time."

"Which one was he?"

"The young intern with the black hair."

"Oh, he was dishy. I liked him. He's the one I asked you about, and you got mad at me. I couldn't tell if he's a sister. Architects are a weird bunch. I met this one guy, I think he works in your firm, and we were talking about the Mattachine Society, because he'd been to a meeting in San Fr—"

"You were talking about the Mattachine Society at the book party?"

"Yeah, I—"

"How many times do I have to tell you I don't want you to mix that up with my professional life?"

"This isn't just about your professional life."

"These are my colleagues. Some of them I see every single day." A thought crossed his mind. "How were you introducing yourself to people?"

"I don't want to talk about this."

"Tell me how you were introducing yourself. What did we agree?"

"*We* didn't agree to anything. You *told* me what you wanted me to do and say, like I'm supposed to obey you because you're older and more established or something."

"We have talked about this over and over, and you still don't understand, do you?"

"It's pathetic the way you pretend to be someone you're not. I'm not saying you have to announce to everybody you're homosexual, and I'm not saying you have to introduce me as your lover, and for your information I told people I'm your friend, okay? 'Friend.' Can you live with that?"

"'Friend' isn't good enough. You know some people interpret 'friend' as something more than a friend. We said you're a distant cousin, staying with me until—"

"I can't read people's minds and I'm not about to start trying. It's legitimate to talk about the Mattachine Society just as it would be if I were a member of the fucking ASPCA. It's not gonna make their heads explode."

"You're making *my* head explode!"

"Well, good, go ahead and explode. I'm fucking sick of this!"

Curt jumped out of bed and went to his closet.

"What are you doing?"

"What does it look like?"

Frederick watched him slip on a pair of dungarees and a sweater, then sit on the floor to put on socks and sneakers. Next be began stuffing some extra clothes into a duffel bag.

"Where are you going?"

"What do you care?"

"You always walk out when there's any kind of conflict."

"You try to control every word I say, every move I make. You're not my father!" With that, Curt exited the bedroom.

Frederick decided to let him go this time without further argument. He heard him rustling hangers in the hall closet. He heard the front door bang.

Damn Curt and his outbursts! He reached for a sleeping pill on his night table. Something had to be done. Things couldn't go on like this. Already he suspected Deborah knew the score between them ("How did you and your friend meet?" she asked at the book party—no one asks that unless they're prying into the relationship itself—unless they assume there's a "relation-ship" to begin with). She was urging him to join a network of preservation activists who, at a moment's notice, could be called upon to run to the rescue of buildings under siege, at least until—if, when, it wasn't clear—a landmarks law was passed. Never! He was an architect, not an anarchist. He'd rather design his country house than run all over town making a spec-tacle of himself. He could feel the pill starting to take effect. He pictured a bunker. A pyramid, half-submerged underground. He could hear the rain outside, the pyramid sinking deeper into the ground, a building that, in the event of an air raid or a Soviet attack, could, with the flick of a switch (Curt left the light on in the hallway, but he was too tired to get up and turn it off) sink into the earth out of sight, all its treasures safe from bombs falling and the rain falling, and he slept heavily, and the next morning woke with a hangover—what with the pill and the wine at the party and—a sick feeling welled up in his gut.

Curt was gone. The bed was empty. It was a grim, gray late-October morning. He might never come back this time. He'd said he was sick to death, or words to that effect. He opened the drapes and saw the spire of Grace Church. A landmark. Hundreds of years would go by and it would still stand. Or would it?

He opened his front door and saw a picture of one of the Penn Station eagles cut loose from the façade, harnessed and lowered to the ground with a trio of men in hard hats looking up as it made its descent. "Beginning of the end of a landmark" the caption read. "Marked the start of transformation of Pennsylvania Station yesterday morning." He stood in the kitchen, his bathrobe falling open, exposing his nudity, but no one could see, he was on such a high floor, and if someone from a neighboring building were perverted enough to spy through binoculars, what did he care? Curt was gone this morning and, to tell the truth, it was hard to care about much of anything at all.

> *At 9 A.M. electric jackhammers tore at the granite slabs of the side of the terminal near the 33d Street entrance, crushing the hopes of a band of architects who had rallied to save what the Municipal Art Society called "one of the great monuments of classical America."*

There was mention of the protesters with armbands and signs reading "Shame," along with the inevitable other side of the story.

> *Morris Lipsett, president of the concern that is preparing the site for the new center, said: "If anybody seriously considered it art, they would have put up some money to save it. You always have half a dozen societies around trying to preserve everything."*

Frederick threw the paper down on the table in disgust. "Trying to preserve everything." It was an insult, as if their opposition to the demolition of a masterpiece of American architecture was nothing more than a naïve wish that nothing change. "What we were trying to do…" he started to say out loud, but the sound of his own voice was too real, too frightening—he much preferred to stay inside his head and not have to confront the real world in any of its forms, even the reality of his own speaking voice. At least not yet, not now, at six o'clock in the morning, before his first cup of coffee, and Curt was gone, and when would he come back?

Frederick pushed through the day and night, and the next morning dawned much as the one before. He opened his front door, picked up the *Times*, made himself a cup of coffee, sat at the table and glanced over the front page, then turned to the editorials, as was his custom (how quickly he reverted to custom with Curt gone—but he would gladly forego his daily habits to have him back, to wake up next to him).

Farewell to Penn Station
Until the first blow fell no one was convinced that Penn Station really would be demolished or that New York would permit this monumental act of vandalism against one of the largest and finest landmarks of its age of Roman elegance.

He could barely stand to read it. The description of the station's rich grandeur—its Doric columns, vaulted concourse, opulent detail, and precious materials—was painful. And to think New York, with all its resources and tens of thousands of artists and intellectuals—to think New York City couldn't save it… *The final indictment is of the values of our society.* Hear, hear! Frederick thought as he lit a cigarette. He'd read recently that a group of doctors warned cigarette smoking could be dangerous to one's health. He used to think such warnings foolish, a bunch of eggheads whistling in the wind, but what was the difference between a group of architects saying, This old building has value, though most people couldn't care less, and a group of doctors saying, Our research shows what you always thought was good may in fact not be good after all, and now whom do you believe, and what do you do? Who has the answer? *Any city gets what it admires, will pay for, and, ultimately, deserves.* He began to feel sick. He shouldn't smoke on an empty stomach first thing in the morning. *We want and deserve tin-can architecture in a tin-horn culture.* In Europe, time weathers and dignifies what's old and makes it venerable. The cathedrals that survived the bombing, even in their ruined condition, have a nobility no new building, no intact building, could approach. But here in the United States…

He rushed to the living room and pulled the sketchbook from his brief-case. He had an idea for his country house. Take an existing building in ruins—a barn or even just the foundations of a building. He thought of the shell of the old Summit Hotel at the top of Mount Penn in Reading. Build on top of it. Incorporate the remnants of the old into the structure of the new. It had been the basis for his inspiration to re-use the portico from the old Rheinlander mansion on the façade of Two Fifth Avenue. Someone had proposed doing something like this with Penn Station, but then someone else objected, saying Penn Station is total architecture, you can't just save one piece of it. So now we'll have nothing, he thought, and wondered if Curt would call him at the office today. Or perhaps when he got home tonight he might find Curt sitting on the sofa, or asleep in bed, all wrongs forgiven, all fights put to rest, a new day dawning.

In any case, all of his things were here. He'd have to come home some time. *And we will probably be judged not by the monuments we build but by those we have destroyed.* "I'm getting married," Jon had said. "I can't talk to you now," Frederick replied and still hadn't spoken to him to this day. It was all he could do to fight back tears, with his entire family sitting there watching, listening (he felt tears coming on and fought them back). And where had Jon gone? What had become of him? Had his marriage turned out well? Did he have children? Or did he come to his senses and admit who he is? And if so, had he found another man, and was he, even now, living somewhere in New York City? Some days he was sure he saw him, on the subway, passing on the street, and he would hurry on up ahead to get a better look, but discreetly so as not to disturb whomever it might be. And if it *were* Jon and he had the chance to approach him, speak to him, would he do it? What would he say?

I miss you. I need you. I have never stopped loving you.

1964

CHAPTER ELEVEN

THE ALCOHOL FLOWED MORE FREELY THAN USUAL AT BAILEY FAMILY GATH-
erings. Frederick looked dazed as Curt and his mother sat among the aunts
at the dining table. The women had staked out their usual positions. Not
even the death of their beloved baby brother could change certain habits.
What he couldn't get over was that Clare and Curt had taken a liking to
each other.

"What did she say?" she repeatedly asked him as the aunts told stories
about Fritz dating back to the '90s.

"Something about Brown's Cove?"

"Brown's Cove, Clare," Hilda shouted, even though Clare was sitting four
feet away from her. "Where Papa used to take us in the summer."

"There was no running water!"

"Just the bucket."

"And the stream!"

The women erupted in squalls of laughter. Death seemed to have opened
some hitherto untapped reservoir of hilarity.

How he and Curt had come to be here together was still a matter of
astonishment to Frederick. It all began with their big fight last October,
the night of the book party. Curt left in a huff and had all but decided (he
later confessed) to end it with Frederick. But he soon grew uneasy. Why,

he couldn't exactly say. It became clear a month later, the day of Kennedy's assassination. He was alone at Collin's apartment watching TV. He'd called in sick to the agency. It was a Friday. Around 1:30 in the afternoon there was an emergency news bulletin: the president had been shot. For the next half hour he watched in disbelief as the reports trickled in. At 2:00 PM Kennedy was pronounced dead. Suddenly nothing was secure, nothing was safe. If the president could be shot and killed, anything could happen. Life seemed to hang by a thread. By 3:30, Johnson was sworn in as president. It never even occurred to him to contact Collin. He called Frederick at the office, but the secretary said everyone had already gone home. In a panic, he went directly to Frederick's apartment. Frederick took him in, no questions asked. They hugged and cried and made love, and he ended up staying for the next ten days. Frederick said, Will you come home for good? The first weekend in December Curt moved back in.

"What are they laughing at?"

"I don't know exactly, Mrs. Bailey," he said in a deferential tone Frederick had never quite heard before, "but they're talking about some place they vacationed when they were children, and how they teased your husband."

"Was I there?"

"Clare, honey, we're talking about Fritz when he was a boy, before he met you, long before you were married."

Then last week he got the call from Marge. It's about Papa, she said. He was driving out on Rt. 222. In the rain. An aneurysm. (Everyone thought Clare would go first.) He knew instantly he couldn't face his father's coffin, or his family, alone.

He sat down on the other side of his mother.

"Here's my Fritz."

"Mama, it's me, Freddy."

"I love you, honey. Both you boys." She pulled Curt's chin to hers and kissed him and did the same to Frederick. Curt beamed a wide-eyed smile.

Without giving it a second thought, Frederick asked Curt to accompany him to the funeral, and Curt (quoting Bob Dylan) said almost laughingly, "'Don't criticize what you can't understand!' Sure, I'll go with you. Sure."

And so here he was.

"You want a drink?" he asked Frederick, getting up from the table.

"I'd like another glass of wine," Clare said.

The story was, he was the son of Frederick's friend Sandy, new in town, no place to stay, living with him until he got on his feet. Every time Frederick introduced Curt to a member of the family, there was a split-second of eye contact in which, it seemed, the knowledge was acknowledged. Oh, nice to meet you, thank you for being here, yes it was a shock, and so on. Otherwise no one said a word about it.

Marge appeared suddenly from the kitchen, reached for Clare's glass, and reprimanded Curt. "Don't keep offering her wine, she's had enough."

"He wasn't offering her wine," Frederick whispered so as not to embarrass Clare. "He was asking me if *I* wanted a drink. Marge," he said, getting up from the table and putting his arm around her, trying to escort her out of the dining room, "for once you don't have to be the hostess. Jean and Sally are taking care of everything. We just buried our father. Why don't you calm down and—"

"I know we just buried our father, thank you!" She fended off his touch with an aggressive shrug and walked into the crowded parlor.

Curt arrived with his drink. "So this is what an Irish wake looks like. Cheers."

"Where's my wine?" Clare shouted from behind them.

"Mama, I'm sorry," Frederick said and went to the kitchen to make sure her next drink had plenty of water in it. Curt wandered out to the porch where the youngest members of the family were assembled and slipped easily into their conversation about the Beatles. The boys were taunting the girls about their crushes on this or that band member.

"So now we're gonna spend the next hour talking about which Beatle is the cutest? I'd like to punch Paul in the face."

"Shut up! Just 'cause he's cuter than you."

"Oh, sorry, I don't look like a sheepdog."

"Sheepdogs are sweet!"

"You don't even listen to the music. They could be singing 'Happy Birthday' and you'd be screaming, 'Oh my god, Paul! Paul!'"

The boys laughed in solidarity with each other.

Curt asked everyone what they thought of the Supremes. The conversation shifted to the question of whether or not Diana Ross "sounded black," with Joan admitting she didn't know whether she sounded black or white, all she knew was how pretty she was, setting off a fresh round of teasing, this time about whether any of them would dare go out on a date with a Negro. Curt merely listened, offering no opinion on the subject, leaning on the threshold.

"I still can't get used to seeing you in the house I grew up in, mingling with my family." It was Frederick, whispering in his ear. "I'm just glad you're here. I don't know what I'd have done without you." Frederick wanted to embrace him.

"You would have been fine. Your family loves you a lot. Your aunts keep saying what a wonderful boy you are." He giggled. "I think they want to adopt me."

"Curt, I love you," he whispered, trying not to move his lips. They stood now in the middle of the parlor surrounded by thirty people all talking at once.

"Tell me again tonight," he said at normal speaking volume, "and I'll have a reply for you, okay?" He turned and went towards the kitchen for a refill.

"Why is he here?" Marge said, appearing suddenly at his side. "Who is he?"

"Marge, you're drunk. You've had enough."

"Don't tell me I'm drunk. I'm asking who he is and what he's doing here."

"I don't understand your hostility. I told you he's a friend of my friend Sandy—"

"You said he was the *son* of your friend Sandy."

"I mean, he's the son of my friend Sandy. He's living with me because we just—because he just—moved—"

"You know, it's like you've rehearsed it, only not enough because you're forgetting your lines. And by the way, how long can you go on saying he 'just moved to New York'? He's been living with you over seven months if I'm not mistaken. You told Pop about it in a letter, and in case you didn't know he always shared your letters with me. How long does it take to find a job and a place to live in New York City?"

"He *has* a job, and—it's none of your business, actually. I'm not talking to you unless you sober up. You're a mess."

"I need a favor from you." He was in no mood to give her anything, do anything for her, now. "I need you to stay here with Mama tonight."

"I thought she was staying with you."

"She's been with me since Papa died. But I need a break. I need some help. I can't have her every night, full time."

"Marge, she can't live on her own." Just as he said it he realized he'd given her the opening she'd been waiting for.

"Exactly. What are *you* doing about it?"

"Let's have this conversation when you're not drunk."

"Stop saying I'm drunk!"

"Then stop shouting," he said and pulled her into the hallway by the steps where there were fewer people.

"You can't avoid this. I'm asking you if you'll stay here with her tonight so I can have a night off. I need some time to myself, you know?"

"I've paid the hotel through tomorrow."

"Get a refund. Or not! Who the hell cares, you can afford it!"

"What about Curt?"

"What *about* Curt? You're not his guardian, are you?"

"I refuse to talk to you about Curt or anything else right now." He attempted to walk away.

"Damn you!" she shouted. The few people congregating in the hallway moved with embarrassment into the parlor. Conversations continued, but now the argument reached the ears of everyone in the parlor and those in the kitchen as well. "How many rooms have you rented at the hotel?"

"I think you should go home."

"Are you sharing the same bed?" She said this as she followed him into the kitchen. Frederick called on the first person he saw, his cousin Steve McDevitt.

"Would you take Marge and the kids home? She's had too much to drink. I'd take her myself but I feel I should stay here—"

Steve agreed but then got pulled into conversation with others.

"Steve, she needs to go *now*," Frederick pressed him a moment later. But then the thought of being left here with so many family members, most of whom, it seemed, had heard Marge's outburst, filled him with more panic than the thought of having to spend one more minute with Marge and her outrageous insinuations. He wanted to disappear and never come back. But where was Curt? He announced he would take her home himself.

"I'm not leaving!"

"Yes, you are, you're leaving right now because I'm taking you."

"You don't want to hear it."

"I don't want to hear *you*, that's true. I want you to shut your mouth, do you understand?"

Curt appeared at last. "What's the trouble?"

He told Curt to gather Markie and the baby—but no, there was no time, he'd have to come back for the children. Marge had to be gotten out of the way now. Gripping her hand, he dragged her through the kitchen and down the stairs to the basement.

"You have to hear me!"

"What the hell do you want?"

"I want you to see me and hear me."

"Listen, I don't know what you were insinuating up there, but you must control yourself." The words "control yourself" seemed suddenly to have some magic, calming influence. Perhaps they needn't return to her hideous words in the hallway. Perhaps she'd forget she ever said them. Perhaps everyone who heard would pretend they hadn't heard. "You want me to look after Mama tonight, okay, fine. I'll stay here tonight."

"And then after tonight? What happens when you go back to New York and I'm left here with an old woman who can't live by herself and two children and no husband?" Reluctantly he took her in his arms.

"It's gonna be all right. Maybe not this minute, but we'll find a solution that works for both of us. For all of us. You and me and Mama, okay?"

"I want Papa! Oh God!"

"I know, Margie. I know you do."

She rehearsed the events surrounding their father's death, how horrible it was having to identify the body. "I have to be strong for Markie and take care of the baby, and Mama—oh God—she can't live without Papa."

She will, he assured her, though he had no idea how it would all work itself out.

She grew calm.

"I want to go home."

"Good. I'm taking you home." She was docile. Mercifully, the final preparations for their departure happened quickly, as if everyone knew the best thing to do was get all of them—Marge, the children, Frederick, Curt—out of the house. Frederick was right. More than anything, they wanted not to know.

BY THE TIME THEY RETURNED THAT NIGHT, THE HOUSE AT 13TH STREET was empty except for Frederick's cousin Sally, who was still washing up in the kitchen, and Clare, who was already upstairs getting ready for bed. Curt gave Sally a hand with the remaining dishes while Frederick went to check on his mother. He found her in the dark, sitting motionless on the side of her bed, one shoe off, facing the window with the blinds drawn. He knocked gently on the door frame so as not to frighten her.

"Mama, can I help you?"

"Yes, dear." She said it calmly without turning to face him, as if she'd been waiting for his return and sensed it even before he uttered the words.

He pulled off the other shoe, unrolled her stockings (her legs were streaked with blue and red veins, her toenails were coarse and needed clipping), helped her off with her dress, and started searching for a nightgown, opening drawer after drawer, trying to follow his mother's confusing instructions—"No, not that, the other—no, the one over there—below that one—*below* it!" He found the one she wanted—lavender, though she insisted it was pink—and helped her put it on. Then he tried gently to lead her to the bathroom but she protested, saying she was a big girl, she could do it herself, didn't he know that?

He returned downstairs to find Sally gathering her jacket and purse.

"I'm off. How was Marge?"

"Practically asleep by the time we got her home."

"She needed to blow off steam tonight." She looked at him as if to apologize for what Marge had said at the reception. But Frederick wanted to move quickly onto neutral ground. He thanked her for all she'd done and embraced her. She said she didn't need to be thanked, she loved her Uncle Fritz and Aunt Clare and her Bailey cousins. "And I really do want to bring the girls to New York this summer. We don't have to do anything special, we just enjoy spending time with you."

"I'm sure we can arrange it," he said. Just to spend time with him? It seemed no one in his family had ever wanted that.

He went back upstairs to say goodnight to his mother, but she was already in bed, her eyes closed. When he returned to the parlor, there was Curt, lying like an odalisque on the couch.

"I have a theory about one or two of your relatives." He curled up to give Frederick room to sit, then draped his legs across his lap. Frederick began massaging his feet. "Am I the only one who thinks little cousin Willie is the most beautiful creature in the world?" Frederick wanted to object, but Curt insisted. "There *must* be other queers in the family besides you. They say it's inherited. I read that in *The Mattachine Review*."

"Can we discuss it some other time?"

"Sorry. I guess I should say goodnight. Where am I sleeping?"

This would require some discussion. There were two options as Frederick saw it—Marge's old room, "Where you'll have your privacy," and Frederick's old room. "Where..." But he hesitated to say what he had in mind. "...where the bed is narrow, but at least..."

Curt watched him inch towards his goal.

"…we'll be together."

"And then there's this couch, which is feeling pretty good to me right now."

"If you'd prefer—"

"This is your home, it's the place you grew up. Your mother is asleep upstairs. What do *you* want?"

"What do you think?"

"I don't know," he lied, "that's why I'm asking."

"Why are you forcing me to say it?"

"Why are you *afraid* to say it?"

"So we both know what we're talking about."

"I'm too tired for games, I'll be fine here."

"I can't be alone tonight," Frederick said at last. He reached over and took Curt's hand. "Please. I need you."

That night they lay in each other's arms, holding on to prevent falling out of bed. The unlikelihood of making love in so confined a space—not just the narrow bed of Frederick's childhood, but also the room itself, overstuffed as it was, for Frederick, with memories (the place he retreated as a child to draw, discovering and developing his artistic gift; the place he studied and read, realizing, as the years went by, the full scope of his intellectual powers; the place he happened upon masturbation and then regularly indulged the habit in secret and in shame; the place he deliberately touched his friend Georgey Heizmann while looking at dirty pictures, only to find life-giving acceptance in his friend's eyes; the place he wanted to die the night Jon announced his engagement) and overheated, for Curt, with intimations of violation, even perversion (he pretended, at one point, to be chubby, sweaty, thumb-sucking, well-hung Georgey Heizmann himself, whispering to a trembling, teenage Frederick, Yes, I want it, do it now, yes, yes)—the unlikelihood of making love here in this place was the very thing that made it so overpowering. And brief: Curt came almost as soon as Frederick thrust into him and started to cry out, but Frederick cupped his hand over his mouth and kept fucking and felt Curt's teeth sink into his fleshy palm until he came as well.

When he woke the next morning, he couldn't recall any lag between sex and falling asleep. They must have both dropped off instantly. He felt Curt's arms around his body. His body was warm and strong. He turned to brush the hair from his forehead and…—what was today? Sunday. What time was it? The clock on the dresser said 6:30 AM. He heard a floorboard creak. His mother was awake and might come into the room any minute!

He leapt out of bed and put his ear to the door. It seemed she hadn't come out of her room yet. He opened the door, saw the hallway clear, darted—but softly—down the hall to Marge's old room, entered, turned and mussed the bed clothes, tossed the pillows, then went downstairs to make coffee. Around 7:00 AM, Clare entered the kitchen, washed and smartly dressed. She'd had a good night's sleep, she said, and was ready for church. When Frederick explained that Sally and Veronica would be arriving in a couple of hours to take her, she should have some breakfast in the meantime, she stubbornly refused and sat at the dining table holding her purse and still wearing her veil and gloves, watching Frederick move about the kitchen.

"Where's your friend...what's his name?"

"Curt. He must be..." He hesitated a moment and ran through the story in his mind. "...still sleeping." Then he added, "I gave him my old room and I took Marge's room."

They were silent for a minute.

"How did you two meet?"

He gave his by-now rote answer, the answer Marge had said sounded overly rehearsed.

"So he's living with you."

"Yes..." He felt the need to add some qualification but left it at that.

"I slept better last night than I have in a long while."

"That's good!" He was glad for a change of topic.

"I don't like the bed at Margie's. Too soft. I like a firm mattress." But before he could offer his assent, she continued, "That bed is just too soft. Gives me a sore back. I'm glad to be home again. If you prefer Margie's old room, you can keep it."

Now he must be clear. He was returning to New York, he said, this morning. First they must check out of the hotel, return Marge's car, then catch their train back home. They had a lot of things to do this morning and would be leaving as soon as Sally and Veronica arrived. She was confused, however, and insisted he should stay here, *this* was his home.

"No, Mama, I live in New York."

"You live here!"

"Mama..." He stopped what he was doing at the sink and joined her at the table. "I'm here because of Papa's funeral. My home is New York City now. I've lived there for thirty years."

But she insisted Reading was home, and she lamented his leaving her again, he was always leaving her.

"I can visit you whenever you like, but—"

"I'm staying here."

"I'm sorry, but Sally's coming over this morning to take you to church. If you feel up to it you can visit the aunts after mass, you always enjoy that, but then Sally is going to take you back to Margie's house this afternoon." He knew this made it sound as if she had no say in the matter.

"Good morning."

They turned to see Curt standing in the doorway of the kitchen.

"How're you doing this morning, Mrs. Bailey?"

"Not too good. Frederick wants to send me back to Margie's."

"Mama," Frederick said, now raising his voice slightly, as if she were hard of hearing, "now that Pop is…"—but he couldn't say the word "dead"—"now that Pop is…gone…you…"—and again, the words sounded insensitive—"you can't stay here by yourself. You need help. Someone to look after you."

"But I have you two."

The thought vaguely amused Frederick, in spite of his frustration. Curt joined them at the table.

"Mama, do you know why we're here?" Frederick persisted.

"No, why?"

But Curt gave him a look that said, let me try. "Mrs. Bailey, I was wondering if you could show me your wedding album. I was admiring the picture on the mantel of you in your wedding dress, and I wondered if you had any others."

"Do you remember where you put the wedding album, Mama?" Frederick was happy to take Curt's lead.

They found it in a cabinet in the living room. While Frederick showered, Curt and Clare went through the album page by page. Clare had difficulty identifying faces, other than those of her two children, her husband, and herself.

"That's okay, Mrs. Bailey," Curt said, "it's nice just to look at the pictures. You were a beautiful bride." He remarked at a photo of the just-married couple seated in a horse-drawn carriage outside Saint Joseph's church. Frederick strongly resembled his father, only if anything, he thought, Frederick was more handsome—thanks to his mother, no doubt, whose beauty in some strange way had increased with age. Tucked into the back of the album was a picture of two young men in military uniforms, one seated, the other perched on the arm of the chair, leaning against his companion with his arm around his shoulders.

"Who is this? Is that Frederick?"

"Well, now, let's see. Yes, I believe that's Frederick" Clare said, pointing to the seated man, "and that," pointing to the other, "is...oh, what was his name? Freddy's friend from the army. I must ask him when he comes down."

"May I have this picture, Mrs. Bailey? I'll return it the next time we visit. I'd just like to look at it for a while."

"You can do anything you want. You can keep it." She pulled the photo out of the album, handed it to Curt, and kissed him on the cheek.

They were still looking through the album when Sally and Veronica arrived. Now it was a clash of conflicting agendas and mixed messages—Leaving so soon? I thought your train wasn't until this evening. Can't you stay for lunch? What about meeting us after mass, and we'll all go visit the aunts together?

"No, I'm sorry, we really must get going," Frederick said.

"What's the rush?" Curt said. "I think your mother—"

He insisted they had to return Margie's car, she was waiting for them.

"Well, it was so good seeing you, Freddy," Sally said, "even if the circumstances were..." She looked at Clare. "You know."

"Mom says I can come visit you in New York," Veronica said as she embraced him.

"No, I said we would *ask* Freddy if he would like some visitors. Now is not the time to discuss it." Then to Frederick: "I keep telling the kids you design tall buildings, but I don't think they have any idea what that means. I'd love for them to see what you do."

Frederick replied, "Yes, of course," but again felt it was just the kind of thing family members say, not really meaning it. Then he turned to his mother. "Mama, we're leaving now." He thought to acknowledge his father's death and his now-watchful gaze down upon them (though he wasn't that kind of believer, he knew it would make sense to his mother), but he decided to avoid the subject altogether.

Curt reached out and gave Clare a long, tight embrace. "I'm sorry, Mrs. Bailey," he said, "I'm so sorry." She held him tight in return, but said nothing.

Alone at last in the car with Curt, Frederick felt embarrassed by how abruptly he'd taken leave of his family. He wanted reassurance Curt didn't think less of him. But he felt awful even to hint in that direction. Instead, "I want to apologize for my mother," he said.

"Why? *She's* done nothing wrong!" Curt could have said more but held his tongue. He knew Frederick wasn't in his right mind and didn't want to start a fight.

"I mean, we can still drive around the city if you like. We have some time. You want a little taste of small-town Pennsylvania?"

"Whatever you want."

Sensing Curt's indifference, Frederick decided in a burst of spontaneity, "Well, you know what I *really* want? When I was a kid, I used to prowl around construction sites. I'd love to do that right now!" There was a new development in Wyomissing, he said, on the way to Marge's house. After checking out of the hotel, they could go exploring there. Frederick glanced around to see if anyone was looking. The car was shaded by heavy trees. The porch was empty. He turned to kiss Curt on the mouth, but just then a couple and two children appeared, coming up Perry Street. All he permitted himself was a thank you.

"For what?" (They shouldn't have left the way they did, was all Curt could think.)

"For everything."

After checking out of the hotel, Frederick drove toward Shillington, west of the city, but then took the detour through Wyomissing. They descended a hill at the bottom of which was a corner property where the house was only half finished. The ground was mud. Trucks and large piles of bricks stood between the road and the front door of the house.

"I sort of feel like I'm breaking and entering," Curt said, trying to play along with Frederick's game but still stuck on the way they'd left Clare.

A wood plank served as a ramp leading to an entrance foyer. From there, a staircase led straight up to the second floor. To the right was a large room spanning the entire depth of the house.

"Okay, here's the living room," Frederick said. He could tell because, for one thing, there was a fireplace and the room was large. They stepped carefully amid loose piles of lumber, sawhorses, and wood-cutting machinery. A doorway led to a smaller room at the back of the first floor. "And this is some kind of office or den. See, there's going to be a door that gives onto the back patio, and a door to the basement…" They entered a series of broken corridors. He pointed out the probable locations of the laundry room, kitchen appliances, and dining room.

"And what about through there?" Curt asked.

"The garage."

"You know, Frederick, I was thinking, about your mother. If she needs to move in with you—you know, in your apartment in New York—I could move out."

Frederick was taken aback. "But she's not coming to New York."

"I thought you were considering it."

"What makes you think that? I didn't say anything—"

"Don't get testy, I thought—"

"I'm not testy, I just don't know where you're getting that idea."

Obviously he'd tripped a switch. "Sorry, I was only saying—"

"Saying *what?*"

Frederick was primed for confrontation. But Curt hadn't meant this to be a confrontation. "I'm sorry."

"*Sorry for what?*"

"Sorry for nothing! Sorry I said anything! I only meant to suggest I would move out if she needed to live with you."

"Is that what you want?"

"It seems like a complicated decision, what to do with your mother, and she obviously doesn't want to live with your sister."

"That's not what I'm talking about. I'm talking about you, not my mother."

"Well, I *am* talking about your mother."

"Why should you care what happens to my mother?"

"Do *you* even care what happens to your mother?"

"What business is it of yours what I think or feel or do about my mother?"

"She's your mother!"

"That's funny coming from someone who says if he never spoke to his mother again he wouldn't give a shit."

"My family is fucked up, that's different. But you have a real family."

"Oh, and what is a 'real family'?"

Seeing the scope of the conflict he'd set off, Curt stepped through the door out onto the back patio and sat down on a stack of bricks, his back to the house. Frederick lit a cigarette and watched him. Everything depended on the way he handled this. He knew from bitter experience, Curt didn't like to be confronted. Couldn't be controlled. He went out onto the patio.

"I'm sorry, I'm not myself these days. It's hard for me to think straight about anything, especially my mother, right now."

"What sort of future do you see for us?" Curt asked. Here he was again, posing a question for which Frederick was ill-prepared. He felt a curtain slowly descending. "Frederick, let's be honest. Things have changed in your family because of your father's death, and it could affect our relationship."

"Hello?" A voice came from behind them. They turned to see a young man and a little girl. "I'm Jack McCoy. I own this house."

Frederick apologized, saying they hadn't meant to trespass. "I'm an architect, I was taking my—"

"I closed on it last week and wanted to show my daughter the place. This is Lisa. Say hello to the gentlemen." Seeing how Frederick neglected to introduce his companion, Jack introduced himself to Curt. Then to Frederick, "So, you build houses?"

"Mostly large apartment buildings. I work in New York. I'm originally from Reading, but the firm I work for is in New York." He was babbling.

"I see." Jack looked at Curt.

"You've picked a nice place to live," Frederick said, hoping to distract him from whatever might be going through his head just now regarding himself and Curt.

"Well, my wife saw it first and persuaded me. Seems like too much house to me, tell you the truth."

Frederick took this as his cue to inquire about the rest of his family. Was it just the one child?

"No, we have four, plus a fifth on the way."

Frederick and Jack talked about the need for more space when raising a family, housing prices, lawyers, the development of the Reading area, especially Wyomissing, which seemed to be attracting a lot of young newcomers these days. Meanwhile Curt was coaxing some words out of Lisa, who, little by little, warmed to his attentions.

"I'm seven."

Curt asked which room would be hers. She said she didn't know and tugged on her father's sleeve, but he was talking about the trees. "I don't like the idea of moving into an area without any trees. I don't exactly know how long it takes for trees to grow their full height, but it's gonna be several years."

"They'll probably grow faster than you expect."

"If trees are anything like little girls," he said, sweeping Lisa up in his arms and giving her a loud kiss.

They proceeded carefully up the steps since the railing hadn't been put in place.

"The master bedroom is to the right, I believe," Jack said.

There were three other bedrooms, and Lisa ran from one to the other.

"Can I pick the one I want?"

Jack laughed, "We'll see."

"I want this one," she cried when she entered the front room. "I can see the road and the driveway so I'll always know who's coming to visit."

"You want to be the eyes and ears of the house?"

"Yes," she giggled. "Does Lucy have to share with me?"

"She's your little sister, you mean you don't want to share your room with her?"

"No, I want my own room."

"There aren't enough bedrooms for you to have one all to yourself, Angel. You know we share in this family."

"Do I always have to share with her?"

"All right, that's enough, we're not gonna decide right now. We're just looking around."

"What's up there?" Curt asked Jack.

It was the attic. Jack said, if they continued having children, they might turn it into a bedroom, but for now they would just use it for storage. Then to Frederick, "Amazing how much stuff you accumulate when you have a family," putting extra emphasis on the word "stuff."

"I can imagine," Frederick said, now feeling the strain of making polite conversation. He turned to Curt and muttered, "We ought to be going."

Curt shrugged his shoulders, reminding Frederick their earlier conversation was still a dangling live wire. They said goodbye to Jack and Lisa, but rather than head to Marge's right away, Frederick suggested they walk around the block, for they still had time before their train.

"She was a sweet little girl," Curt said. Frederick wasn't interested in talking about the girl or her father. "And he was kind of yummy. Don't you sometimes just want to fuck every guy you meet?"

Now he seemed to be saying things calculated to upset him. "No, I don't," Frederick said sharply.

"Did I say something wrong?" Curt asked, feeling certain Frederick was burning for another fight.

"You wanted to fuck that guy?"

"Sure, why not?"

"Really?"

"No. I don't know. Maybe. So what? What's eating you?" Frederick hesitated. "Yes, I'd like to fuck him. Yes, I thought she was cute. Yes, I'd love to have a daughter like that someday."

"Well, I hope you get one. But then, of course, it won't have anything to do with me."

"How could it? Two men can't have a child."

"So you're saying you want to go straight now?"

"Don't be ridiculous."

"Who's being ridiculous? You want to fuck every man you meet, and now you want to be a father? Be serious."

"Why does that threaten you?"

"I just think you're showing what a child you really are. And you say you want a child of your own!"

"Why shouldn't I want a child?"

"Since the day I met you, you've never said or done anything to indicate you have the capacity to care for a child, let alone another person, any kind of person."

"I suppose nothing I've done over the past five days matters at all." He was silent for a moment, then said, "Frederick, I think we should talk—"

"Don't say another word. Please don't." Curt thought he was about to cry.

"So you just want me to shut up. You don't like anything I have to say today, and now I should just shut the fuck up, is that it?"

"I'm sorry. Forgive me. I think I want to get out of here, get out of Reading." He looked at the houses under construction, their wooden frames and abstract forms, and the barren hill under the bright sun. Quicker than words could form in his head, he thought of hills with olive trees and red tiled roofs and golden light showering down amid ancient ruins, the dome of St. Peter's on the horizon. "Why don't we take a vacation? Really get away. I think that's what I need."

"Maybe you *should* take a vacation."

"I mean you and me. Let's us go somewhere. Let's go to Europe. Let's go to Italy! This summer!" It had always been a dream of Curt's…to fly…Europe… But was Frederick serious? "Let me take you to Europe. I think two, three weeks in Europe would do us both a lot of good. A whole month! It would give us a chance to really be together. We've never been truly alone together. There's always some disruption. I think we need to have that experience of traveling together. It would be wonderful! Let me take you."

Curt was skeptical. He wanted Frederick in his life, it wasn't that he didn't. He saw how touchy Frederick became if he said anything that suggested he wasn't happy or wanted to break up. But he felt, more than ever, an exclusive relationship with one person was never going to work for him. Not at this point in his life. But to say that now, with Frederick so fragile (for he really did care about the man's feelings), and now when he was offering to take him on a trip to Europe—and if he were to refuse, everything would fall apart—and he *did* care about Frederick, it *was* a nice life they had together, it *wasn't* that he didn't want to be with him—he needed to make sure Frederick understood—

"Well?"

"You know I care about you," Curt said.

Frederick was still waiting for his answer.

"Of course I would love to go to Italy with you." But there are a few things I think we should discuss—that was what he wanted to say, what he should have said. But here they were, back where they'd parked the car. Frederick was already inside, putting the key in the ignition. Curt got in and closed the door. He put his arms around Frederick's neck and laid his head on his chest and rested there without saying a word. He thought of Marcello Mastroianni in *La Dolce Vita* and imagined the handsome Italian men and voluptuous Italian women he was sure to meet in Rome.

Frederick looked out the window for signs of Jack and his little girl. No one in sight. They were safe in the car in their deserted village of the future. "I want you to be happy," he said. "I want us to be happy." He started the car.

Upon their arrival at Marge's, Curt promptly went out back to play with Markie, who was learning to throw a football. Frederick, meanwhile, was bracing for more unpleasantness with his sister. They needed to come to an agreement about what to do, at least for the short term, about their mother. But he needn't have worried. For Marge was tired and washed out from yesterday. The house was a mess, and she looked a mess. Their conversation was brief and restrained. He proposed that Clare continue to live with her until more permanent arrangements could be made. In his mind he'd prepared a statement about how he wasn't going to dignify her comments at the reception by discussing them in any way, they were beneath dignity, if she wanted his financial assistance this was how it had to be, like it or not—but none of it was necessary.

Neither of them was inclined to prolong the visit. He was in a rush, he said, and called for a taxi. He would contact her later this week to arrange the next available weekend—he didn't have his appointment book handy—when he might come to Reading to scout out nursing homes in the area.

When the taxi arrived, Marge called Markie and Curt in from out back, then said a cool goodbye. Markie gave long, impassioned hugs to both men, hanging on especially to Curt like a long-lost brother.

"We'll be back soon," Frederick said to Markie, stooping to his level and brushing the hair from his forehead. It was then he noticed his sister looking at him. Her expression was hard to interpret. It wasn't disapproving, but neither was it warm. For a split second he thought to apologize for everything that had happened, starting with their father's death. But he mustn't keep the taxi waiting.

Frederick and Curt spoke little on the way to the station and then on the train back to New York. Both were glad to be returning to the city. Curt was eager to gain some distance from Frederick and his moods. At the same time he nursed his anticipation of their trip to Italy, which they decided would be in August—only four months away. Frederick, meanwhile, felt he'd gotten a new lease on life. He was already planning their itinerary in Rome. He'd always wanted to visit the Baths of Caracalla, McKim's prototype for Penn Station. That would be a day in itself. A full week in Rome, then. And while they were in Italy, how could they pass up the chance to see Venice?

But how far, Frederick remarked, the demolition of Penn Station had advanced after only five months! Exiting at Seventh Avenue, they passed beneath a sign proclaiming, *"On the way to you…New Madison Square Garden Sports Center, Redeveloped Pennsylvania Station, We are doing everything to hasten completion of the project for your convenience,"* with amateurish drawings of basketball and ice hockey players and a family dressed in traveling clothes, standing by their suitcases. Atop the entrance, a shroud covered the clock, flanked by female figures of Day and Night and the squadron of stone eagles, still maintaining their perch. A group of men peered through the entrance to the 31st Street driveway, now exposed to the light of day as the masonry was torn away to reveal the underlying steel skeleton. *"Sorry, but clear it we must to build your new station."*

Sorry?

An old gentleman hesitated at the stoplight in front of the station. Frederick handed Curt his suitcase and offered his arm to the old man. Escorting him across the intersection, he figured by now Sally and Veronica had taken his mother to Marge's house, and Marge was explaining how she would live there for the time being until a decision could be made for a more permanent living situation.

"You're a nice young fella," the old man said as they reached the Statler Hotel on the opposite corner. He hobbled on his way.

Frederick felt a sickness in his stomach. The news, he was certain, would crush her.

CHAPTER TWELVE

PERCHED ON THE QUIRINAL HILL ADJACENT TO THE BORGHESE GARDENS, the Hotel Eden was a massive wedge of russet-colored stone, stucco, white trim, and green awnings. Having lived with Frederick now for almost a year, Curt was used to a lifestyle a notch or two above what he'd known as a kid, but the opulence of this place was apparent even from the sidewalk. The doorman came to the curb, opened the taxi door, and proceeded to empty the trunk of their suitcases.

"Benvenuti, signori, welcome," he said in a thick accent. Curt felt mildly uncomfortable with the effort the young man was making to serve him. He couldn't have been more than a couple of years his senior. "Your first time in Rome?"

"Sì," Curt said.

"Thank you" Frederick said, handing him an American quarter—"Remind me," he added, turning to Curt, "to exchange some travelers checks once we get settled."

They were shown to a corner room on the fourth floor by a bellboy who carried all three of their suitcases. Curt tried to say he'd be happy to give a hand but made a mess of the Italian, prompting the young man to insist, "No sir, you are the guest, it is my job." Frederick handed him a quarter (his pocket was full of them for this very reason), said "Thank you" again, and shut the door. Curt went directly to the bed and threw himself face down.

"I hate the English language," he mumbled into the bedspread.

"Yes, it's a problem that Americans by and large don't speak foreign languages," Frederick acknowledged, sitting down next to him and stroking his head. He knew Curt was having his first real, if harmless, experience of culture shock. "Understandable," he said, "on one's first trip abroad, but what were you expecting?"

Curt sat up and looked around the room. The furnishings were antique. Two large windows, heavily draped, opened out onto a small cast-iron balcony overlooking the mellow foliage of the Borghese Gardens. In the distance rose the dome of St. Peter.

"I feel like Rapunzel locked away in her castle."

"We haven't even unpacked our bags. You're probably a little distraught from jet lag. Take a bath, you'll feel better. I'll order some drinks."

After freshening up, Curt was in brighter spirits. Frederick proposed going for a walk to one of Rome's most famous spots, the Spanish Steps—get that into his system, he thought, so he'll forget about the politics of being an American abroad. Curt brought along his movie camera, a gift Frederick had given him after he'd made a theatrical show of wanting one for the trip as they passed an electronics store window one day while shopping for a proper suitcase. But the camera now became an unwelcome fifth wheel.

"Frederick, look here, say hi, wave to the camera." Curt attempted to film Frederick walking away from the hotel down Via Francesco Crispi towards Via Sistina.

"Why don't we just enjoy our surroundings?"

"But this is my first time in Europe," Curt said. "You've been here before, you've seen it all, I haven't."

"All the more reason to look with your eyes! When you look through the camera, you're not really looking, and *you're* supposed to be the one who doesn't want to behave like a tourist!" He turned away dismissively and continued walking a few paces ahead.

"Fuck!" Curt shouted.

What was the matter now? Frederick wanted to throttle him and feared this was going to be a long three weeks.

"A pigeon just shat on me."

They spent the next several minutes, on the corner of Crispi and Sistina, wiping the bird droppings off of Curt's shoulder with tissues and spittle.

"Did any of it get into my hair?"

Frederick checked perfunctorily and assured him his hair was clean but felt it would serve him right if the bird *had* shit in his hair.

"Which way is Via Veneto?" Curt asked.

"I thought we would walk to the Spanish Steps first. It's one of the greatest public spaces in the world. You'll love it." He described the way the steps spilled forth from the foot of the church of Trinità dei Monti, how storied a location it was, the setting for movies and operas, where Keats—

"I don't think I could handle going into a church or a museum right now."

"I'm not proposing we go into any church or museum."

"I just want to walk and experience the city."

"With a movie camera stuck between you and the city you're so keen on experiencing?"

"I don't need you to be my tour guide. I'll figure it out on my own."

Frederick stopped in his tracks. "Then why have we come here? Why travel together?"

"We don't always have to do the same thing all the time."

"We just arrived!"

"You think because you're paying for everything you can dictate what we do?"

"I think you're seriously overreacting—to what, I don't know. Maybe you need to rest."

"Stop telling me I need to rest. I'm fine. Maybe *you* should go back to the hotel and rest."

But this was absurd, Frederick thought, arguing on a street corner in Rome. It was the height of embarrassment, and Curt didn't seem to have any idea how ridiculous the whole thing looked. Frederick realized he had to offer a concession and fast. He proposed a *brief* visit to the Spanish Steps and then returning to the hotel by way of Via Veneto, along which they could find a place to have some lunch.

The Spanish Steps worked their magic on both of them. It was a little past noon, the sky overcast, the steps carpeted with people lounging and talking, couples embracing (Frederick and Curt were both reminded they were forbidden such intimacies in public), musicians playing, tourists taking pictures, old men selling flowers. Frederick pointed out how the shape of the stairs alternated between convex and concave arcs, how movement down the stairs was retarded at intervals, like the flow of a melody, or a dance, by the numerous landings. They walked down several flights until they found an unoccupied spot along the wall and took a seat on the steps. A flock of birds swooped down low over their heads and then up again. Curt began to notice young men, not so very well dressed, drifting up and down the steps, now and then approaching a solitary man or woman.

"Prostitutes," Frederick explained. They'd been noticing and thinking, apparently, the same thing.

"Hey, look at him," Curt said, discreetly pointing to a ruffian with baggy pants, suit coat, and no shirt underneath. Then a skinny blond fellow. Then a curly-headed Adonis.

Frederick regretted what he'd started.

"There's nothing wrong with saying we find someone attractive, is there?" Curt asked, but though it took the form of a question, it really was a declaration.

"It's not that I don't find other men attractive—" Frederick started to say.

"We see men every day, everywhere we go. We *look*. I look, you look. Everyone looks. That doesn't mean I'm going to pounce. It doesn't mean you're gonna run off with the first attractive man you see." Frederick scowled but Curt, undeterred, looked him square in the eyes. "Would it be so terrible, for once, to have an experience together with a third person?"

"Are you proposing it?"

"Not necessarily right now, I'm just saying, in general…" Curt hadn't quite intended to broach the subject, but there it was. Frederick thought, This is the first of twenty-one days together, how am I going to get through this? He almost looked forward to their return to New York and the resumption of normal, everyday life. Now he really did want to step inside the church at the top of the steps, cool his thoughts and dry his brow (the clouds were breaking up, the day was getting hot).

Instead he suggested they go somewhere for a drink. Via Veneto seemed the best place to kill two birds with one stone—Curt's wish to have a taste of the street made famous by the recent Fellini film and Frederick's need for alcoholic refreshment. They retraced their steps along Via Sistina until they came to the Piazza Barberini, at the center of which Bernini's muscular god Triton, borne aloft on the broad tailfins of four flapping dolphins, blew into a conch shell, sending a single jet of water spurting high into the air. Curt might never have noticed the fountain, however, had Frederick not drawn his attention to it and explained its significance (something to do with a passage from Ovid, and transforming a common feature of the urban scene—a public fountain—into a work of art), for he was preoccupied with figuring out which of the several streets that fed into the piazza was Via Veneto and how to get there from here, as several lanes of cars and buses whipped around the circle.

Frederick let Curt take charge, and he steered them to Harry's Bar. It wouldn't have been Frederick's choice—sumptuously (some might say ostentatiously) decorated, it was also crowded and noisy with tourists. They were brusquely ushered to a table indoors near the back next to a large, loud American family. "Looks like they put all the Americans near the kitchen," Curt muttered, and Frederick thought he might be right. It was only once the drinks arrived they began to relax (neither of them bothered to attempt Italian—the waiter begrudgingly spoke English, quickly took their order, and was back surprisingly soon with the drinks). Alcohol and cigarettes lit them up and calmed them down, enough to discuss what their next move should be. Curt wanted to wander back down Via Veneto, admitting Harry's Bar was bullshit but determined to get the full flavor of the street if possible. Frederick felt a need for sketching and for solitude. He thought there might be a bad omen in agreeing to part so soon only hours after their arrival, but he expected the first day for both of them to be a blur of fatigue and astonishment rolled into one, and so he accepted his urge, made sure Curt had enough lire in his pocket, agreed on a time to rendezvous back at the hotel, and with his sketch pad in hand set off to the Borghese Gardens and the Borghese Gallery.

Half an hour later, he was wandering alone among paintings and statues, the best company, he thought, when there in the middle of the room stood Bernini's *Apollo and Daphne*, her hair and hands turning to laurel branches and leaves as young, delicate Apollo, his limbs and posture musically complementing hers, innocently, naïvely, achingly strained to capture her. He sat on a bench in view of the statue and began to sketch. He didn't try to make an exact copy but, instead, focused on her strange, alien hands, half human, half vegetable. Those who love to pursue fleeting forms of pleasure (he read the Latin inscription at the statue's base) in the end find only leaves and bitter berries in their hands. He grew more and more fascinated by this freakish girl whose body had become her own enemy as well as the enemy of the boy who loved her. Apollo didn't interest him except in a purely sexual way—it was Daphne who roused his imagination—and he soon ran free with the idea of all things, not just hands, but the entire human body, male and female, and buildings—walls, rooftops, staircases—overgrown with vines and weeds, rude bushes and trees sprouting up in the midst of corridors, crashing into bay windows, disturbing the peace, nature brutally taking back what man had only briefly won for himself. He reverted to ruins, as all things do eventually, he said to himself, and thought anew of his country house, but something more modest this time, a cabin, secluded in the woods, perhaps, like Thoreau's cabin at Walden Pond...

Curt, too, sat staring at love's pursuit. A bearded man and a severe, stylish woman without makeup, seated at the next table, kissed and whispered in each other's ear, laughing (he'd found a more modest, and therefore, he realized, more suitable café farther down Via Veneto). They sat against a mirrored wall, so he was able to watch them and watch himself watching them at the same time. Soon the couple was joined by another man. Curt couldn't tell if he was expected or a surprise guest. The man leaned down and kissed the woman, then the other man stood up and the two men kissed each other on both cheeks. He sat at the table and placed his arm around the man's neck. The woman reached across the man in the middle to touch the newcomer's face as the three of them laughed warmly in unison. The lines of affection and desire were impossible to interpret and, for that reason, utterly and forever appealing. The freedom and beauty of Italian men! The way they held their bodies. The way they expressed themselves, groomed themselves, combed their hair—their clothes, their shoes, the rings on their fingers—you would never see two American men approach each other, relate to each other like that, not in full view of other people. He almost wanted to cry.

He finished his drink and ordered another...

When Frederick returned to the hotel room, Curt was in a deep sleep. He stepped out onto the balcony and lit a cigarette. The setting sun was shrouded in mist. It was hard to tell from looking at the sky, the city, the shadows, the soft light, what time it was. The Victor Emmanuel Monument, its long row of pillars gleaming whiter than white, hung suspended in air like an opium eater's dream palace or a phantom Penn Station. He began to count the columns but quickly lost track. The delirium of jet lag, he thought, and ordered room service before turning in for a long, drugged night's sleep.

The next morning both Frederick and Curt felt reborn. They made their apologies upon waking, admitting "Jet lag will do that to a person." The ceiling in the restaurant at the top of the Hotel Eden was lower than on the other floors, but its compensating feature was a set of wide windows giving panoramic views over the spires, roofs, and treetops of Rome. Awnings sheltered tables on the terrace, which ran the perimeter of the building. Frederick and Curt took a table outside. The morning air was like nothing either experienced in New York. There was a heavenly aroma in it, they agreed, but of what—jasmine? Eucalyptus?

"Buon giorno, signori, volete un caffè?"

Before them stood a tall young man with a transcendently open smile. They could almost have laughed for joy over his stunning, easy beauty. What is it about Italian men? they began to wonder aloud once he'd taken their order and left, and this time the conversation about the attractions of other men didn't unsettle Frederick. This was vacation, he would try to think and feel and act differently. The waiter brought the coffee, and as he took their food order, they seized on little opportunities to ask him questions and to engage him in light conversation (how late was breakfast served, could they purchase cigarettes here in the restaurant, had this always been a hotel or was it something else before?), which he sunnily, obligingly answered (until 11:00 AM, yes, of course, he didn't know for certain but believed originally it was an apartment building, he would be happy to inquire of someone at the hotel who knew its history better than he, if the signori wished). All through breakfast (the coffee was incredibly good, the rolls and jam better than anything you could get even at the best bakery in New York—Frederick was pleased to see Curt catching travel fever, but he felt it too—it was indeed good to be out of New York, out of the US, for a while at least) they talked about what they might do for the day. The waiter overheard and stopped at their table.

"Is this your first visit to Rome?"

No, they explained, Frederick had been here before but, yes, it was Curt's first time—actually, his first time anywhere outside the US.

And today? What were they planning to do? They looked at each other and said they hadn't decided.

"Don't go to the Vatican. It's Sunday and the crowds will be horrible. Better go tomorrow. How long will you stay in Rome?" At first he suggested the obvious tourist sites—the Trevi Fountain, Piazza Navona, the Pantheon, the Colosseum—but as the talk continued, he became friendlier and began to refine some of his earlier suggestions. "Where are you from?" When they said New York, he raised his eyes to the sky and shifted his weight onto one leg, the better to settle into conversation. "I have been to New York, it is my favorite city in the world. I will go again and maybe live there. Americans come here and wish to live the life of the old world, but I want to go to America and live in the new world. It's funny, isn't it?" He then suggested an itinerary "if you want to see another side of Rome. Go to Tivoli and see the Villa d'Este and Hadrian's Villa. You will see beautiful gardens and ancient ruins and a small town but not so many tourists." He had to dash away to tend other customers, but every chance he got he returned to their table, each time introducing some new topic. "What do you think of Steve Mc-Queen?" or "What is the popular opinion of President Johnson?" and "Will there be a great war in Vietnam?" Both Frederick and Curt were surprised and impressed by his knowledge of the US, how closely he'd followed recent events, but also the range of what he knew. He could touch upon seemingly everything from local cuisine ("New Orleans gumbo I would love to try") to popular television shows ("unfortunately the drive to Pompeii is not so easy as touching your nose like Samantha Stevens"—it took even Curt a moment to catch that reference) to current political events ("There will be a great society because of the Civil Rights Act, no? In Italy we do not have this problem with the races"). But again he had to wait on other customers. Finally he returned as Frederick and Curt were preparing to leave. "Please, what is your name? I am happy to meet you. I am Angelo." They introduced themselves, thanked him for his suggestions, and wished him a good day. But then Curt lingered a moment longer, as Frederick headed toward the elevator, to ask Angelo which days he worked and to remind him they'd be here until Friday, when they must leave for Florence.

Angelo smiled. "See you later, alligator." He extended his hand. "Americans shake hands, they do not embrace like Italians. Very manly," he said laughing.

Curt found it hard not to think of Angelo that day, but thinking of Angelo made him an unusually easy companion, Frederick found, though he didn't know the reason. All he knew was that whatever he suggested, Curt went along with it. They visited the Colosseum after breakfast, and Frederick eagerly pointed out the various orders of columns on the façade—Tuscan, Ionic, Corinthian—the Corinthian pilasters at the top (a later addition), the numerals over the entrances, the genius of the Roman arch, the centuries of decay and damage, fire and earthquake, the numerous reconstructions, its use and reuse as amphitheater, church, monastery, cemetery, squatters' den, factory, stone quarry, Liszt's joke that it would make a fine concert hall, what Goethe and Byron, Hawthorne and Dickens and Henry James would have seen when they visited, and what they wrote. The saga of Daisy

Miller, and her untimely death from malaria after an ill-conceived tryst one night in the Colosseum, was told in riveting detail. Curt was surprised one building could have meant so much to so many people, could have figured so prominently in so much famous literature, and then the thought of those ancient spectacles, the scenery rising from chambers beneath the arena, the dressing rooms, the slaughter of animals and humans—he allowed himself to be drawn into the coils of history and fantasy as Frederick deftly maneuvered him around groups of tourists and droning tour guides, and Curt felt privileged to have his own personal guide.

Amazing, he said to himself afterward, as they sat on a low wall opposite the entrance, enjoying a cigarette and keeping an eye on two young Italian men sitting nearby, and their fascinating physical camaraderie (one minute arm-wrestling, the next laughing, smoking, then lying on their backs, their shirts riding up their torsos)—amazing how a person like Frederick lives every day of his life, he thought, with so much knowledge in his head, and this is just one old building in one European city! He was filled with awe at how little he himself knew and how much he must learn even to come close to Frederick, but the thought, as such thoughts often did, made him churlish, and so he retreated to the equal and opposite position—all authority, all expertise is bullshit, it's *experience* that matters, and…the thought inevitably trailed off into deserts of its own, and then the sight of those two handsome young Italians, or a speeding Vespa, distracted his attention, and he imagined racing seventy miles an hour. But how lucky I am, he thought (for Frederick was standing over him, offering a hand to pull him up), that Frederick loves me. And mixed with thoughts of Angelo, and wondering if there might be some opportunity to see him outside the hotel, or even *inside* the hotel when Frederick wasn't around (maybe when he goes to the Vatican, for really Curt didn't care if he never saw it)—the best thing, he decided, was to go along with Frederick today, humor him, because what he gives in return is so great. He took hold of Frederick's hand and rose.

From the Colosseum, they wandered towards the Monte Capitolini, bought sandwiches from a street vendor, and sat in Michelangelo's plaza, surrounded, Frederick explained, by some of the most perfectly proportioned buildings in the Western world. But the more Curt observed the Italians and other European tourists around them (it was easy to spot the Americans, and both Frederick and Curt shrank from their shrill voices, their imposing ways), he felt, I look too much like an American, I need new clothes, and so they spent the afternoon, closer to the hotel, in the shopping streets around the Spanish Steps and along Via Veneto, going from one store to another, outfitting Curt with clothes to make him look the part of a world traveler. In the dressing room of Brioni's, Frederick stood before him buttoning a shirt, his fingers brushing the skin of his chest, and on an impulse Curt threw his arms around him, kissed him, grabbed his crotch until he felt the erection, opened his pants, knelt down, and proceeded to give him a blow job, and Frederick knew it was madness to do this in a dressing room where their feet could no doubt be seen, but this was Rome, they were far from the lives they normally led, and he submitted to the pleasure and it carried him up until he came inside Curt's mouth, and Curt, his mouth full of cum, stood up and kissed Frederick and the cum spilled down their chins and Curt said, Thank you, thank you, Frederick, I feel—

"Signori, signori."

"Oh, shit!" Curt whispered laughingly, thrilled with the excitement of doing something so incredibly transgressive. In Rome, he was starting to notice, half of what he himself did and said struck him as rude—he wanted to change his personality, change his manners, really wished in some ways he were European instead of American—even began inflecting his statements and questions differently, almost with the touch of a British accent. He knew, once he got back to New York, it was all over with Collin. For Collin could never make possible experiences like this.

The next morning, Angelo noticed something different about Curt. "Already you look Italian," he said as he placed the coffee before them. He smiled and gave Frederick a wink.

"New threads." Curt described their shopping expedition.

"Maybe we exchange clothing. You look more Italian, I look more American."

They laughed and teased as Curt continued his narrative of their travels the day before. As Frederick listened and observed the two young men's interaction, he sensed something unspoken amidst the chatter ("Stand up and see if my shoulders are as broad as yours"—"But you're taller than me"—"Maybe not in bare feet"). He felt he'd missed a beat in their story, that, indeed, they were playing out a story, some new narrative unfolding before his eyes.

"And the volcano is quite nice, still active. It is dangerous to live there, but it is the most populated volcanic region in the world. You will love to see it."

"It sounds great," Curt said to Angelo while looking at Frederick, as if silently to ask, Wouldn't it be great?

"So Wednesday morning early I pick you up at the hotel. We go to Pompeii, and maybe later we drive to Positano. The Amalfi coast is magnifico, and it will be inconvenient to get there by coach or by train. Much easy to drive by car."

"Maybe," Frederick said, hoping to delay a decision and, eventually, talk Curt out of it. He looked at Angelo, who now seemed less the image of an heroic Mediterranean god and more the seductive, threatening, dangerous type of the Roman street hustler, the sort they'd seen prowling the Spanish Steps.

They argued over the invitation as soon as they got back to their room. Curt had his heart set on going. Frederick, though disinclined to tell Curt the real reason, felt equally sure it was a bad idea. He said there were too many other things to do in the city and they couldn't really afford a day out of town.

"I don't need to see everything in Rome. This is a chance to experience the real Italy with a real Italian. I hate always being surrounded by tourists." Frederick felt insulted, but to insist would only inspire further, stronger resistance. He mustn't appear jealous. "You don't have to go, you can do what you want. But so can I, right? There's no law saying we have to be together every minute of every day, is there?"

Of course not, he said, but now felt he *must* go, for surely something was afoot. "Unless you'd prefer I didn't."

"What are you talking about?"

"Oh, I don't know, sometimes when you're young…I'm just trying to figure out—"

"It's up to you, I have nothing to figure out. I'm going."

"All right. I'll go." Curt didn't respond. "I mean, I would *like* to go." Still Curt was a blank. "Okay?"

"Yes, okay. Fine. Good."

But Frederick knew it wasn't fine and good. Once on the road with Curt and Angelo, he experienced the full oddity of his position. He felt like a chaperone, the elder parent who insists on riding along with the kids on their first date—and being given pride of place in the front seat next to Angelo, as they drove south from Rome toward Naples, didn't mitigate the strong feeling he was nevertheless taking a back seat to the friendship—or something more than friendship—blossoming between the younger men.

Everything Angelo said—about the geographical differences between the Lazio and Campania regions through which they passed, the most common Italian surnames, famous locals Sophia Loren and Enrico Caruso, the Neapolitan origins of pizza—seemed a performance, a bone thrown to the old man, with the real communication taking place sotto voce. And to some extent he wasn't wrong. For he never saw, as Angelo careered down the highway at top speed, how Curt, sitting directly behind Angelo, passed his left hand forward alongside Angelo's hip, slid it into his pants pocket, spread his fingers, and squeezed Angelo's thigh through the fabric, nor how every time Angelo gently removed Curt's hand from his pocket, all the while carrying on the conversation, Curt put it right back in.

"Most New Yorkers do not own a car," Frederick explained. "The island of Manhattan is so narrow and congested, a car is more a hindrance than a convenience." But Angelo wasn't familiar with the words "narrow," "congested," "hindrance," "convenience"—nevertheless he caught the drift of what Frederick was saying and managed to hold his own while feeling Curt's fingers pressing his thigh, as if on cue, each time Frederick made a remark.

"I would feel like a dog—how you say 'al guinzaglio,'" he murmured to himself knowing neither of the Americans would be able to supply the words. He raised his right hand from the stick shift to indicate the collar around the neck and the long cord attached from the neck to the hand of the owner, and he let drop his hand momentarily onto Frederick's hand.

"Leash."

"Leash," Angelo repeated but pronounced it "lish," which made both Curt and Frederick smile. And for a moment Frederick felt included in the circle of friendship. For this was something that united him and Curt beyond any doubt—their fluency in English only.

"The world is forever changed because the automobile—" Frederick started to say philosophically, but Angelo cut him off to point to the silhouette of Mount Vesuvius rising in the distance. Frederick imagined a column of fire shooting up, the top of the mountain exploding, raining down lava on the valley below, drenching all civilization in molten rock. It was powerful, vivid, real as nothing thus far on their vacation had been. It wasn't art, it was nature, it was life, and life, Frederick felt, was terrible. But the road bent towards the sea and the mountains flattened out as the perspective changed and Vesuvius disappeared. Now Angelo was talking about Positano and the beautiful coast and the fishing villages and the food and sun and palm trees and beaches, and wouldn't it be nice to spend the night in one of those towns? Curt explained the proximity of beaches to New York City, "But it's nothing like this," he said, and now Frederick felt he must put down New York in order to praise Rome, say how much better everything in Italy was—the food, the physical beauty of its women, the clothes people wore, the compact automobiles they drove, the climate, the mountains, the history.

"Everything in the US is new. We have no history," Curt said. The thought was novel and interesting to him.

"But this is why I like the US. You begin the world all over again and you can be whatever you want. You are free."

"But only some people are free. That's a myth about the US," Curt said.

"What is the word?"

"Myth. M-Y-T-H."

"A-hah, myth," Angelo said. "Mitologia."

Frederick grew quiet as they approached their destination. The boys, meanwhile, grew more animated. Angelo warmed to the discussion of differences between the old world and the new. Clearly he'd given the topic a great deal of thought, and he enjoyed theorizing about it. Occasionally Frederick would interject a few words ("Something many Europeans don't realize about the US is how religion dominates our society—how Puritanical we are. We are seen by the rest of the world as the standard-bearers of freedom, but our values are provincial"), but more often than not it had a stifling effect on conversation. His sentences were too long, his syntax too complex, his vocabulary too sophisticated, so much so that Curt was moved to make a joke or change the subject or ask a question about some passing sight. He knew Frederick was making an effort to connect but too often failing in the attempt. Now and then he felt chastened and came to Frederick's rescue. "How are you?" he asked once they'd parked the car after filling the tank.

"Fine," he said, wishing he could pour out his insecurities to Curt, knowing it was entirely uncalled for.

"You sure?"

"As long as I'm with you, yes."

"Well, here I am."

"And how about you?"

"Good," he said with a diffident tone, masking, Frederick was sure, his real feelings; he's trying not to show how much he prefers the company of Angelo, right now, to mine.

"Ready?" Angelo stood before them and put one arm around Curt's neck and the other around Frederick's and pulled them towards him and growled. "I am hungry. Will you like to eat now?"

It was left to Curt to say he was starving and to decide for the group they should eat.

Frederick was glad to be out of the car, glad to be moving his legs, a few steps apart from Curt and Angelo. Naples, however, was a disappointment—noisy, dirty, choked with automobiles, graffiti everywhere. He never imagined an Italian city could be so unbeautiful. But he had to persevere. Get through the day. Time was merciful. It only moved in one direction. Eventually it would be evening. Eventually they would return to Rome, to the hotel. After all, he thought he heard Angelo say something about work tomorrow afternoon. His sketch pad! That was the answer. He told them he wanted to go off to do some sketching and would meet them later. He wasn't so hungry anyway. Angelo protested—out of politeness, no doubt— but then assented, as if sooner or later he'd expected Frederick to peel off, leaving the two of them alone. There was the complicated business of re-calibrating plans—whether to tour Pompeii, "But I thought you wanted to see the ruins," "How far is Pompeii from here?" The longer it took to resolve, the more impatient Frederick became to venture out on his own.

They agreed to meet in front of the Central Station in Piazza Garibaldi. Just east of the square was the old city, so Frederick figured since he was here already, he might wander through. The cramped, dusty streets and seedy establishments held little appeal, however, and, to make things worse, he quickly lost his way in the labyrinth. After half an hour going in circles, he found himself back at the main square, at which point he decided to cut his losses and head toward the Capella Sansevero to see Giuseppe Sanmartino's sculpture of the Veiled Christ. He spent the rest of the afternoon in the cha-pel, sketching and contemplating the otherworldly figure of the dead Savior draped in a transparent veil, the incongruous sound of a radio broadcasting song after song by Nino Soprano, the young, handsome Italian crooner of the moment, coming from somewhere seemingly within or perhaps just outside the chapel. The last to leave the chapel, he was ravenously hungry and ate an awful pizza near the railway station. The station, he noted, was an angular, modern monstrosity recently erected in place of its venerable ancestor.

When they rendezvoused that evening, Angelo and Curt seemed com-fortable, casual. They had gone to Pompeii after all, driven to the foothills of Vesuvius. Curt embraced Frederick when they greeted each other. "You would have loved Pompeii," he said. He seemed eager to show Frederick how much he'd learned, as if he'd been storing up information and images just for him. Whatever really happened between them, Frederick thought, they weren't showing it.

"How was your afternoon? Did you make some good sketches?"

"May I see?" Angelo asked.

Frederick opened his sketchbook and began flipping the pages. He passed over a sketch he'd done of Curt the day before.

"What is this?" Angelo asked. Frederick reluctantly showed him the page. It was a drawing of Curt, nude, on the bed in their hotel room.

"When did you draw that?" Curt asked incredulously.

"Yesterday morning. You were asleep." He wanted to turn the page, but Angelo held it open and scrutinized it.

"You sleep with no clothes?"

"Sometimes."

Curt sounded contrite as he said it. Frederick couldn't understand why he was pretending to be so modest. And then it hit him: it wasn't Angelo's gaze that embarrassed him, it was Frederick's.

CHAPTER THIRTEEN

THURSDAY MORNING CURT WOKE TO FIND FREDERICK'S BED EMPTY. A NOTE on the dressing table said he'd gone to catch the sunrise from the Spanish Steps. But it was odd he hadn't taken his sketchbook with him. He sat up in bed and opened the sketchbook. He found the drawing of himself asleep in the nude. He marveled at Frederick's skill. His body wasn't nearly so good, he thought, but if that's how I look in Frederick eyes, who am I to argue? It might be nice, actually, to frame it and hang it in the bedroom back home. "Our bedroom," he said to himself as he got up and opened the drapes, admitting a flood of light. He swung open the doors to the balcony and breathed in the fresh morning air. The day was cloudless. He returned to bed and paged backward through the sketchbook. There were drawings of the train station in Naples, Mount Vesuvius from a distance, a man draped in a veil, lying on his back, the bay of Naples, then the Colosseum, the Arch of Constantine, the Spanish Steps, then pictures of trees and bushes growing out of body parts, a human head with leaves and branches covering the face, hair made out of moss, hands that tapered to flowering branches, a girl half human, half tree. Then pages with drawings of Penn Station in New York, not demolished but ruined, as if it were an ancient Roman ruin, with broken walls and vegetation growing on top, cattle grazing in the waiting room, sheep roaming the concourse, skyscrapers in various states of decay, some crumbling as if made of dirt, then more pages with images of the station as it actually appeared, with dump trucks, cranes, scaffolding, whole sections torn away, buildings, automobiles, pedestrians glimpsed through shattered windows and skeleton walls.

He closed the sketchbook and lit a cigarette. He thought of Angelo. He might have been up for something, especially since Frederick had left them alone for several hours, but he was different when Frederick wasn't there. He became elusive, hard to get, less talkative, less willing to translate things into English. Curt felt he was merely tagging along as Angelo chatted with shopkeepers, restaurant owners, people they encountered in the park. He wasn't nearly so attentive a travel companion as Frederick. He began to think he'd done something wrong, said something inappropriate, to make Angelo lose interest. He'd wanted Angelo to kiss him. Tried to touch him, find opportunities when they were alone, or when no one was looking, to initiate some physical contact, like the contact they'd had in the car. But Angelo wasn't going for it. He was merely polite. It was a relief when they finally reunited with Frederick that evening. But by then Frederick seemed to have gotten into a funk.

Well, he didn't understand any of it. He lit another cigarette and paced the room. He was scrutinizing his naked body in the mirror when Frederick entered.

"Good morning," Frederick said somewhat shyly and gave little more than one-word answers to Curt's questions—Did you see the sunrise? How come you didn't take your sketchbook? Is something wrong?—until Curt had to press him to find out exactly where he'd gone and what he'd done. "I went to mass at Trinità dei Monti. A whole group of nuns prostrated themselves before the altar. When I first saw them, I thought they were sculptures, they were so still."

"Strange."

"Beautiful…in a way, that kind of life."

"What kind of life?"

"Contemplative. Religious."

Curt, still nude, lay across Frederick's bed, vaguely hoping to seduce him. "Do you wish your life was more contemplative?"

"My life already is rather contemplative," he said and turned to enter the bathroom.

All day long Curt noticed the change in him. He was present but withdrawn. He didn't need Curt, apparently, in the same way he did yesterday and the day before. Nothing overt, nothing he could put his finger on, but there was a detachment. He didn't touch Curt the way he normally did. Didn't check to see how Curt liked his coffee or how he was feeling. Often he could be annoyed by Frederick's constant "wifely" attention, but now that it was taken away he missed it. But he didn't want it back, exactly. To be honest, he welcomed the extra breathing space. There was less talk, less analyzing things, less effort to enter into each other's thoughts, and as a result less conflict. They bickered less than ever. He felt washed clean of something. As the day unwound, and they walked around St. Peter's Square (Frederick convinced him he couldn't leave Rome without seeing the Vatican, and passively he agreed), waited in line to enter the Sistine Chapel, wandered the long halls of the Vatican museum (standing before Raphael's *Transfiguration*, Curt found the figure of the walleyed boy, possessed by demons, oddly disturbing, and for the rest of the day he was unable to get the boy's face out of his mind), they moved like sleepwalkers in a kind of narcotic state. Around 4:00 PM, Frederick proposed a quick visit to the Galleria Doria Pamphilj before it closed. He wanted to see Velazquez's portrait of Pope Innocent X and started to say something about how it occupied its own intimate corner gallery, and the scene in *Daisy Miller* when Daisy and her Italian boyfriend are discovered there together, sitting beneath the stern gaze of the old pontiff. Curt wasn't really interested, especially after the long day in the Vatican Museum, so he proposed instead meeting Frederick later back at the room.

Upon reaching the hotel he decided to go up to the restaurant and see if Angelo was still working. He found several waiters washing up, setting tables, when Angelo emerged from behind the bar already in his street clothes. He asked jovially for a report of Curt's day. As Curt enumerated the things they'd seen, he realized tonight would be his last night in Rome and his last opportunity to see Angelo outside the restaurant. He wondered if there might still be a chance for something physical between them. Angelo looked spectacular in his leather jacket and sunglasses, a pair of perfectly polished mirrors. He hadn't removed them when Curt appeared.

"What are you doing right now?" Curt asked.

"I am going to meet some friends. Would you like to come?"

Curt admitted, frankly, he had something more intimate in mind. Angelo laughingly dismissed the proposition. "Come with me and meet my friends. Where is Frederick?"

"At a museum," he said, and remembered his promise to meet him back at the room. He said he could join Angelo and his friends for an hour or two, perhaps, but Angelo was driving up to Tivoli and wouldn't be able to bring him back until quite late. Curt knew it would be wrong to disappear on Frederick like this. Despite Frederick's coolness with him all day, he'd been a perfect gentleman, and to abandon him now—he imagined Frederick standing innocently before a building, looking intently, not hurting anyone, moved, as he always was, by architecture—he knew it was a comfort to Frederick to come home at the end of each day, to fall into his arms, feel human flesh against flesh, forget about architecture for a while, not think too much, just feel, touch—he knew Frederick wanted that from him, needed that from him—and he was happy to give it, and often such intimacy, innocent as it was, turned into something more, something fiery, ferocious—he imagined Frederick fucking him—they might spend the rest of the evening in the hotel room fucking, they could order room service, watch Italian television, and he would feel safe, not chasing after Angelo, who at bottom really didn't seem all that interested anyway... To abandon Frederick now, he admitted to himself with reluctance, would be a show of ingratitude beyond all imagining. "Well, I guess I better go. I promised Frederick—"

"Then I see you tomorrow, yes? You will leave for Venice tomorrow?" He was already heading toward the elevator.

Florence, *then* Venice, Curt explained as he trailed him like a puppy. Holding the elevator door open, Angelo scrawled onto a slip of paper the name and address of his Venetian friend Paolo—"An artist, he will love to meet you I am sure"—and tucked it into Curt's breast pocket, giving him a pat on the chest. "Sorry, are you coming down?"

When the elevator door opened onto his floor, there wasn't time for more than a brief, rather impersonal "Ciao."

Curt let himself into the room, closed the door behind him, fell onto his bed, and cried. Eventually his tears subsided, and he dozed.

By the time Frederick returned, he was gone.

As a result he was forced to entertain himself on his last night in Rome. Of course he knew well how to do this and was, to some degree, just as happy to eat a quiet dinner in the hotel, enjoy a cigarette and a Scotch in the hotel bar after dinner, then read and retire early, for the train to Florence left first thing in the morning—but that was the problem, for the pleasures of his dinner, drink, cigarette, and book were attenuated by the anxiety that Curt might not come back at all that night, might force them, by his irresponsibility, to miss their train, or worse that something might have happened to him. He bit the nail on his thumb. After a few more glasses of Scotch, he was able to fall asleep with the hope that Curt would turn up in the morning.

Curt, meanwhile, went out wandering the cafes of the Via Veneto one last time but failed to make contact with anyone Italian or tourist (he wasn't in a mood to socialize—why, then, had he come here in the first place, he asked himself, sitting at a café on the Piazza Barberini, watching the cars drive by and the people passing along the sidewalk, a group of drunken friends loudly singing "Stormy Weather," couples enjoying the warm night air and the festive atmosphere of the street, but it had none of the allure of *La Dolce Vita*, and there was no Marcello Mastroianni or Anouk Aimee or Anita Ekberg to sum it all up in one glamorous personality), and so finally he trudged back to the hotel at 2:00 AM, drunk, depressed at his failure to find a home in fashionable Italian society, even as an exotic outsider. Frederick's suitcase was already packed, he noticed, when he slipped into Frederick's bed. He pulled the sheets over the two of them and wrapped his arms and legs around Frederick, who only half-responded.

Frederick had little to say in the morning, though he didn't show displeasure. He was oddly neutral. He seemed more concerned about the business of checking out and securing their transportation to the train station, finding their way to the train, to their seats on the train, and getting settled in for the journey to Florence. Conversation was light, intermittent, consisting mostly of straightforward observations—look at that church tower over there, probably a fortress, see those clouds, must be a storm coming... It was only as they were approaching Florence, and the excitement of entering a new city melted away their resentments and anxieties, that Frederick was able to ask, as if his uppermost feeling all along had been one of concern for Curt and Curt alone, "How was your night last night?"

"You were asleep when I came in."

"Actually I was awake, but I wanted to be well rested for this morning, so I just tried to remain still."

"Well, my night stank. I went to a few cafés and came home."

"What were you looking for?"

The question could have been taken a number of ways. But the station was approaching, the red roofs of Florence and then, suddenly, an enormous dome came into view. Already Frederick was taking down the suitcases, and passengers were filing off the train.

Forty-eight hours was all they had in Florence—just enough time, they discovered, to see a few of the major sights, have a few splendid and one or two mediocre meals, walk the Ponte Vecchio, stroll around the center by night (they were staying at the Hotel Savoy, another grand establishment chosen by Frederick), and leave feeling they'd only just gotten acquainted and would have to return someday. They spent most of Saturday at the Uffizi. It wouldn't have been Curt's choice, but he was getting used to Frederick's routine. Superficially they had never seemed so compatible in all the time they'd been together. And yet they were not as physically affectionate as they had been in Rome. Curt, for all the excitement and beauty of foreign men, was not feeling particularly sexual in Florence. While Frederick was occupied in the bathroom, prior to their venturing out on their last evening, Curt masturbated, making sure Frederick couldn't hear his heavy breathing as he reached orgasm. It was a relief to get that out of his system. This must be what marriage is like, he thought. It wasn't unpleasant, but it wasn't exciting. By the time Frederick emerged from the bathroom, Curt had managed to wipe away all traces of his moment of ecstasy and to control his breathing. The only giveaway was his temperature. His body was still warm, and if Frederick should touch him he would know at once. He rolled out of bed and walked to the window. Frederick asked him if he would be ready soon and what he was hungry for. Curt reached for his pants and, slipping them on, heard something crinkle in the pocket—the note from Angelo with the name, address, and phone number of his friend in Venice. He hadn't mentioned it to Frederick. Down below Giuseppe Square was alive with the sound of bells, laughter, and the occasional high-pitched roar of a motor scooter.

"Curt?"

He turned from the window to face Frederick.

"What are you hungry for?"

"Anything."

FREDERICK INDULGED CURT'S WISH TO USE THE MOVIE CAMERA IN VENICE. How could he not? Every vista, every corner, every piazza, every bridge afforded a picture like a stage set. Everyone was an expert picture taker in Venice. He went so far as to film Curt sitting contentedly, like he'd just gobbled the mouse, in the gondola from the train station to their hotel on the Grand Canal. At dinner that evening—the restaurant spilled out onto the veranda overlooking the canal (Frederick made the reservation as soon as they checked in to ensure they got dibs on one of the tables outdoors)—Curt was in a receptive, listening mood, unusual for him. During their meal, a couple sat down behind Curt. Frederick choked at the sight of the man. He could have sworn it was Jon. He had to watch him closely to be sure one way or the other—but even then he had his doubts. A person could change a good deal in five years, and married life had a way of transforming some men into chubby Buddhas from the slim, fit, younger men they had been. To say nothing of hair loss. But this man—even his laugh sounded like Jon's.

"What is it?"

"Sorry, it's rude of me, I know. The man behind you looks…like someone I know."

Curt turned.

"No, don't look!" Frederick said under his breath.

"It's all right, I'm pretending to look at the scenery." Turning back to Frederick, "He's handsome. Someone you…?"

Frederick hesitated to explain. Not long after Curt moved in with him, he had described the bare outlines of his relationship with Jon, though he'd been careful not to use his name. Curt, he remembered, seemed quickly to lose interest in his story and, apart from the portrait photograph of him and Jon during the war, which Curt had requested from his mother, certainly never, in the months since then, showed any further curiosity about his wartime love. But maybe it was the air in Venice—the water was inky and glittered with reflected lights from the palaces along the canal—gondolas and vaporettos and the occasional utility boat glided by—maybe it was the wine, or the way Curt had made himself so agreeable these last few days—or the realization there needn't be any secrets between them now because, in a way, there was little left to lose…

"Yes, as a matter of fact."

Curt slouched a couple of inches lower in his chair. He wasn't sure he wanted to hear after all. Frederick took his posture to mean, *I'm all ears.*

He'd been drafted, Frederick said, by lottery in January of '42 at the age of twenty-seven. He was sent to Fort Dix, New Jersey, for basic training. Immediately he was perceived by the other men at the base to be an intellectual—sensitive, delicate, a smooth-handed, white-collar worker from New York. They nicknamed him "The Professor." He soon fell in with a group of men known as the "college crowd," one among them in particular, Jonathan Foley, variously nicknamed "Pinup Boy" and "Billy Budd" because of his extraordinary physical beauty. Frederick was riveted by him—the perfection of his features, the poise of masculinity and femininity in his body and carriage. Eight years younger than Frederick, he had dropped out of college in his third year to enlist. He'd gotten bored in school—too smart, perhaps, or too lazy, or too much of a snob to work hard to succeed. He had a girlfriend back home—Cathy—and the real reason he enlisted, Frederick always suspected, was to get away from her, though just about everyone was joining the war effort, one way or another, in those days. It was universally understood in the barracks that the men in Frederick's circle were homosexual or at least not staunchly, conventionally masculine and heterosexual. Not normal in some way. Frederick was surprised, however, to discover that there was a place for him in the military, that he fit in, that he wasn't ostracized for being queer. He grew strong. He had to admit he marveled at his own physical abilities, his strength and agility during training. Though grueling, basic training was rewarding, and Frederick was eager to prove to himself and others he wasn't a helpless fairy.

There was an unwritten rule among his friends in the barracks that they would never have romantic relations with each other since that would jeopardize the all-important camaraderie they'd built up. But Frederick and Jon did engage in an intense, quiet flirtation. Much eye contact and allowances for seemingly trivial physical intimacies—a brush of hands in passing, a touch on the back to get the other's attention—but they were immensely significant. Warily they allowed themselves to come closer and closer until, around the seventh week of training, they were transferred to Camp Hulen, Texas. In a Pullman car of the troop train, they saw to it they shared a berth. During their first night, Jon flung one leg, then an arm over Frederick, and Frederick responded. They had furtive sex, quick and passionate. From then on they were lovers. They seized every opportunity to be alone together. They were recklessly in love, though Jon frequently expressed ambivalence about his homosexuality, spoke often about Cathy, told Frederick he saw marriage and children in his future, though he also said he couldn't imagine not being with Frederick now that they'd found each other.

One weekend they got passes to leave the base. They stayed with a local family and shared a small guest bedroom, squeezing themselves into one of the two beds. Frederick didn't know how to kiss—his knowledge of kissing came mostly from the movies, and he'd never seen two men kiss. Jon, however, was a natural at it. Frederick didn't like it at first. He turned away. But Jon was patient. That weekend, Frederick learned how to kiss. The world was a hostile place, but Jon was safe and warm, and nothing else mattered except the two of them, together against almost cosmic forces. They found a volume of Whitman's Civil War poems, some of them vividly homoerotic, lying on the table by the bed and wondered if their hosts knew of their relationship and, inexplicably, wanted to show their approval by leaving it there for them.

"Is that when you discovered Whitman?" Curt asked.

"I'd known his work before, but…that's probably when I changed from just reading it for the intellectual kick to actually living it."

Curt looked down into his lap, almost as if, at that moment, it would have been immodest not to do so. He seemed to be taking the idea of *living* Whitman and going somewhere with it in his mind. But Frederick continued: At the end of training they were assigned different duties. Because of his typing skills, Jon became an Army secretary in Washington, while, because of his design skills, Frederick was made a camoufleur with combat troops in northern France. While apart, they wrote letters in code to evade military censors. They managed to see each other whenever Frederick got leave, and their meetings were brief and unforgettable. One meeting in particular was seared into Frederick's memory. It was November of 1943. Frederick was home for two weeks but had to ship out the day after Thanksgiving. They'd hoped to spend a full week together in New York, but Jon was detained and couldn't leave Washington until Thursday night. It snowed that Thanksgiving, and all the trains up and down the east coast were either canceled or delayed. Their week-long vacation had been scaled back to a mere twenty-four hours, but now even that was leaching away as afternoon turned to evening and still no sign of Jon's train. Frederick spent Thanksgiving night in the station. Finally, the next morning around 7:00 AM, the train pulled in. Frederick looked and looked and didn't see Jon and thought with a panic, He's not here, he's not coming, I'll never see him again, my life is over, when someone grabbed his shoulders from behind, spun him around, kissed him on the lips, and embraced him. It was Jon, he was home, and they stood beneath the soaring glass roof and steel columns in the middle of the concourse of Penn Station holding each other tight as crowds of people poured through the gate, and for once in his life Frederick didn't give a damn if anyone saw or what they thought.

But there was no time to lose. They had only a couple of hours before Frederick must report to the dock at 42nd Street, so Jon said, "Let's go!" They pushed their way through the waiting room, raced up the staircase skipping steps, through the arcade, across Seventh Avenue (Jon shouted "Watch out!" as Frederick nearly ran in front of a bus barnstorming down the Avenue), into the Statler Hotel, not blinking an eye as they asked for any room that was available, they were willing to pay extra since check-in wasn't for several more hours, then up the elevator to the 18th floor, inside the room, kicking the door shut as they kissed and groped and Frederick just managed to set the alarm clock before they tore off their clothes and made love for exactly two hours.

"Having sex like that in the Statler Hotel was…" Frederick paused to choose his words carefully. "It was unforgettable because…" He fingered the stem of his wine glass. "Because everything we meant to each other was summed up in it. Everything. I can't even describe it as sex. It was…love-making." He took a sip of wine. "When the alarm rang we jumped out of bed, jumped in the shower, and I fucked him in the shower, and I didn't care if the chambermaid heard all the noise we made." He looked at Curt. "We were discharged in December of '45."

Again Curt seemed to be revolving a thought and was on the verge of ar-ticulating it when Frederick explained how, during the war, Jon had hinted he might move to New York when it was all over, but when the war ended he returned to his hometown of Lexington, Massachusetts. From then on, he and Frederick made frequent visits back and forth between Boston and New York. At first, Frederick enjoyed his visits to Boston. They spent weekends wandering Beacon Hill and walking along the Charles River. But instead of getting closer, they seemed to settle, little by little, into what Frederick came to feel was an unfair arrangement. Jon continued dating Cathy yet never made clear, either to Cathy or to Frederick, whether he intended to marry her (during the war Jon would show Frederick his letters before sending them off—lines like "I am so full of love" made them laugh because they were really about Frederick, but she'd never know—and yet, Jon said, he wasn't exactly lying to her either). Five years went by and still no commitment from Jon. Cathy grew tired of waiting and left Boston for the west coast. It was at this point that Frederick tried to pressure Jon to make a decision—come to New York, or Frederick would move to Boston. But by this time Jon felt no need for a change. They had the best of both worlds, he kept saying—the days apart made weekends and holidays together mean so much more. Besides, everyone knew Jon as "Freddy's friend"—why raise eyebrows by setting up house together? Frederick wasn't sure but Jon might be right. Still, he persisted in the hope that one day they would live together. Become a real couple. So he waited, hoping there would be a change of heart. A few years later, Frederick wasn't sure exactly when, Jon began seeing Rachel, an old acquaintance and friend of the family. He also began having occasional romantic trysts with an old school chum, Philip, who'd always seemed content to play second fiddle in Jon's life. And he continued seeing Frederick on weekends and sometimes for week-long vacations. He found a secretarial job in a law firm but didn't much care for the work. It was as if he was biding his time until the right person came along, made him an offer he couldn't refuse, "made him a wealthy woman," as he sometimes joked. Frederick hated sharing him but had long accepted the fact that Jon could not be forced to change. It would have to come from Jon, at his own pace, in his own way, or not at all.

Their twisted, frustrating, long-distance affair went on like this for several more years, until Christmas of 1959. They'd made plans to spend the holiday together in New York, but at the last minute something came up—some family emergency, was how Jon put it—and Frederick ended up going to Reading instead. The call came Christmas Eve. "Freddy, it's for you," his mother said. It was Jon, phoning to tell him the "good news." He and Rachel were engaged. It was Rachel who'd proposed. He wanted Frederick to be his best man. He said this didn't mean anything had to change between them, he would always have special feelings for Frederick. In some way, Frederick would always be "the one."

Curt was stone silent. Frederick thought he detected tears in his eyes. Or was it the reflection of lights from the canal? He refilled their glasses. He didn't ask if he should continue.

When he put down the phone, he was in shock but couldn't let it show. He said, Excuse me, went upstairs to his old room, and shut the door. He sat on the edge of the bed and began to cough, a dry, aching, hacking, choking cough. And then the tears came. He cried, and the more he cried the more fierce his sobbing became. Then he grew angry and put his face to the pillow and screamed. He pounded the bed, then slapped his thighs, his arms, and when that wasn't enough—when the pain didn't sting enough—he slapped his own face. He cried and raged so long and so hard he was out of breath. At length he grew calm, composed himself, and came downstairs again, trying to act as if nothing had happened. But he was all nerves. He went out for a walk Christmas morning. He crossed paths with a couple he knew from the neighborhood. He struggled to be cordial. They could tell something was wrong—everyone knew something had happened—but what could they do or say? Some things you just don't talk about.

He dated other men after Jon, but it never went beyond a few outings. One or both of them sooner or later lost interest, and usually it was sooner than later. Gradually he only wanted brief, impersonal, sexual encounters. These became his steady diet. Until he met Curt.

"So you really were in love with him," Curt said, but Frederick didn't seem to hear the tone of resignation in his voice.

"Yes," he replied simply.

Curt lay awake that night, hearing the lapping water of the canal and the occasional boat going by in the dark. He thought of the picture of Frederick and Jonathan during the war. Of the way Frederick had spoken about Jon. He needed to find somebody who would speak about him like that one day. Someone to whom he would be everything. For all his ability to wrap Frederick around his little finger, he realized there was something about him he would never be able to touch. Never lay claim to. He got out of bed and reached for his pants. Again he felt the crinkle of the piece of paper in the pocket (Tomorrow, he decided, the first thing I'm gonna do is pay this guy a visit). He slipped out of the room, left the hotel, and walked all the way to St. Mark's Square.

The vastness of the empty square at night—no café orchestras, hardly a person in sight, even the pigeons were gone—opened up before him. He peered in the dark at the arches and mosaics, the domes and flagpoles of St. Mark's Basilica. Frederick was so in love with old buildings. And old boyfriends. If he couldn't get what he wanted from Frederick, he'd have to look elsewhere. It wouldn't be the first time in his life he was driven to that. He was a cat with nine lives. He liked Frederick—maybe even loved him (who the hell knows what love is anyway?). But he was still a young man. He had his whole life ahead of him. No way was he ready to settle down. He would never want the kind of life Frederick described with Jon. He had too much living to do, places to see, people to meet, worlds to change.

He walked back to the hotel feeling something had changed in him. Tomorrow, he promised himself, and thought of Scarlett O'Hara lying across the red-carpeted stairs at the end of *Gone with the Wind* proclaiming, "Tomorrow is another day." "Silly queen," he said to himself, "I hope Paolo is good looking."

After breakfast the next morning, he mentioned casually that Angelo had given him the name of a friend and he thought he'd look him up. To Curt's surprise, Frederick said he'd like to go with him. The address was near their hotel in the Dorsoduro district, across the canal from the ramshackle Squero di San Trovaso, the gondola construction and repair yard. The number was painted on a metal garage door, seemingly the only modern feature in the entire row of buildings fronting the canal. Upon pushing a buzzer next to it, they stood back as the metal door was pulled up to reveal a short, bearded, rather burly man, somewhere between Curt's age and Frederick's—it was hard to tell—and, behind him, an enormous painting of Angelo in the nude. To be greeted with what was unmistakably Angelo's face, and the body neither of them had seen but had, each in his privacy, speculated about, aroused Curt and made Frederick uncomfortable—he felt instantly revealed as a homosexual, standing there next to Curt, before Paolo and the painting of Angelo. Paolo, Curt dimly felt, might yet be a conduit to Angelo.

They introduced themselves as friends of Angelo's. Paolo welcomed them in and led them up a flight of stairs to a large, glass-roofed studio. Paintings mostly of nudes, male and female, covered the walls and leaned against every available surface. Their talk initially revolved around Angelo—how they'd met, what was he doing now—does he still work in the hotel restaurant? Does he still drive that broken little Cinquecento?

"The green Fiat?" Frederick said, "Yes."

Curt was bowled over by the larger-than-life-size nudes on display. Paolo's hard-edged, almost cartoonish style emphasized the extreme physical power and beauty of his subjects, especially the men.

"Excuse my asking, but…" (looking at Curt) "…did Angelo give you my name as a recommendation for subject?"

There was no way of saying no. The question already implied an interest.

"I've never been painted by a real artist," Curt said but then recalled Frederick's innumerable sketches of him, including the one of him in the nude in the hotel room in Rome. He felt a quick thrill at the thought, just then, of wounding Frederick and knowing he was in no position to object.

Paolo showed them his work. Each painting was the occasion for a story about the sitter—his name, age, place of origin, occupation, but also things less tangible—a charming habit, a vocal eccentricity, an aura—none of which, Frederick noted critically, had any traceable connection to what dominated the canvas—feet, calves, buttocks, thighs, penis, abdomen, navel, nipples, shoulders, underarm hair. Paolo then led them into the garden out back. He served coffee. His English was stilted and polite. He asked their plans while in Venice, what they'd seen so far, whether they'd been to the Lido ("beautiful people there, you will see"), and recommended a few restaurants, churches, and shops near their hotel.

"Completely vulgar," Frederick said of Paolo's work once they'd left the studio.

"I didn't think so at all."

Frederick queried him as to what he liked about it, what he thought good about it. Curt knew he couldn't converse about art on Frederick's terms, so he merely said he didn't know—all he knew was, he liked it.

"You hear that so often. 'I don't know anything about art, I just know what I like.'"

"Are you insulting my intelligence?"

Frederick felt chastened. "I'm sorry, I didn't mean… He made me uncomfortable, that's all."

"Well, don't worry, *you* won't be posing for him."

Frederick let it drop and hoped Curt would do the same. They'd paid their visit, sent good wishes from Angelo in Rome, done their friendly duty, and that was all. But Curt was hugely flattered by Paolo's interest in him and announced to Frederick the next morning he was spending the day at Paolo's studio.

"Why?" he asked before he'd had time to think about how best to handle the situation.

"He wants to paint me."

"Did he say so?"

"Even if it wasn't explicit, who says I can't offer my services to him?"

Frederick laughed. "What services do you have in mind?"

"Whatever he wants, you have a problem with that?"

"He's a pornographer!"

"So what? It could be fun. Angelo wanted me to meet him, he obviously wants to paint me, and there's no reason he shouldn't."

Frederick didn't press the issue any further. He only asked when they might rendezvous later.

"I have no idea how long these things take."

"You expect to spend the entire day and evening with him?" As he said it, he feared he'd planted the idea in Curt's mind.

"Maybe. I don't know."

"So you're prepared to separate for the rest of the day."

"I'm just gonna see what happens."

"If I don't see you by 7:00 PM, should I assume you'll be having dinner elsewhere?"

"Yes. You should assume that."

It was one thing, Frederick realized, to feel that love had been lost between them, but to feel Curt no longer needed him… He began picking at the cuticle on his thumb. "Very well," he said with resignation. "Are you planning on having breakfast before you go?"

"I'm not very hungry."

Clearly he wanted to be left to his own devices. "Make sure you have your key."

"Frederick, I'm fine," he said with exasperation and reached out to embrace him. Frederick flinched. "All right, if you don't want to touch me. Have a nice day."

As Curt turned to leave, Frederick reminded him they were scheduled to go to Munich on Thursday. This made Curt angry. "Do you really think I'm just gonna ditch you for the rest of our vacation?" he asked and left without waiting for a reply.

Frederick spent the morning at the Accademia Gallery. He found a café at lunchtime and, afterward, made the rounds of some churches by Palladio he'd wanted a closer look at. He thought an excursion to Palladio's La Rotonda outside Vincenza might be a pleasant way to spend tomorrow. But mostly he was just worried about getting through the next forty-eight hours. He had an uneasy feeling about the way he and Curt had parted.

Not only did Curt not return to the hotel by 7:00 PM but he didn't come back to the hotel at all that night. On Wednesday morning Frederick took a gondola to the mainland and boarded a bus to Vincenza. All his professional life he'd wanted to see the mansions of the Renaissance master architect whose name was a byword for beauty and elegance of proportion. La Rotonda in particular interested him as one of the buildings that inspired Jefferson's Monticello. But he was distracted with thoughts of Curt. As he approached the small villa, its isolation amid sweeping lawns making itself more keenly felt with every step, Frederick thought Palladio's austere design—the perfect symmetry of pediments and columns, stairs and statues—almost barbaric in its simplicity, crude in its directness. No one, he felt, could live in a country house so rigidly perfect as this. And he only became more morose as the day wore on. What could have happened? Was

Curt having an affair with Paolo? Was he punishing him for something he'd said, something he'd done?

He ate alone in the hotel room that night. Packing his bags for the next day's trip to Munich, he felt as miserable as he'd ever felt. He knew if anything he should be worried on Curt's behalf, but self-concern trumped all other feelings. It was like their first date all over again. He was being stood up, and he could hardly believe Curt still had the nerve to do it. The same old game of cat and mouse. Making up only to break apart. The same old conflicts, the same old arguments, over and over.

Frederick returned to the room after breakfast the next morning to find Curt soaking in the tub. He said nothing but waited for him to emerge. He was determined to avoid an argument. They greeted each other casually as if nothing had happened, Curt especially playing it cool as he emerged from the bathroom, wrapping a towel around his waist. Frederick thought his golden torso looked particularly beautiful still dripping from the bath. Curt inquired about checkout time and, saying nothing else, proceeded to gather his things. Frederick sat at the table by the window and lit a cigarette. He watched and waited for an explanation.

Once his suitcase was packed, Curt, still dressed only in his bath towel, sat at the table opposite Frederick—"may I?"—and lit a cigarette for himself. "I'm not going to Munich." Frederick looked at him in disbelief. "Paolo asked me to stay on in Venice. I'd like to spend more time here, not live so much like a tourist. I can stay with him and it won't cost anything. I just need some spending money to get me through until the eighteenth."

Frederick waited several beats before speaking. "You're leaving me for the rest of the trip?"

"There's something I've been wanting to say to you and I didn't know when was the right time." Frederick saw his mother approaching him, telephone receiver in her hand, snow falling outside the dining room window. *Freddy, it's for you.* "I need to be free. Make my own decisions. Sometimes I feel you own me. Like I'm dependent on you for everything. That's not good for me and it's not good for you."

"Please don't tell me what's good or not good for me." He picked at the cuticle on his thumb.

"I need some time to myself. I'm sorry this had to happen here. You have your work and I know that will occupy you in Munich."

Again Frederick asked him to stop making suppositions about him.

"I'd like my plane ticket and some money. I'll meet you in Rome next weekend."

Frederick continued to stare at him. Finally he asked, "Why?"

"Why what?"

"Why are you doing this?"

"I don't believe in monogamy. Not between two men. It doesn't work for me. I'm sorry. I care about you, but right now I need to be on my own. This week. I want to be free to do what I want this week. It doesn't mean I never want to see you again. But I need to be on my own for a little while. I don't know what else to say."

But he didn't need to say anything more. Frederick reached for his brief-case and retrieved the ticket. He wanted to make sure Curt had his passport—wanted to advise him to be careful, don't let anyone, Paolo included, take advantage of you... But it was clear Curt didn't want parental attention. He saw the waters of the canal behind Curt's head, the sparkling mosaic of the Palazzo Barbarigo. A gondola drifted by. Venice was the most sordid, the most grotesque, the most vulgar place he'd ever been. *You and I will always...it's just that with Rachel—*

So be it. He had a train to catch. He'd made plans to continue on to Munich. He'd corresponded with a German architect, Reinhard Riemerschmid, a professional acquaintance of Seymour's and Deborah's, and arranged to see firsthand how Munich had rebuilt itself since the war. He wasn't going to let the man down now. He'd made a promise, and he was not one to break a promise ("fifty, a hundred, a hundred fifty, two hundred" in travelers' checks—that should be enough for the week).

His only worry now was how to stand up, cross the room, and make his exit while still maintaining his dignity.

REINHARD RIEMERSCHMID STRUGGLED TO FIND WORDS TO EXPLAIN THE shocking extent of the destruction after the war. "The sight of our dear city in ruins went straight to my heart, and I felt..."

As if the idea of Munich in ruins triggered some movement in his bowels, Frederick felt a sudden urge to defecate.

"...obligated to do something."

He looked up at the twin towers with matching onion domes of the Frauenkirche (must have been those sausages he'd had for breakfast), but felt perilously distracted from what his companion was saying. Where was Curt? How had he spent the last twenty-four hours? He imagined him posing nude for Paolo. Then the two of them making love, right there in the studio, under the skylight. He hated to think of it and tried putting it out of his mind. Just concentrate on this, here, now. He wondered how long he could last before making an escape to the nearest toilet or at least a bench to sit down upon. He was sweating and beginning to feel faint.

"One stood horrified, horrified, and then again horrified. Everything was strange. The sight of the broken Victory Arch on Ludwigstrasse was so ghastly one did not realize it, although it was right before our eyes. We thought we were wandering through an absurd dream. To perceive it as real was completely devastating. It was difficult for our sadness to be selective. We had to deny it. So we no longer experienced anything at all."

Ever since his arrival yesterday evening, Frederick had been struck by the cleanliness and orderliness of the city. So little trace of war damage remained, especially here in the historic center, one might think the clock had actually been turned back forty years. But perhaps some buildings looked *too* well-kept, too clean, the edges too straight, the roofs too sturdy, the whitewash too white—evidence that what one saw *wasn't*, in fact, an historic building but a modern replica. New materials, new methods of construction inevitably tipped their hand. *Real* old age was a sagging of the flesh, a redistribution of the hair, a protrusion of the bones, a shifting, however subtle, in the original, underlying structure. (Had Curt given him up because he was too old? But Paolo, though younger, was surely nothing to look at. He pictured Curt in the arms of Paolo—squat, hairy, paint-splattered Paolo! Concentrate, he demanded of himself.)

"It must be difficult for Americans to understand. You have never suffered this kind of damage."

Not since the Civil War, Frederick said, which was confined largely to one underdeveloped region of the country. True, there was Pearl Harbor, but that never touched the places people live. "The only thing that comes close," he supposed, "for those who live in a city like New York, is the sight of new buildings under construction everywhere you look. The tearing down of the old and the putting up of the new" (Curt had discarded him for someone new), "even when there was nothing especially wrong with the old."

"But there is an essential difference between destruction undertaken in war and demolition in peace time."

Frederick sensed the debating instinct and shrank from it. He picked at the cuticle of his thumb. He thought the only real difference was the one between buildings that fell by accident and those brought down by deliberate intention. But before he could decide even to withhold his opinion, Reinhard was heading toward the entrance to the church, explaining along the way the difference between the restoration of this church and that of the Peterskirche, just off Marienplatz (focus, Frederick insisted with himself once more—the discomfort in his stomach seemed to have subsided for now).

"When the war was over, there were plans to tear it down, until Cardinal von Faulhaber said 'I cannot imagine Munich without the Peterskirche,' and this helped to inspire public opinion. The people of Munich were very attached to Peterskirche. It is our oldest church. The reconstruction was a popular success because it was as close to an exact reproduction of the original as possible, and this gave confidence to other projects throughout the city."

Once inside the Frauenkirche, Reinhard stopped in front of a bulletin-board display of several photographs showing the bombed-out church as it appeared at war's end. The twin towers were remarkably intact, but three quarters of the roof was gone, revealing the interior stripped entirely of ornament, matching the surrounding buildings, all of which appeared not only damaged but decayed as if from millennia of steady, constant erosion, like ancient ruins.

"The exterior was generally rebuilt to its prewar appearance, but the interior required a simpler solution. Too much was lost." He described various proposals put forth for how to rebuild. He himself had proposed a plan that was "appropriate for the ruins." He'd wanted to express the departed greatness of the building. "Not to blend in the old with the new but to show the *difference* between old and new. Make it stark. As a reminder. A constant visible reminder." There had been other ideas—to subdivide the interior into various rooms for meetings and worship, to leave the roof open and damaged as it was but simply add a flat concrete ceiling underneath, not to rebuild the high altar but to replace it with the figure of a dove. Frederick had now irritated the cuticle of his thumb to the point of bleeding. He put his thumb to his mouth and sucked. Poetic ideas, he thought, and looked at the clean, white interior with its relief-encrusted pulpit ("made of reinforced concrete," Reinhard explained), modest stained-glass windows, and modern lighting fixtures. As such it was a disappointment, he thought, compared with almost any church you might stumble across in Italy. And to leave the roof broken, unrepaired, he thought—you might as well have abandoned the whole godforsaken city. (Should he cut short his time in

Munich? Go back to Venice? Make amends with Curt? It would be too humiliating…)

"'Without the Frauenkirche, Munich would not be Munich!'" Reinhard mimicked those conservative Münchners, architects and laymen alike, who lacked vision. "Pretty soon you come to the conclusion that you must re-build everything as it was before the war—but why stop there? Why not resurrect the medieval fortifications? Then you have, excuse me, Disney-land. Hollywood. You do not have a real historical city. You have childhood fantasy and illusion. You have Neuschwanstein—a nineteenth-century building constructed with the latest technology but decorated to look like a medieval castle" (Neuschwanstein, indeed! Frederick thought, remember-ing his boyhood fascination with King Ludwig and his architectural folly in the Alps—he would *not* go back to Venice and lower himself to Curt—he would stand his ground, take a day next week and make an excursion to Neuschwanstein…).

They walked the aisles of the church and compared notes on the state of historic preservation in Germany and America. The Germans were, of course, decades ahead of the Americans, but Reinhard was critical, it seemed, of all sides of the question: the moderns had no respect for the past; traditionalists, on the other hand, buried their heads in it; reconstruction was, more often than not, a fraud. "Works of art are *meant* to be destroyed." The idea was almost incomprehensible to Frederick. "One must confront a disfigured work of art. In the same way one faces old age and death."

They had come full circle and stood now at the exit. Frederick put out his hand and braced himself for a grip sure to exacerbate the pain in his thumb. "It was a pleasure to meet you."

"Must you go? I was hoping we might have lunch. I wanted to introduce you to one of my colleagues who is very much interested in urban plan-ning. She has visited New York and spoken with some of those people who protested the tearing down of your train station. They are called—what is the name?"

"AGBANY. Action Group for Better Architecture in New York. It's an acronym."

"Yes, exactly. My colleague—"

"Perhaps some time next week, I'm here until the seventeenth" (he won-dered if Curt would be there to meet him in Rome).

"I don't know if she will be available." Reinhard seemed to sense some-thing was not right. In a final show of collegiality, he urged Frederick to take a look at the Siegestor on Ludwigstrasse, directing him to walk north, past the Hofgarten on the right. "You will see the kind of restoration I am talking about. I would be much interested in your opinion of it."

Glad to be free of Reinhard (his thumb had stopped bleeding at last, but the queasiness in his stomach had returned), he proceeded up Ludwigstrasse as suggested. But almost immediately he regretted his quick, capricious departure. Deborah had gone to some trouble to help facilitate their meeting because she'd been curious to learn more about historic preservation developments in Europe, especially Germany, which had sustained so much damage. Well, there was still a chance they might meet once more before he returned to Rome. Unless he made a detour to Venice en route and had to leave Munich early. But intruding upon Curt and Paolo—he imagined actually walking in on them in flagrante delicto—unthinkable! Picture the scene Curt would make. He almost wished he never had to face Curt again.

There, up ahead, was the triumphal arch whose reconstruction Reinhard so admired. Nearly the entire top half of the arch had been blown off. But rather than simulate the original using comparable stone and replicating the moldings and sculpture, the missing pieces had been filled in with plain, poured concrete. No adornment. Just the original outline of the structure was indicated, nothing more. If anything, it looked like a temporary solution until the right craftsmen and the best materials could be located to finish the job. But the job, according to Reinhard, was finished, it looked exactly as intended. A brutal reminder of war, a withering commentary on the very idea of "triumph." A triumphal arch left in defeat, like a head gone bald, he thought, instinctively running his fingers through his hair and picturing Curt and Paolo making love under the skylight in Paolo's studio.

Suddenly he felt a rising in his gorge. If he didn't get back to the hotel immediately, he knew, he was going to vomit.

CHAPTER FOURTEEN

This law would bring much-needed order and control to the now-chaotic process by which New York City undergoes change.

THE LANDMARKS PRESERVATION COMMISSION, AFTER MUCH NEGOTIATION and many revisions, had finalized its Landmarks Preservation Bill and forwarded it to Mayor Wagner. It had been sitting on his desk since early May, and now it was mid-September. In a city of perpetual change, Wagner was the king of deliberation. Would it take *another* disaster like Penn Station to wake him up? All he had to do was send the Landmarks Bill on to the City Council, just get it off his goddamned desk!

But he mustn't let anger seep into his prose. *We need historic buildings in order to understand how people lived at a time so very different from our own.* Mustn't sound strident or hysterical. *The materials, techniques and styles of these buildings are virtually extinct.* Antagonizing the mayor was the last thing this letter should do. He was already, presumably, on their side. The idea was to keep it that way, build on that good will. He had to choose his words carefully. *Though obsolete in terms of maintenance, housekeeping, and function, such buildings provide irreplaceable variety to the cityscape.* But when he thought of the Brokaw Mansion, exposed there on the corner of Fifth Avenue and 79th Street, a fine, fragile gem from an earlier era, stripped of its ornament, hacked to pieces, raped (he'd once thought it squat and pudgy but now that it was on the road to extinction, he saw it in a different light)... *The apartment towers that replace them are all stamped out of the same mold—a routine economy model, using standard brick on steel or concrete frames, standard plans and fenestration, dictated purely by the speculative formula of maximum profit to minimum investment*...he wanted to stand up and shout Stop, don't do this, it isn't right! Leave things as they are!

Frederick slumped in his chair and looked up at the cloud fresco on the ceiling of the reading room at the New York Public Library. He had received a telephone call from Curt last night. Why now, he wondered, after two months of complete silence? Nothing at all for two months, then suddenly, out of the blue, he telephones. And not just once, but five times in a row. He thinks he can lure me back with his tantalizing ways, his promises—probably needs money. Or he's had another fight with Collin and wants a place to sleep.

But he hated being insensitive. What if Curt really was in trouble? What if he truly needed help? Why *not* help him? In spite of the way things ended, he did mean something to him. The past counted for something, didn't it?

Nothing between us has to change. It's just that with Rachel...

Who was he kidding? How long before he got it through his skull? Curt was a user, a manipulator, a seducer. A sadist and a liar. Never again! Never would he be taken in again.

Chewing the nail on his middle finger, he surveyed the piles of books and papers before him. He had amassed more information than he knew what to do with. His notes filled several legal-sized pages: "Built between 1887 and 1889 for Isaac Vail Brokaw, multimillionaire realtor and founder of Brokaw Brothers, well-known clothing manufacturer...one of seventy large mansions built around turn of the century along 'millionaire's row'...modeled after early-sixteenth-century Chateau de Chenonceau in Loire Valley... Interior: blend of Italian and French influences...lavish entrance hall, Italian marble and mosaic, ornate carvings...foyer illuminated with sunlight through stained glass windows by day, electric globe by night...rooms unusually large for their time...ceilings lined with stone and wood...sevenfoot-tall safe concealed behind panel in library, opened by pressing hidden catch in moulding...originally had its own moat but Brokaw enclosed with stone wall after runaway horse fell in... June 10, 1896, daughter Elvira married in sumptuous ceremony in mansion, reported by New York Times..."

It was nearly closing time and he'd spent far too long drafting his letter.

Part of two flanking blocks of "Golden Age" architecture, the house belongs to an historical enclave and a total area of unusual civic urbanity. Hence, in the case of the Brokaw Mansion, the loss would be double, he concluded, starting to bite the nail on his index finger, *the loss of a precious architectural master-piece and of the larger ambience of that part of the city.*

Frederick switched off his light and stood up. The reading room was emptying out. Packing papers and sketchpad into his briefcase, he pictured his empty apartment. What if Curt phoned again tonight? What if he *didn't* phone? He hardly knew which was worse.

He decided to get some fresh air and walk up Fifth Avenue to Central Park. His steps unwittingly brought him to the corner of 79th Street, diagonally across from the Brokaw Mansion. He found a vacant bench, took a seat, and opened his sketchpad. He heard a couple of kids playing roughhouse behind him in a sandlot. He decided to sketch the house he'd spent the afternoon studying in the library. He observed the lines of its gables and turrets, its pinnacled dormers and chimneys. Though the pain in his fingers mitigated somewhat his control over the pencil (the flesh around the fingernails had become infected as a result of constant biting and picking, and he'd had to bandage the finger tips), he tried sketching what he saw. But something wasn't right. The pitch of the roof, was that it? Or the proportions of the whole?

"*Heeelp!*"

(The boys behind him were playing tag and yelling bloody murder.)

He turned the page and faced a blank. This time he concentrated on the low stone wall around the base, the sidewalk, the station wagon parked in front of the entrance. A woman came out onto the porch and looked across the street in his direction. For a moment she looked like his mother forty years ago, standing on the porch of their house on 13th Street. ("I'm dying!") He was just a kid playing on the slope across the street, Pop's Model T parked out front, Georgey Heizmann nipping at his heels. It appeared she was looking straight at him.

"Freddy, it's getting late! Come home right now!"

"I'm coming!" he screamed.

("You're it! You're it!")

But Georgey grabbed him by the waist and pulled him to the ground and stuffed his mouth full of grass. He tried to break free, but Georgey's full weight was upon him. At last he managed to roll over, and still Georgey hung on, and they rolled and rolled back down the hill with the grass in his mouth and Georgey's hot, sweet breath on his face and the setting sun burning in his eyes.

"Right now!"

"I said I'm coming!"

Whatever became of Georgey Heizmann? he wondered. They'd stopped being friends after their sexual encounter in Freddy's bedroom—once they both realized their friendship was something more than friendship. They were children, but already they were making existential decisions to last a lifetime.

Now two men came out onto the porch and down the steps, carrying a sofa.

He turned the page and began drawing freely, a castle part Brokaw Mansion, part Neuschwanstein, perched on an Alpine cliff. In the distance he drew the slightest suggestion of a Japanese temple (Marge had given him their father's painting of the Reading Pagoda after all; he put it over the credenza in his office—"Freddy's Pagoda"). For years he'd fantasized having a country house close to the city. He might find the right plot of land somewhere upstate or in Connecticut, but now there seemed no point in designing it himself. He'd run out of ideas. The truth was, he had little to say as an architect, never really having developed a style of his own. He'd adapted himself well—too well, some might say—to the corporate style of Emerson, Root. Maybe he'd never really wanted to invent new buildings. Maybe all he ever wanted was to inhabit the old, pay homage to the tastes, proportions, and manners of an earlier era. Instead of designing a country house from scratch, or combining parts of the old with something new, maybe he should look to buy an old house and renovate it, restore it to its former glory.

("Now it's my turn! You said it was my turn!")

He turned the page and saw the face of Curt. It was a portrait he'd drawn their first day in Florence. Curt stood at the open window of the hotel room, a sliver of the Arno River behind him, with heaps of buildings, two towers and a dome, a suggestion of hills and trees, beyond. His hands gripped the windowsill. He looked stiff and uncomfortable in his shirtsleeves. Frederick had begged him to wear something more formal than a t-shirt. For once, he said, do this for me, I want to see you dressed up. And Curt had obliged.

Had he been too harsh with the boy? When they reunited a week after the separation in Venice, Frederick hardly spoke to him. Could barely look him in the eye. By a kind of perverse, negative energy, he maintained his aloofness the entire flight back to New York, and then the long taxi ride from the airport to the city, and all the rest of that first night at home. The next morning Curt tried to bring up the subject of what had happened in Venice. I will not discuss it, Frederick said, what's done is done.

"But we *have* to discuss it. Why can't we discuss it?"

"Because it's in the past," Frederick said. "Do you understand? It's finished. I'm finished!" There was a finality to his outburst that surprised even himself.

Curt collapsed. "Then I guess you'll be wanting me to leave."

Frederick had no trouble saying it: "Yes, that would be best. As soon as possible."

But his compassion for the boy rose up. He hated to think of him standing on the sidewalk, his few possessions at his feet, nowhere to go. He watched while Curt telephoned Collin to confirm it was all right for him to move back. He offered to drive.

"Don't bother, I've taken care of it."

"But I want to."

"Never mind, *please*, Collin is coming to get me!"

When the buzzer rang later that afternoon announcing Collin's arrival, and Frederick said "Send him up," Curt fell to his knees and cried. "Paolo didn't mean anything to me! He never meant a thing! You have to believe me!"

Frederick was flabbergasted to see him groveling on the floor. He felt at that moment tremendous power, as if he might put his foot upon Curt's chest and shove so hard it would catapult him clear across the room.

"Why did you leave me in Venice?"

"I didn't realize what I'd done until after you'd gone, I was miserable the whole week, I couldn't wait to see you again."

He didn't believe a word of it. It was only now Curt faced eviction he saw what he stood to lose. He would never be taken in again. He wanted to break him, beat him until he bled. Never, never again!

The doorbell rang and there stood Collin. Without saying a word, he propped open the door with his shoulder bag, strode purposefully into the apartment, and started grabbing Curt's things, carrying them out to the hallway. Curt called downstairs to have a luggage wagon sent up, and as soon as it arrived he began loading it by the elevator. Frederick stood by the credenza with his arms crossed, watching the operation, a sick feeling in his stomach. When the wagon was loaded, Curt headed back toward the apartment, his eyes still red from crying. For a split second, Frederick hoped he would ask once more to be forgiven, say it was all a colossal mistake, promise to be faithful. But then he saw Collin leaning against the cart out in the hallway, an insolent look on his face. Frederick's pride stiffened. He took one step backward at Curt's approach. At the same moment, as he was about to cross the threshold, Curt stopped in his tracks and looked at Frederick with incredulity and contempt. He reached inside his pocket, pulled out his key, and tossed it into the dish on the credenza. He grabbed Collin's shoulder bag, turned, and walked away toward the elevator.

The door slammed shut.

Frederick looked around the apartment. The stillness was palpable. The spire of Grace Church rose up white outside the living room window. He felt tears coming on, but held them back. He'd been here before. Solitude, loneliness. He could certainly survive it again. Much better than being cuckolded, wasn't it?

The men had finished loading up the station wagon in front of the Brokaw Mansion, slammed the rear door shut, got in front, and pulled away from the curb. The old woman stood looking out across the street for another moment, then turned and went back inside.

The children playing behind him had gone away.

There was something particularly desolate about a solitary Saturday evening in New York. The rest of the city was embarked on errands of mystery and play, but Frederick was alone with his sketch pad, nowhere to go, no one to see (he'd arranged to meet Deborah at the protest, but that wasn't until next weekend—"I doubt we'll have any more luck than we did with Penn Station," she'd written in a note, "but what I really want is to hear about your trip to Europe").

Tonight he might read or clean the apartment. He felt a rising panic. Neither of those things appealed to him. He could, of course, go to a bar. The Snake Pit, perhaps. But the thought of meeting someone new—conversing with a stranger—taking him home—undressing him—all the unknowns of an unfamiliar person, an unfamiliar body (there was no more nail left to bite on his pinky, so he began picking at the skin alongside)—none of it appealed to him in the least. He thought of Curt's bizarre string of telephone calls last night. Each time he answered, Curt tried to speak: "Frederick, it's me, I need to—" "Frederick, don't hang up, there's something—" "Frederick please don't—" Each time he put the receiver down. The last time, Curt said only one word. "Frederick..." For several seconds he stood with the receiver to his ear, listening to the sound of Curt's breath. Then he put his finger on the hook. Like dropping an atomic bomb merely by pushing a button.

He wondered if there would be a message from Curt on his service when he got home tonight.

He closed his sketch pad and looked one last time at the Brokaw Mansion. It was hard to believe within a year it would be gone. The surrounding buildings didn't flame up in protest. Cars wheeled by. Pedestrians strolled up and down the avenue. Birds glided down, alighting on ledges. An airplane soared majestically—but no, it was a bald eagle! How fine and strong its silhouette as it rode the air, its broad wings outstretched. He'd read there were fewer than four hundred and fifty bald eagles left in existence.

Beautiful creature. Someone should protect it. Trap it. Never let it go.

THE SIGNS PEOPLE CARRIED AT THE RALLY IN FRONT OF THE BROKAW MAN-sion the following Saturday were less witty and imaginative than those at the Penn Station protest two years earlier. And the crowd was different. Noisier, angrier, less well-dressed, and younger. A speaker's platform had been erected on the 79th Street side of the building, and protesters and passersby gathered around to hear one person after another make speeches on the importance of landmarks to the urban scene, the value not just of the Brokaw Mansion but of many other venerable buildings, the atrocity taking place before our eyes day after day down at Penn Station, the break-neck speed of tearing down and building up in the city, the need to enact legislation already submitted to the mayor, the irony that next Monday begins "American Landmarks Preservation Week," announced one day be-fore the *Times* broke the story of the impending demolition of the Brokaw Mansion, and how fitting it would be for the mayor to send the bill to City Council next week to ensure this elegant old building, which has graced the corner of 79th Street and Fifth Avenue for seventy-four years now, will not be harmed. The vicar of All Saints Church and representatives of the local planning board, the Lexington Democratic Club of the Ninth A.D., the Village Independent Democrats, the Committee on Parks and Playgrounds, the staff of the Park East newsletter—all were out in force.

"Kind of takes away the fun, doesn't it, when everyone gets in on the act," Deborah said laughingly after the rally, as they crossed Fifth Avenue and entered the park. "But I guess that's what progress means. It's not so much like *home* anymore." She had asked Frederick to walk her to the IRT on the west side. They hadn't seen each other in over two months since his return from Europe, and there was a lot of catching up to do. But she was bursting with something important to tell him.

"Columbia University is starting a certificate program in restoration and preservation, and I'm thinking of enrolling!"

"You are?—they are?" Frederick was skeptical. He wondered if she were really qualified for an advanced degree.

She said it was being spearheaded by James Marston Fitch, whom she and Seymour knew socially. She'd worked with him in the campaign to stop Robert Moses from building the Lower Manhattan Expressway. She was especially friendly with his wife Cleo. "She's an archaeologist—do you know the Fitches?"

"No—but—why are you thinking of doing this?"

"I'll be forty-two next year, the kids'll both be in college, and I'm looking around and thinking, what do I do now? I can't just stay home and keep Seymour's dinner warm. You know, I still ask myself what I want to be when I grow up!"

Frederick protested she *was* grown up.

"On the outside, yes, but not on the inside. Never on the inside!" She described the program, the courses she would take, the hours she would spend, the resources the city offered, and most of all the excitement of being part of something at its inception.

"I didn't know you cared so much about preservation."

"That's a funny thing to say."

"I just mean—"

"Of course I care! It's what I care most about, apart from my children and my husband."

"Yes, of course, I know, I know… How does Seymour feel about this?"

"He doesn't know yet. I've been researching it on my own. I wanted to wait until I was one-hundred-percent sure before telling him."

"What do you think he'll say?"

"Oh, I don't know. Sometimes I think he wouldn't notice if I put a paper bag over my head. He eats, sleeps, and breathes his work."

"And what about the children? Who'll take care of—I mean, things… around the house…while you're in school?"

She stopped walking and turned to face him. "Frederick, I'm surprised at you." He squeezed the thumb and forefinger of his right hand together to see if the pain from the infection had abated—not at all.

"I hope this won't change our friendship," he blurted out. Her silence was full of indignation. He tried to right himself. "But really, this sounds good. Good for you."

"You think it's a bad idea."

"No—did I say that?"

"I can hear it in your voice."

"My voice? I'm hoarse from shouting to save the Brokaw Mansion."

"No, that's not it." But with men, she knew when to concede defeat. "Is something wrong?"

He hadn't wanted to speak personally, but neither did he want to entertain too seriously her idea to go back to school. He simply couldn't see her in an intellectual environment.

"It's just that—I'll be interested to know what Seymour says."

"Well, it's not really up to him." She resumed walking.

"Who'll pay for it, then?"

"Let's not talk about it anymore. You haven't told me anything about your trip to Europe."

How to avoid the truth? "You know, oddly, there isn't much to tell. It was wonderful." (Again, he squeezed his thumb and forefinger together and felt stabbing pain.) "I mean, who wouldn't love Rome, Florence—"

"But give me details! What did you do, where did you go? Did you see Reinhard in Munich?"

He briskly summarized their itinerary and described his meeting with Reinhard and the couple of hours they'd spent touring churches. "By the way, thank you," he said, "for making the arrangements." Interesting fellow, he said. She pushed for more details, but they weren't forthcoming. Again she stopped and turned to face him.

"Frederick, dear, something *is* wrong, I can tell. What is it?"

"Nothing."

"You don't sound enthusiastic about the trip."

"Perhaps not. It was months ago and so much has happened in the meantime. It actually seems years ago." (Once more, he pressed his fingers together to feel the pain.)

"How is your friend?" There. She'd said it. She felt on fire. But what are friends for?

"Fine." His answer was practically an invitation to probe further. He started walking again, and she followed.

"What does he do, actually? I just met him that one time at the book party. I didn't really get a chance to talk with him."

"He's..." Suddenly Frederick couldn't remember what he'd told Deborah about Curt. He needed to remember so whatever he said now would be consistent. But he had absolutely no recollection of what he'd said. There were too many stories to keep track of, too many different people with different degrees of familiarity. Since Curt had moved out he'd spent much less time having to keep track of his stories, and now his story-telling was getting rusty. "He's not living with me anymore."

"I didn't know you were living together."

He was making things worse with each utterance! Had he not told her, or had she forgotten? Surely he'd told her. "He's the son of an old friend. He'd just moved to the city and I was doing my friend a favor by putting him up for a few months. Until he could get on his feet. So now he has his own apartment and a job."

She was pensive. He was sure he'd gotten tangled up in his stories. No doubt she was piecing it all together and deciding how or whether to respond to his lies. "And how did he like Europe?"

"He loved it. His first trip abroad."

"And do you still see him now that he's moved out?" He hesitated. "I mean—how is he doing now? What kind of job does he have?"

He said he works for an ad agency.

"Well, I didn't, as I said, get much of a chance to talk with him at the book party." They had reached Central Park West. The light was red. She was heading uptown to use the library at Barnard. She looked him in the eye. "But I liked him. He seemed so..."

As she searched for words, Frederick had the dreamlike sensation she was speaking to his heart of hearts. He wanted so much to know what she thought of Curt, what she thought of him and Curt together, but he would never ask.

"...alive."

He hung on the word.

"I'm sorry I won't be seeing him again," she added.

It was only after they'd parted that he realized: she knew everything. He pulled off the bandage and sucked the blood just starting to ooze from his thumb.

CHAPTER FIFTEEN

THREE WEEKS LATER, FREDERICK STOOD AT THE TOP OF THE STEPS OF THE Eighth Avenue Post Office, facing the back of Penn Station, reluctantly anticipating the trip to Reading and delaying his departure for as long as possible. Except for the sign mounted on the columns above the entrance—"On the Way to You…NEW MADISON SQUARE GARDEN SPORTS CENTER, REDEVELOPED PENNSYLVANIA STATION"—from this side of the building you might never know it was in the midst of being torn down.

The scene inside the concourse, however, told a different story. Red steel beams, marked "BETHLEHEM" in large white letters, jutted up through the floor. Temporary waiting benches crammed what little floor space was left, along with makeshift ticket booths, magazine stands, a snack bar, temporary stairways, barricades, and cheaply-made signs, "Pardon Our Appearance," redirecting passengers. The clock, suspended over the Eighth Avenue entrance, was wrapped ignominiously in a white sheet. He would almost be glad once the whole thing was razed. The congestion and confusion and, God help us, the noise—drilling, hammering, grinding, pounding, shrieking, all the way up to the glass ceiling and echoing back down again, but magnified a hundred times! Sheer bedlam!

The train ride, by comparison, was blessedly tranquil, and it afforded Frederick a chance to catch up on his correspondence (nothing from Curt—but why bother to hope? Curt wasn't the letter-writing type, and even if he did write, Frederick wasn't at all sure he would deign to respond). After a while he dozed. When he awoke, he looked out the window at the brown hills and cornfields of Berks County. His mother had taken another fall. Nothing serious, Marge assured him, but clearly it was time to start looking at nursing homes. He hoped nothing would come of it, ultimately. For Clare, despite her initial resistance to leaving the house at 13th Street and moving in with Marge, seemed to have adapted to the new arrangements just fine, as had Marge by all accounts. But she was insistent they look at nursing homes in the area, and rather than put up a fight, which for sure would provoke another confrontation over who should be looking after their mother, and God knows what else (he still cringed whenever he thought of her outburst at the reception after Pop's funeral—but it was all in the past and should be forgotten—certainly no one in the family brought it up, never said a word, and that included Marge)—he realized the best approach was the path of least resistance.

Marge was there to meet him at the Outer Station. Almost the first words from her lips were, "How is your friend?"

"My friend? Oh, you mean—"

"Curt."

"He's not my friend. I mean, he's the son of my friend…" He quickly repeated the story of why Curt had been living with him, how he'd come to New York, and so on. Marge had called him my "friend," he thought. Right back where we left off at the funeral.

"How is he?" she asked again.

"I wouldn't know. Fine, I guess. He's not staying with me anymore. He found a job and a proper place to live rather than living—rather than my living room couch. And you know how young people are. Here today, gone tomorrow" (he tried to pick the cuticle on his thumb but the bandages on his fingers made it impossible).

"Markie always asks about him," was all she said before Frederick changed the subject to Clare. There were three nursing homes in the vicinity of Reading. The next morning they made their rounds. What quickly emerged was their differing perceptions of Clare's needs and capacities at this point in her life. Frederick was sure she would hate the Phoebe Home, way out there in Wernersville, at least half an hour from downtown Reading, because, as he reminded his sister, this is a woman who's spent her entire life in the same town, in the same place. Practically the same neighborhood. It's all she's known. But in fact, Marge corrected him, she *hasn't* been living in Reading for the last six months, she's been living in Shillington, and she's used to it. Frederick wanted to ask, then why are we moving her yet again, but he knew Marge would protest. And again, at the Topton Home, when they learned their mother would almost certainly have a roommate, Frederick said to Marge as they were leaving, well that rules out Topton. Why? she asked. Because Mama will never tolerate a roommate. She'll want her privacy. Not at all, Marge countered. You should see how much she loves having people around now. I think she might actually prefer it.

Frederick wasn't in a position to argue—Marge ought to know. She took a businesslike attitude towards the proceedings. Her decision had been made and now it was just a matter of finding a place good enough for Clare. She was ready to move on with her own life. Next week she would be starting her new part-time job as bookkeeper at a radio station in town. Markie was in middle school and seemed to be finding his way with some new friends. The baby was eighteen months, old enough, she said, to leave her with her friend Dorothy in the mornings and not feel guilty. She was dating someone (she didn't say much about him, as if the subject weren't fit for Frederick's ears, or as if she assumed he wouldn't be interested), but she'd also begun speaking to Chuck again, who spent every other weekend with Markie.

Indeed, she was moving forward with her life. Amazingly so, Frederick thought. Just six months ago she was headed for rock-bottom. And maybe she did hit rock-bottom. Maybe that's where one has to go before coming up again to the surface (he thought how long it had been since the last time Curt phoned). Anyway, that was what he understood people to say who'd suffered through some great difficulty in life. He wouldn't know, he told himself, his life, his temperament had been, on the whole, so steady, so even-keeled (again he tried to pick the cuticle on his thumb and was prevented by the bandages—he pressed his thumb instead with his forefinger and felt pain). And it was fine if Marge didn't want to tell him about her new beau. Best to keep away from intimate subjects all around. She doesn't talk about her personal life, I don't talk about mine. We don't ask questions. It's cleaner that way.

That night at Marge's house, Frederick couldn't sleep (he was sharing Markie's room, and Markie, it turned out, was a snorer). He went to the kitchen for a glass of milk. Turning on the light, he found Clare sitting on the sofa in the living room. She turned her head like an owl but kept silent. It wasn't clear if she knew who he was or even if he was there.

"Mama?"

"Yes?" she grunted, as if jolted out of sleep.

"Mama, are you all right?" He entered the room, sat down next to her, and repeated his question.

Now she looked him square in the face. "Where's the man of the house?"

"Who do you mean?"

"The man of the house. Where is he?"

"I don't know… There is no man of the house."

"No?" She seemed worried.

"I'm the man of the house, I guess." He took her hand and began to stroke it. He noticed her fingertips were crusted, the fingernails bitten away. They sat in silence for a few moments. "I'm having a glass of milk. Would you like one? How about if I warm it up for you?"

While he prepared the milk in the kitchen, he heard Clare murmuring.

"Were you talking to someone?" he asked as he brought the glasses of milk into the living room.

"I told him I wanted more children but he wouldn't allow it. Mama and Daddy didn't approve, you know. 'Something about the Baileys,' Daddy used to say. 'Something cold about Fred Bailey.'"

"You told—who?"

"Mama used to sing to me when I was a girl. Did you know I had long, brown hair?"

Now she seemed on steadier ground. "You were always so pretty."

"I'm not pretty anymore."

"Yes, you are, Mama."

"I'm bent and ugly."

"Everyone changes as they get older."

But she continued to insist on her ugliness, and he continued, gently, to contradict her.

She looked at him. "You just say that 'cause you're biased."

"Maybe I am."

They sat in silence and sipped their milk. Clare's hand shook as she brought the glass to her lips. Frederick reached to help her steady the glass.

"I can do it."

He withdrew his hand. He asked her why she was awake at this hour. She answered by saying how glad she was he'd come home. There followed a familiar series of questions and answers about where he lives, what he does for a living, how long he would be visiting.

"I'm just here for the weekend." The thought of telling her the real reason for his visit, and for its short duration, nauseated him.

"Why can't you stay longer?"

"Mama, you know I have my work."

"You're an architect."

"Yes, Mama."

She thought for a moment. "I could have worked. I could have gone to college. Traveled. Seen other countries. But when you find love you take it no matter what."

He wondered what the connection was between not working, not studying, not traveling—so much deprivation, as he saw it, so much self-sacrifice—and finding love.

"I could have designed dresses," she continued. "I had a flair for fabric."

"I didn't know that." Frederick figured she was lost in pure fantasy.

"But I never pursued it because of the children. When I die I want you to tell everyone I could have been a dress designer."

"Okay, Mama, I'll—"

"Say it at my funeral."

"Let's not worry about your funeral, that's a long way off."

"If I die before you, make sure you leave something for the children."

"Mama, I don't—what children?"

"Our children. Freddy and Margie."

Was it possible? "Mama, *I'm* Freddy." Pointing to himself, "this is me, it's me, Freddy. Your son."

She looked at him. "No. Freddy's an architect. He lives in New York."

"That's right. I'm Freddy!" He felt a burning in his sinuses.

"Fritz!" She uttered the name like a burp.

"No, *Freddy*. I'm Freddy." He laid his head in her lap and saw their reflection, turned sideways, in Marge's television set. He closed his eyes. "Remember, Mama, I'm your son. I'm Freddy."

She fell silent for a minute.

"Where is your friend? The young man you brought to the house last time." How could she have remembered? "Where is he?"

In a voice almost inaudible, he said he didn't know.

"Did you lose him?"

It sounded like her customary black humor, only she didn't chuckle as she used to do after making a dry remark. Yes, he wanted to say, I've lost him. He went away and he's never coming back.

"He's fine" was all he could say. He tightened his lips.

She waited, then asked, "What was his name?"

It was all he could do to say it without choking.

"He was a nice young man. You seemed very fond of him."

Frederick smelled the fragrance of her sweater, the nightgown underneath, her belly, her lap.

"Yes," he said, his face buried in his mother's lap, the word sounding a mile away, even to himself. "Very fond of him," he said to stop the heaving of his chest.

ON THE WAY INTO TOWN ON SUNDAY MORNING, FREDERICK AND MARGE went over once more their impressions of the nursing homes they'd seen the day before and came to a tentative agreement on which would be best. The Phoebe Home in Wernersville seemed to get the highest mark—the staff was professional but kind, it was clean, however modest, the grounds well kept and pretty, and it wasn't so very far out of town if you thought about it—Really, what's half an hour? Marge asked.

They embraced in front of the station, said their parting words, and Frederick watched as Marge's car disappeared down Spring Street. Why he didn't want her to know he was going up to the Pagoda, he couldn't have said, exactly. After depositing his case in a locker at the station, he continued south on Sixth Street, then east on Washington Street to City Park. He headed for the water fountain in the middle of the park. He took a draft and looked up. There was the Pagoda perched on the side of the mountain. *His* Pagoda. He hadn't visited it since the war.

Hailing a taxi, he found himself, ten minutes later, leaning against the railing at the edge of the cliff. He felt the enormity of the drop. The city of Reading spread out beneath him. There was Penn Street running through the middle of town, crossing the Schuylkill River, continuing through West Reading, Wyomissing, and Wernersville where eventually it would head out west across the state of Pennsylvania into Ohio and the Midwestern plain. It was strange to think of his humble little hometown, nestled at the base of the mountain, as the first step towards anything so magnificent as the wide open spaces of the American Midwest or, further on, the seething, jutting canyons of the Rocky Mountains. His mind roved further—out over the

Pacific, to Hawaii, Japan, Korea, China, India, Arabia, Africa, then across the Atlantic, over Hudson's Bay, the rail lines crossing into New Jersey, and then further, into Pennsylvania, and back again to the Outer Station in Reading. He spotted the station amid blocks of red-brick factory buildings and tangles of cables and innumerable tracks converging. There was St. Joseph's Church, a few blocks from the train station, its yellow stucco glowing as if lit from within like a lantern. His parents were married in that church. He was baptized in that church. He'd gone to grade school in the building next door to it. From there he could easily trace a path along Eighth Street, up Perry to 13th, to the house he grew up in. It was like looking at a child's model train yard, a miniature village where everything was shiny and new and clean and there was no sorrow or pain or anger. Mom and Pop gave me life, he thought, nursed me, raised me, educated me, and he had taken it all and made something of himself. Did he now owe it to his mother to care for her at the end of her life? He looked down over the edge of the cliff. He'd never asked to be born. Honestly, he'd never felt particularly grateful to be alive. Once he'd thought of killing himself, after the breakup with Jon. Curt couldn't hold a candle to Jon. He looked at the Pagoda, its stone base and white portico, its red-tiled roofs, the yellow trim and golden lion heads at the corners, its brick chimney, the dragon dolphins on the roof.

"Great view from the observatory. Sixty miles on a clear day." He turned. Standing before him were a young man and woman holding the hands of four little girls—it was Jack McCoy, the owner of the house in Wyomissing, and his family. "I thought I recognized you! What a coincidence! Dolores, this is—sorry I've forgotten—"

"Bailey. Frederick."

"Yes, Mr. Bailey."

"How do you do?" Dolores seemed shy.

"Lisa, you remember Mr. Bailey. And this is Lucy, Wendy, and Charlotte. Oh, say, you mind taking our picture?" He handed Frederick his Kodak and lifted the smallest of the girls onto his shoulders. Dolores was visibly pregnant. "Try to get as much of the Pagoda in the background as possible."

Curt was right, Frederick thought as he snapped the picture, he was handsome in his gawky, unselfconscious way. He had a gentle demeanor, and his wife was sweet. Even the children were appealing, like little lambs. For some reason, the sight of this young family, out on a day like today enjoying the sights, filled him with sadness.

"Let's go, princesses," Jack said as the girls ran toward the Pagoda. "Watch the steps!"

"Okay, Daddy!" Lisa chirped, already disappearing down the stairs toward the entrance with the others right behind her.

"Your friend not with you today?"

There was that word again.

"No, he's…" But what to say? "He's not with me."

"This sure is a coincidence! Well, enjoy the day. Maybe we'll see you up top." And they went inside the building. A minute later, Frederick followed.

"Like to visit the observatory?" the elderly desk attendant asked. She must have been older than Clare but obviously still had her wits about her.

"Yes," he said, hearing already the girls stomping up the stairs, their mother admonishing them, Be careful, no running. "Tell me, do they still blink the lights of the Pagoda on Christmas Eve?"

"Beg pardon?"

"On Christmas Eve, when I was a child—this is going back a ways—they used to flash the lights of the Pagoda on and off at 9:00 PM as a signal to the children of Reading that Santa was on his way and it was time to go to bed."

She thought for a moment. "I believe they do." Then looked at him and smiled.

The observatory was small, made all the more so by the large bronze bell mounted over the stairwell and the presence of four excitable children.

"You made it!" Jack said to Frederick.

"Mommy, can you see all the way to China?" Lucy asked.

Frederick pivoted in place to look out the windows on all sides in one sweeping glance. In every direction undulating mountains of green, gold, orange and red spread out and away into blue horizons. Majestic Mount Penn, the mountain of his childhood, with its Pagoda raised high above the city, a beacon and perpetual point of reference, was sunk in waves of color that carried him over, erasing borders and names and places and people, a shimmering golden world. Down in the valley, Reading looked more miniature, more negligible than ever, and yet at the same time, riding the back of this great particolored beast, like the whole world carried on the back of an elephant standing on top of a giant turtle swimming through space, it seemed greater than any place on earth. He hadn't wanted to come to Reading this weekend, had looked forward to his departure all the while he was here, but now, inexplicably, he hated the thought of going back to New York. At that moment he could almost have cried.

TWO DAYS LATER A LETTER ARRIVED FROM CURT. "*THE LAST FEW MONTHS HAVE given me a chance to get things clear. I phoned you back in September to tell you about a picket I helped organize at the Whitehall Induction Center to protest the military's exclusion of homosexuals. It was very small. There were six of us, plus a woman none of us knew pushing a baby in a stroller. Crazy! There were no spectators. I tried to phone you because I hoped you might be willing to participate or at least be an observer. Frederick, I know you are the only man who has ever really mattered to me, but what I want is not 'marriage' but something more free. I do not belong to you and you do not belong to me. If we ever get back together, it will be by choice. We are free to be involved with other people, but that doesn't change the way we feel about each other.*"

Complete nonsense. Almost word for word what Jon had said! Did he really think such an arrangement could ever work? Had he no understanding of human nature? Wasn't it obvious he just wanted to come back to a lovely, comfortable apartment, live like a prince, dinners out, nights at the theater, trips abroad, and the guidance, the wisdom of an older man—Frederick looked at himself in the mirror—who isn't at all bad looking for his age?

But he couldn't escape the thought of Curt and the words of his letter. It was hard to concentrate at the office. That night he took himself to see the new motion picture version of *My Fair Lady* at the Criterion in Times Square. He had ordered his ticket weeks before, and the timing couldn't have been better. Curt's letter had thrown him off balance. He needed an escape, and this promised to do the honors. The line of ticket holders outside the theater wound around the corner. Anticipation was in the air. In front of him stood a young man with wavy auburn hair, smoking a pipe and chatting with a pretty young woman holding a parasol. He couldn't help overhearing their conversation—she worried her husband didn't earn enough money to support their lifestyle in the city. He, meanwhile, had just lost his job but thought it all for the best as now he had time to pursue his real love, jazz music. Every now and then he looked Frederick's way, and Frederick wondered if he might be flirting. At one point, however, he locked eyes with Frederick and frowned, dampening Frederick's attraction (anyway, the nose was too blunt) and embarrassing him on top of it.

Inside the theater, the seat next to him remained vacant until moments before the lights went down. Patrons to his left stood up as someone pushed his way through the row—he looked up as if miracles really did happen—but an elderly gentleman excused himself and took his seat.

The opening credits were extravagantly beautiful, a montage of giant close-ups of peonies, daisies, and carnations in rich satiny creams, pinks, purples, yellows, reds, and blues. But the fantasy fell to pieces as soon as Audrey Hepburn opened her mouth to sing (bad enough, he thought, she was utterly unconvincing as a cockney girl of the streets): her singing was dubbed, and the voice was shrill. Competent no doubt, hitting all the high notes, but without warmth, without luster, without soul. And there was no concealing the fact, not only was the voice not really issuing from Hepburn's mouth, but Hepburn herself possessed no real musical instincts. The *body* was the singer's instrument, and what Hepburn lacked was body. She was a thin, breastless, ladies' store mannequin. That, apparently was why women and men alike adored her: they could imagine dressing her up like a doll. For every moment he thrilled to the elegance of the production, the beauty of the songs, the complete expertness of Rex Harrison's performance (a perfect replica of the one he'd given on stage)—for everything one could put in the asset column, there was Hepburn racking up the deficits. And the tragedy was, she was good, but with Julie Andrews he'd seen great.

Only near the end did Hepburn seem suited to the role. Eliza, now a "lady," has found her tongue. She's abandoning Higgins, for now she knows he will do anything, say anything not to admit the depth of his devotion to her. Frederick felt the power of Shaw's myth accumulate over his head like a thundercloud ready to burst. *I shall miss you,* he tells her, not knowing the half of it. *I've learned something from your idiotic notions. I confess that humbly and gratefully.* She is defiant. *I'll marry Freddy, I will, as soon as I'm able to support him.* He lashes back. *Freddy! That poor devil who couldn't get a job as an errand boy even if he had the guts to try for it! Woman, do you not understand? I have made you a consort for a king!* And for the first time in the film, Frederick didn't notice the inadequacy of Hepburn's voice (he'd always had a weakness for musicals—indeed, he often worried he came across as "too musical") when she sang how the country would still be ruled, how Windsor Castle would continue to stand, how they would all muddle through *without him.*

Frederick drifted west toward the Port Authority after the movie let out, feeling how great an opportunity had been squandered. A great director. A fine star. All the resources and good will of the studio, of audiences across the country and around the world, all except for the most important thing, the one essential ingredient (he didn't believe a word of Curt's letter—*I know you are the only man*—not a single word of it).

On the corner of 42nd Street and Eighth Avenue a group of seedy young men, their hair oiled, loitered near the subway entrance. Frederick lit a cigarette, leaned against the railing along the stairs, and watched them. Eventually, a boy with doe eyes separated from his companions after sharing a private joke, glanced almost imperceptibly at Frederick, and went down into the subway. Frederick followed, extinguished his cigarette, and hoped his bandaged fingers wouldn't interfere with sexual pleasure.

1965

CHAPTER SIXTEEN

FREDERICK HADN'T FELT SO EXCITED IN MONTHS. THE SENSATION, HOW-
ever, was disagreeable in the extreme. He stood by the base of the statue of
George Washington in front of Philadelphia's Independence Hall amidst a
handful of spectators. Facing north across Chestnut Street, he watched as
Curt, along with thirty-three other men and ten women—for he had taken
a precise head count (counting always helped to calm his nerves)—marched
silently, solemnly, in a wide circle on the lawn. The men wore suits and ties,
the women wore skirts and carried purses. All but Curt and one other man
wore sunglasses. They carried neatly-printed signs whose blunt messages
belied the apparent decorum of the proceedings.

HOMOSEXUAL AMERICANS DEMAND THEIR CIVIL RIGHTS
STOP DISCRIMINATORY PRACTICES AGAINST HOMOSEXUALS
GOVERNMENT BY THE CONSENT OF THE GOVERNED
SEXUAL PREFERENCE IS IRRELEVANT TO EMPLOYMENT
HOMOSEXUALS ARE AMERICAN CITIZENS TOO
15,000 HOMOSEXUAL AMERICANS ASK FOR EQUALITY
OPPORTUNITY
DIGNITY

Small groups of men and some women congregated near the picket line.
One of the protesters mingled among them, handing out leaflets. A reporter

and camera crew arrived and stationed themselves at the edge of the lawn. But this blasted afternoon sun! It was starting to bother Frederick's eyes. He pulled a pair of sunglasses from his breast pocket and put them on, maneuvering to keep directly behind two men, tourists apparently, who had stopped to see what all the hubbub was about.

"I still don't believe it! Somebody's got to be kidding!"

"If Negroes can do it, why not sexual deviants?"

They chuckled and walked away, leaving Frederick an unobstructed view of the demonstration, at which point he noticed a somewhat larger group of spectators congregating beneath a tree at the other end of the plaza, near Sixth Street. He headed towards them (more comfortable, he thought, in the shade), but before he could reach his destination the protester handing out leaflets, who had crossed over to this side of the street, intercepted him. It was Harold.

"Hello there!" he said, offering a leaflet. "You made it after all."

"Well—no, I—" Frederick began, feeling obliged to accept. "I was visiting my mother in Reading and thought I'd stop on my way back to New York—I have some friends in town and—"

"The more support, the better," he said reassuringly, as if he knew Frederick was merely coughing up excuses. They exchanged small talk about their respective journeys to Philadelphia. Then Harold bid him good day and proceeded with his task.

Frederick disliked using his mother as an alibi. He hadn't seen her in over a month, even though he'd promised to come back before the end of June. But she'd probably forgotten his promise by now, along with everything else they talked about. "Say hello to this nice young man," she crowed to the residents and nurses at the Phoebe Home, and he covered up for her confusion, saying, Yes, I'm Clare's son, Frederick, but suspected she just as soon forgot who he was. He unfolded the leaflet Harold had given him.

FIRST ANNUAL REMINDER DAY
July 4, 1965
The Declaration of Independence says: "ALL MEN ARE CREATED
EQUAL." But in no walk of life, and in none of his dealings, whether
with his fellow citizens or with his governments (federal, state, or local)
is the homosexual American citizen treated as equal to others; he is
always placed in a status of inferiority. Systematically and unrelent-
ingly, he is placed into and kept in the category of a second-class citizen.

*That the homosexual American citizen is a homosexual is always noted;
that he is also an American citizen, with all that goes with that status,
is always forgotten.*

Discomfited with what he considered the pamphlet's exaggerations ("*no*
walk of life, *none* of his dealings, *always* placed, *always* noted, *always* forgotten"), he merely skimmed the rest—

> *...denied the equality of opportunity which...denied jobs which...
> given a less than fully honorable discharge...denied a security clear-
> ance...subjected to unceasing official harassment...hunted down and
> ferreted out...feels himself disowned and outcast...we now try to bring
> our case directly before the public...*

Not what you expect on a sunny Fourth of July, he thought, watching
Curt and the other protesters, hoping, as he stood among the mostly silent
witnesses, that anyone looking at him today ("They look so normal," a
teenage girl with a beehive hairdo said to her companion as they passed by)
might think he was just another ordinary American.

"You should all be married and have a family!" a woman shouted as she
pulled a child along by the hand.

"Hold your nose, it's dirty here," an elderly man said to the woman he
pushed in a wheelchair.

"I can't read this filth," a man muttered as he tossed a leaflet to the
ground.

Curt as yet seemed unaware of his presence. Frederick wondered when
they might have an opportunity to speak. He daren't approach him on the
picket line. But at some point he would have to risk association with the
group if he wanted a word with him. But what would he say? Why, indeed,
had he come?

Harold was back on the other side of the street again. Mighty awkward
moment that was. He thought of their recent evening together. He'd forgotten himself, about two weeks ago, while heading up Fourth Avenue toward
the subway. Harold summoned him as he passed by the antique shop and
invited him to dinner. Frederick assumed he was "interested," and though
his feelings weren't reciprocal (he half expected Harold to answer the door
dressed in kimono with fan, then proudly show him around a junk-filled
apartment—really, he had no tolerance for homosexuals like that)—none-

theless he thought the acquaintanceship might be worth exploring if only to get a good look at one of those Victorian doll houses. But when the door opened, there stood a tall, rather fit, not unattractive younger man. "I'm Marshall, we've been expecting you." All night it was "we" this, "we" that: "we" like to go for walks on Sunday mornings, "we" tend to watch television before going to bed, "we" sometimes visit my nephew and his family in Rochester or Harold's favorite sister in St. Louis. And the apartment was nothing like what he'd imagined. It was in surprisingly good and surprisingly modern taste. He didn't know why, by the end of the evening, he felt quite so alone—after all, he reminded himself, I am not nor have I ever been interested in Harold in *that* way, and Marshall, while a perfectly nice enough fellow, wasn't exactly his type either (what *is* my type, he asked himself, watching Curt on the picket line. He looked adorable in his suit and tie, his hair cropped short and neatly combed. The look really became him). It was Harold who'd told him about the protest of military policies against homosexuals in front of the White House in May, the thrill of that experience, the belief they were doing something no one had ever tried before, the feeling they'd made a real breakthrough in consciousness, and the discussion afterward at the restaurant in Chinatown, how everyone was sorry the protest was over, everyone, that is, except Curt, who was still buzzing from the event (small as it was—just thirteen of them altogether). And then suddenly Curt stood up, right there in the middle of the restaurant, absurdly holding a pair of chopsticks, and said, "It doesn't *have* to be over!" He proposed a picket in front of Independence Hall, every Fourth of July, "and we'll call it the Annual Reminder, like a gay holiday," to remind people there exists a group of Americans who still do not have the basic rights to life, liberty and the pursuit of happiness.

"And you know Curt," Harold laughed confidingly, "there's no stopping him when he gets an idea up his bonnet."

"I didn't know *you* knew him so well," Frederick said.

But *so what* if he knows Curt better than I! he muttered as he walked home from dinner that night. So what if they're *lovers*, for that matter! Something must have come over Curt since their breakup in Venice. He hadn't disappeared, gotten sucked back with the tide of young people crashing every day onto New York City's shores. He had survived. More than that, thrived. Didn't seem to need Frederick's apartment or money, his intelligence or wisdom, his concern or care, anymore. Maybe a trip to Society Hill, he thought suddenly, in Philadelphia, would give him some fresh sense of the kind of apartment tower they were designing on Park Avenue. It was meant as a sort of homage to the Federal-style townhouse—all red brick and white trim—and Society Hill, of course, was a treasure trove of such houses. He wouldn't tell Harold, though, for he had urged him to come with them to Philly for the Fourth of July picket. The more support, he said, the better. Frederick wouldn't cause *further* friction between them by saying he felt uncomfortable joining a picket for homosexual rights—indeed, that he quite *disapproved* of such an idea as homosexual rights. Let Harold think—let all the radicals think—he shared their point of view. No one need know what he really thought. But he would go to observe, and if someone asked, he would say he was stopping off on his way to New York—had been to Reading for the weekend—had some business to take care of in Philly—he'd think up some excuse.

And so here he was. How could he *not* have anticipated how uneasy he would feel attending a homosexual rights demonstration, in broad daylight? And yet he wanted to speak with Curt—say something to him—though it wasn't clear what he should say. Perhaps he only wanted to hear the words from Curt—the words he wrote in his letter—*You are the only man who has ever really mattered to me.* The rest of it ("What I want is not 'marriage' but something more free, I don't belong to you, you don't belong to me," and so forth)—the rest of it he only wanted to forget. And maybe Curt had forgotten it too. Maybe that was just a young man's protest in the face of onrushing maturity. In the face of reality.

"When you're as disliked as homosexuals, it takes a lot of guts to stand up for your rights." Frederick realized the man who spoke was directing the comment to him, apparently assuming he was *not* homosexual (thank God). "I give them credit for what they're doing."

"Yes," Frederick said half-heartedly but turned away without further comment, heading toward Sixth Street. He'd had enough. Just when he reached the corner, however, thinking he'd hail a taxi to the Museum of Art, end this mad escapade altogether, he heard a woman's voice call out his name.

Bev came running across Chestnut Street. He hardly recognized her in a dress and heels. Trying not to show discomfort at being seen in the company of one of the demonstrators, he embraced her. He asked her whether the protest was going well.

"I'd say so. The drill is, you smile and you smile and you offer a leaflet to everyone, whether they take it or not. We're getting the message out, that's the most important thing. How do you like my dress?" She swiveled her hips.

"If I didn't know better, I'd swear you were a girl."

"You've no idea how much we fought the dress code. Curt especially. He kept saying, 'we have to tear off our ugly frog skins and release the beautiful Fairy Prince underneath!' I think they were ready to expel him from the organization."

"Well, the man in the suit is still the overwhelming norm in this country." He said it without a trace of irony.

"We thought sheer numbers of *all kinds* of people were more important," she said a little combatively, "than projecting an image of 'quality folks,' but the conservatives won. And, brother, did they lay down the law: they said, 'Picketing is not an occasion for an assertion of personality, individuality, ego, rebellion'"—she laughed gently—"'generalized non-conformity or anti-conformity. The individual picketer serves merely to carry a sign. Not he but his sign should attract notice.'" Again she laughed. "'No smoking or talking on line. If you're interviewed by the media, you're supposed to say 'homosexual citizens'—"

"I don't see how you can make fun. Don't you realize" (now his blood was starting to boil) "you run the risk of finding your picture in the paper, losing your job, getting arrested, winding up on an FBI list—"

"I don't like to picket, but we have to, we just *have* to. And the truth is, a weight has fallen off my shoulders. Today I think I lost my last bit of fear."

Frederick was sure it was a mistake to have come, the whole event a tactical error. And yet he couldn't deny, there was something sweet about Bev. He'd always thought so. "How is Kay?" he asked.

"She's fine. Doesn't she look cute in her dress? She can get away with it more easily than I. God, we're so conscious of appearances, aren't we?"

"You have to be." Now *he* was speaking imperatives.

"Have you seen Curt?"

"Yes—right behind you in the picket—"

"No, I mean have you talked to him?"

"No—I'm in Philly on business." She looked skeptical. "Something I'm working on—a building—I wanted to see some houses in Society Hill, and I thought as long as I'm here—"

"I think you should talk to him." He wanted to ask why, but she made to leave. "I've got to get back. Come to the next Mattachine meeting in New York."

"We'll see," he said and thought, almost for her sake, it might be worth doing. Seeing her now was a good reminder of how fond he was of her. It was too easy to put people out of sight, out of mind. He looked at the leaflet still in his hand. "Annual Reminder." People needed to be reminded homosexuals were persecuted. That homosexuals existed. But it wasn't just homosexuals, he thought. Sometimes we need to be reminded *our own loved ones* exist. That was what had brought him here in the first place. Not that he wanted to *talk* to Curt necessarily. He had nothing to say to Curt. It was over between them. It ended the day they drove to Naples. The day he realized he might be Curt's "home base" but never the one, true love of his life. No, now he just wanted to see him, be reminded of his presence. Even if only from a distance. For he has been part of my life, he thought. Things have changed, of course. I've changed. Gotten back to normal. And in the end it's probably better this way (he scratched his thumb with his middle finger and began peeling off the nail). But when Harold told him about the demonstration, and that Curt was one of the main organizers, Yes, he felt, I have to see what my young man has accomplished for himself.

Bev had returned to the protest. She and Curt were standing to the side of the picket line, talking or arguing, it was hard to know. He wondered if she was telling him of their conversation just now. Curt still wasn't acknowledging his presence. Either Bev wasn't speaking of it, or, if she were, Curt wasn't interested. He wondered if what he'd said in his letter was still true ("*I know you are the only man who has ever really mattered to me*"). But why did he care? That was almost a year ago. He retraced his steps towards the plaza in front of Independence Hall. There was something foolhardy about the protesters, he thought. But also heroic. And the two things, no doubt, went hand in hand. Me, I've never been that kind of person. Never belonged to any party, subscribed to any creed (Catholicism?—he'd abandoned it years ago—now he just went to Mass on Sundays in tribute to the past—"once a Catholic..."). No, my contribution to society is in the things I make. I do what I can do. He took off his sunglasses. Anyway, he added, I'm here to show my support (the more support, the better—that's what Harold kept saying). Isn't that enough?

His heart began to race. Curt was crossing the street. Curt was coming towards him.

Now here he was, standing before him. Here he was.

Curt.

He opened his arms and embraced Frederick, the way he'd done that first night he showed up on Frederick's doorstep—what time was it? Eleven? Twelve? After midnight? He felt Curt's body fit perfectly into the cradle of his own. They stood holding each other tight, under the blazing sun, on the plaza in front of Independence Hall, as spectators stood all around and pedestrians came from every direction. He was terrified to think what a pretty picture the two of them presented to the world at this moment. He let go.

"How are you?" Curt asked without smiling. Somehow he looked more youthful, if it were possible, than ever before, dressed so handsomely in his suit and tie. At the same time he looked more serious than ever. He'd gotten a crew cut. It was a different Curt. But the feel of his body, the strength of his touch, the forthrightness of his gaze, the low, burnished quality of his voice—none of that had changed. It was the same young man he'd fallen in love with three years ago.

"I'm here on business this weekend. We're designing an apartment building on Park Avenue, and I wanted to see Society Hill because we're aiming for an early-nineteenth-century look. Red brick, coach lamps—"

"I mean, how are *you*?" Curt asked again.

"Busy with work. I've been involved in the Landmarks Preservation Commission. The law was passed in April, I forget if you knew that."

"I didn't."

"Well, not before we lost the Brokaw Mansion. It was a free-standing house on Fifth Avenue and 79th Street, just a couple of blocks south of the Metropolitan Museum. We rallied, wrote letters, did everything we could, but there was no way to stop it." Curt was listening intently but with a puzzled look on his face. "I forget why I started telling you this."

"I asked you how you are."

"Oh. Well—so, I've been very busy with that, and…" He was embarrassed by everything he'd said.

Curt, on the other hand, had no difficulty telling about his work for homosexual rights. He described his involvement with the Mattachine Society, how New York Mattachine joined forces with other chapters to form the East Coast Homophile Organizations, his constant fights with the conservatives in New York, "and this whole thing about dressing up."

"You look like a prince."

"I look ridiculous. But you just have to have faith. I've promised to be a good boy."

Frederick wanted to know everything. And yet he wanted to know nothing. He didn't want to be reminded how much Curt's life carried on without him, how well Curt had survived him, how, for all his volatility, his unpredictability, his mercurial ways of acting and thinking and feeling, there was solid ground beneath him, solid rock at the center of him. For he had emerged. Blossomed. Frederick was a mere antechamber to but one room—one room in one wing—of the mansion of Curt's life, that seemed clear. Frederick tried to hold steady his breath, as if he'd been sprinting and stopped abruptly. Damn Curt for making him feel this awful excitement.

"What do you think of the picket?"

"I think it's probably best to work quietly on an individual basis."

"What good will that do?"

"We've had this debate before. I don't think you can really talk about 'homosexual rights.' That's not to say homosexuals should be persecuted or further stigmatized, but—"

"I'm just as good as the next person. Why should I be treated like a second-class citizen?" Frederick held back. What was the use of further debate? "Homosexuality is not an illness, we are not sick. It's the rest of society that defines us that way. How can I argue for my rights if I see myself as a sick, immoral person? And why should I have to wait for other people to decide to stop persecuting me? Why is it up to everyone else but me?" But still Frederick hesitated to respond, and Curt gave up. Instead he said, "You never answered my letter."

Frederick looked in his eyes. In that moment, everything he'd ever felt for him cascaded through his brain, shot through his veins, and clutched his heart. "No…" he said.

Curt waited for him to continue.

Just because I'm getting married doesn't mean—

Never again.

Frederick looked down to the ground, avoiding further eye contact.

Curt took a deep breath. "So, 'if you want me again look for me under your boot-soles,' is that it?" He too looked down and noticed Frederick's bandaged fingers. Instinctively he reached out and gently took his hand. "What happened here?"

Embarrassed, Frederick withdrew—"Nothing, it's nothing"—and put his hand in his pocket. "I burned myself on the stove." Again he looked down.

"Okay," Curt said. He was about to go when he remembered one last thing. "How is your mother?"

Frederick's throat went dry. "She's fine. She's in a nursing home."

"Oh, I'm sorry. Is she sick?"

"Just old."

"How sad."

"Not really. No, she's…" He swallowed. "Content."

"Well, I guess that's all that matters. If she's content."

Their parting words came suddenly—take care of yourself, good luck, see you sometime. Curt opened his arms for one final embrace, but Frederick abruptly thrust out his hand for a handshake instead.

Watching Curt return to the picket line, he wondered if he should have been warmer. Maybe explained his position about the letter. But Curt obviously had gotten the message. What more was there to say? "If you want me again look for me under your boots-soles"—wait a minute. Where had he heard that before? "I bequeath myself to the dirt to grow from the grass I love"… Whitman! Curt had just quoted Walt Whitman. It was near the end of "Song of Myself." After many hundreds of lines, Whitman had said everything he'd come to say and at long last was taking leave of the reader (Curt now crossed Chestnut Street, heading toward the other protesters on the lawn), never to return, at least not in the flesh. *I depart as air, I shake my white locks at the runaway sun, I effuse my flesh in eddies and drift it in lacy jags. I bequeath myself to the dirt to grow from the grass I love. If you want me again…*

So Curt had been reading Whitman on his own, to the point that he knew it by heart. Frederick remembered reading Whitman to him on one of their first nights together.

He turned and began walking away from Independence Hall. He didn't know how to get to the Museum of Art from here. He only knew he had to leave.

CHAPTER SEVENTEEN

BY THE TIME FREDERICK'S TRAIN PULLED INTO NEW YORK THE NEXT DAY, Penn Station was hell on earth. Jackhammers, bulldozers, welders, sparks flying, a wrecking ball smashing the north wall of the waiting room like an exploding bomb, hordes of office workers, shoppers, commuters, tourists, police sirens, ambulance horns, fire engines roaring down Seventh Avenue, traffic backed up through the intersection, pedestrians shouting obscenities, hot dog carts, soft pretzels, chestnuts for sale, secretaries rushing to get back to work, starting a new week, no time! I haven't got time! dodging barricades, bewildered passengers pointing this way, no, that way, you have to go through there, down the steps, then up again where you'll find the ticket booths. "Believe me, trains are still running!" a man shouted as he walked past, his dog pulling at the leash, growling, barking at another dog, a woman in high heels tripping across the avenue, cars barreling toward her, Bitch, get out of the way before you get hit! Did you see that? How rude! Are you all right? I'm fine, he was just about to run me over! She picked up her dog and checked his paws to make sure he wasn't hurt. "Bastard!" she shouted and let the dog drop to the sidewalk as she tottered past the construction site, where workmen sat on cement blocks eating their lunch, whistling and shouting Come to Papa, hey baby, you and me, waddaya say?

"Bastard!"

Exiting the station, Frederick felt a choking sensation. Ever since yesterday in Philadelphia, he'd been having difficulty breathing. The air in midtown only made it worse. Why on earth does anyone ever live in New York City? he wondered, just making it to the sidewalk across the street from Penn Station as the light changed, the sign flashing DON'T WALK, and the traffic springing forward. He felt faint. He pushed his way across the busy sidewalk towards the Statler Hotel and leaned his shoulder against the building. He pulled the handkerchief from his pocket and mopped his forehead.

He turned to look back at what was left of Penn Station. One, two, three, he counted the remaining columns, eight, nine, ten...They'd already demolished the carriage entrances at 31st and 33rd Streets. The arcade was completely gone. The façade of Penn Station was now little more than a screen with nothing back of it. But Day and Night, their gowns black with grime, still stood over the entrance, propping up the shrouded clock that told No Time, their minions, proud stone eagles, still maintaining their lookouts. Clouds of smoke and dirt and the sound of engines howling rose above the station, and he could now see bright red steel spikes jutting up behind the shell of the waiting room, the soon-to-be Madison Square Garden, Coming Your Way, For Your Convenience, a gigantic, futuristic drum taking shape. Twenty-two, twenty-three, twenty-four... He remembered the protest three years ago—now there was hardly enough room on the sidewalk for a man to stop and catch his breath, much less a protest of five hundred. That was all in the past now. It was all too late, what's done is done. Time flowed in one direction only, carrying everything and everyone with it, like lava flowing down the slopes of Mount Vesuvius, so much noise and confusion he couldn't hear himself think. His head ached as if metal plates were screwed to the sides of his skull, an invisible hand cranking them tighter and tighter—when a bomb dropped—*Curt would never come back to him again*—exploded in a million pieces—*they would never see each other again*—spreading shock waves out from the center. Before his eyes a monumental wall of granite began to crack and then crumble. He looked up and saw pieces of stone falling from the sky, coming toward him. A fiery mushroom cloud rose over Penn Station, a blinding burst of light, then darkness. He turned to face the wall of the Statler Hotel, put out his hand against the building to steady himself so he wouldn't fall, a red pagoda teetering on the edge of a cliff, *Frederick it's for you,* his mother said, snow falling through the dining room window, his own mother didn't recognize him anymore, burning rocks falling, his father was dead, and he would never forget where he stood that day the bomb fell, everyone frozen in mid-stride, buried in rubble, burned to death stepping from a taxi, bending over a jewelry counter, dancing salsa on a front stoop, playing tag, jumping rope, running through an open hydrant, feeding ducks in Central Park, sitting on a bench eating a sandwich, reading a newspaper, walking the dog, lovers kissing, caught in the revolving door of the Statler Hotel, kissing, embracing, he and Jon, right there in the middle of the concourse in Penn Station, so in love they didn't care if everyone stopped and stared at the sight of two men embracing in public, holding each other tight.

Then he heard someone choking, an aching, hacking, coughing, choking sound, and it was the sound of his own throat, it was the sound of his own tears—*what have I done*—erupting from the open wound of Mount Penn, weeping, standing and steadying himself with one arm against the wall of the Statler Hotel, across from the ruins of Pennsylvania Station, *On Its Way To You, Coming Soon, All-New, Ultra-Modern, For Your Convenience,* weeping for the dawn of a new day he wished would never come, as first one, then another, then another person stopped and stared at this queer fellow standing alone there weeping, steadying himself against the building, his suitcase at his feet, his face buried in his hand.

AUTHOR'S NOTE

PENNSYLVANIA STATION IS A WORK OF HISTORICAL FICTION. IT DRAMATIZES the intersection of the mid-twentieth-century historic preservation movement with the Civil Rights movement using mostly invented characters and situations as well as some actual events and a few cameos.

My sincerest thanks to publisher Steve Berman for his belief in the book and his patient editorial guidance. Thanks to Franco La Russa (aka Thion) for his inspired artwork on the cover and inside the book. Jill Dearman and the members of her writing workshop played a crucial role in getting the book off the ground. Without the camaraderie and intellectual support of Marcy Arlin, the book wouldn't exist. For generous feedback on the manuscript, thanks to Margie McCarthy Ferro, Cris Gleicher, William Burgos, Gilbert Cole, Amy Pratt, and Janet Rosen. Thanks also to copyeditor and interior designer Alex Jeffers. John Dever shared with me his knowledge of the history and geography of Reading, Pennsylvania. Robert Grobstein and Simon Levine gave me invaluable insight into the lives of gay men before Stonewall. My depiction of the early years of the contemporary gay rights movement owes a lot to Martin Duberman's book *Stonewall*, especially Duberman's profile of activist Craig Rodwell. Anthony C. Wood, along with his indispensable book *Preserving New York: Winning the Right to Protect a City's Landmarks*, helped me understand the history of the historic preservation movement and the role that the demolition of the old Penn Station played in it. Laura Pedersen at the New York Preservation Archive Project gave me access to some rare, early-1960s documents. The idea for the novel occurred to me in the spring of 2004 as I was teaching a seminar at Columbia University on post-World War II lesbian and gay fiction; thanks to the wonderful students in that class for helping me more fully appreciate the power and pain of modern "protest" fiction. And thanks to the Trustees of Long Island University for granting me sabbaticals in 2009-10 and 2016-17 during which I was able to make sustained progress on the manuscript.

Above all I am grateful to my husband, Eduardo Leanez, for being such a reliable sounding board and faithful reader from the moment I started working on the book. I dedicate it to him with love.

ABOUT THE AUTHOR

PATRICK E. HORRIGAN was born and raised in Reading, Pennsylvania. He earned a BA from The Catholic University of America and a PhD from Columbia University. He is the author of the novel *Portraits at an Exhibition* (Lethe Press), winner of the 2016 Mary Lynn Kotz "Art in Literature" Award, given jointly by the Library of Virginia and the Virginia Museum of Fine Arts. His other works include the memoir *Widescreen Dreams: Growing Up Gay at the Movies*, the play *Messages for Gary: A Drama in Voicemail*, and (with Eduardo Leanez) the solo show *You Are Confused!* He has written artists' catalogue essays for Thion's *Limi-TATE: Drawings of Life and Dreams* (cueB Gallery, London) and Ernesto Pujol's *Loss of Faith* (Galeria Ramis Barquet, New York). His essay "The Inner Life of *Ordinary People*" appears in Anthony Enns' and Christopher R. Smit's *Screening Disability: Essays on Cinema and Disability*. He and Mr. Leanez are the hosts of *Actors with Accents*, a recurring variety show in Manhattan's Lower East Side. Winner of Long Island University's David Newton Award for Excellence in Teaching, he is Associate Professor of English at LIU Brooklyn. He lives in Manhattan.

www.patrickehorrigan.com

CPSIA information can be obtained
at www.ICGtesting.com
Printed in the USA
BVHW031421090719
552969BV00001B/78/P